A BRILLIANT DEATH

A
BRILLIANT
DEATH

A NOVEL

ROBIN YOCUM

SEVENTH STREET BOOKS®
AN IMPRINT OF PROMETHEUS BOOKS
59 JOHN GLENN DRIVE • AMHERST, NY 14228
www.seventhstreetbooks.com

Published 2016 by Seventh Street Books®, an imprint of Prometheus Books

Cover image © Wendy Stevenson / Arcangel Images
Cover design by Nicole Sommer-Lecht

Inquiries should be addressed to
Seventh Street Books
59 John Glenn Drive
Amherst, New York 14228
VOICE: 716–691–0133 • FAX: 716–691–0137
WWW.SEVENTHSTREETBOOKS.COM

20 19 18 17 16 • 5 4 3 2 1

Library of Congress Cataloging-in-Publication Data Pending

ISBN 978-1-63388-128-0 (pbk)
ISBN 978-1-63388-129-7 (ebk)

Printed in the United States of America

For Melissa

PROLOGUE

I never met my Grandfather Kaminski. He was only forty-two when he dropped dead of a heart attack at the Nickel Plate Railroad yard in Dillonvale. He had just finished his coffee break and was putting together a train of empty coal cars to be filled at the Youghiogheny and Ohio Coal Company mine in Barton when he turned to Nippy Borkowski and said, "Dammit, Nippy, I think I'm dead." Before Nippy could take the cigarette out of his mouth, my grandfather dropped like a felled pine between two coal cars. They called Doc Barnes, who ran down from his office over the Miner's Bank & Trust Company, but my grandfather was likely dead before he hit the gravel ballast.

Doc Barnes said it was a massive heart attack, but my father said that anyone who knew my grandfather realized he died of acute estrogen exposure.

Walter Kaminski was five when his family immigrated to Ohio from the Oder River basin town of Bukow in western Poland. They settled in the coal mining community of Piney Fork, about ten miles west of the Ohio River Valley. He was fourteen when he began working on the railroad and twenty-six when he saved my grandmother from becoming an old maid, marrying her when she was nineteen. Over the next eight years, she gave birth to six children—all girls. She was ready to stop at four, but agreed to keep trying in order to give Grandpa Kaminski a son to carry on the family name. Alas, another girl—my Aunt Bess. When she became pregnant with baby number six, she announced that upon delivery of the child, son or no, it would be the last. Before she left the hospital with Aunt Victoria, she had her tubes tied and the baby factory closed.

Or so she thought.

Apparently, tubal ligation in its infancy wasn't that effective, and six months later she was pregnant again. She was furious; he was delighted, as it gave him one last chance for a son. The fates were against him, however, and she delivered not one daughter, but *three*. Triplets! This was extremely rare in the 1930s, long before the advent of fertility drugs. There were big stories in the papers, and the girls became local celebrities, known as "the abelles"—Annabelle, Marabelle, and Rosabelle.

He had a wife and nine daughters born within ten years of each other. My father said Grandpa Kaminski took the coward's way out, choosing to drop dead and cede all responsibility to my grandmother.

The triplets grew up, and in a six-week stretch in the fall of 1952, each gave birth to first-born sons. Marabelle gave birth to me on October 7. Rosabelle gave birth to Nicholas on October 30. Annabelle delivered Johnny on November 21.

We three cousins grew up in the same Upper Ohio River Valley region, dreaming of fame on the athletic field and hoping to escape the steel mills and coal mines. I was not the equal of my cousins in athletic ability or good looks, but I'd like to think God evened the score by granting me a modicum of common sense, which sometimes seems to be sadly missing in most descendants of Walter Kaminski, who have shown a tendency to live for the moment and think with their peckers.

My name is Mitchell Malone, and I grew up in the river town of Brilliant. Nicholas, who was known as Duke, grew up in Mingo Junction. Johnny, who in junior high insisted that he be called Giovanni, even though he was more Polish than Italian, grew up in Steubenville. We were bonded by family blood and the gritty air and muddy waters of the Ohio River Valley. Never in my vivid imagination did I dream we would ultimately have another common bond—murder. Duke and Johnny would see their adult lives knotted like spinning rope, and they have their own tales of intrigue, but not just yet. First, there's my story. It begins in the summer of 1953, when a river barge crushed a pleasure boat—*Lady Luck*—on the Ohio River. The disappearance of the boat's passengers would launch a mystery that would fuel the gossip mill and perplex authorities for decades.

And I am the only one who can tell the entire story.

CHAPTER ONE

From the Steubenville, Ohio, *Herald-Star*, June 7, 1971.
Brilliant Senior Class Salutatorian
Missing After Car Plunges into River

BRILLIANT—Rescue workers from five local fire departments searched the Ohio River today for the body of the Brilliant High School senior class salutatorian believed to have died shortly after midnight Sunday when the car he was driving plunged 110 feet over a cliff and into the murky waters beneath Hunter's Ridge just north of town.

Authorities identified the man as Travis Franklin Baron, 18, of 138 Nichols Drive, Brilliant.

Baron, who only hours earlier had addressed his fellow seniors at his commencement, was fleeing police when he crashed through a barrier and went over the cliff. A police spokesman said Baron was last seen driving at a high rate of speed on Jefferson County Road 19 near the entrance to Hunter's Ridge Park.

By the time pursuing police arrived at Hunter's Ridge, the car was sinking into the Ohio River. There were no witnesses to the accident.

Sources said Baron had reportedly been drinking at several graduation parties before the chase began shortly before midnight.

"Obviously, we don't hold much hope of finding him alive," said Brilliant Volunteer Fire Chief Delmar Bernoski, whose son James also participated in the graduation ceremonies. "With all the rain, and the river flowing so swiftly, his body could be 20 miles downstream by now."

Ironically, Baron's mother drowned in the river 18 years ago this fall, not far from last night's mishap. Amanda Baron was on the family's cabin cruiser the night of Oct. 17, 1953, when it was rammed by a coal barge.

Her body and the body of a male companion were never found.

Shortly after noon today, divers located the car, a black, 1957 Chevrolet show car owned by Travis Baron's father, Francis M. Baron. However, the body had been washed free of the vehicle.

The senior Baron, a truck driver, was out of town at the time of the accident.

Brilliant Police Chief Steve Maurer said Baron had reportedly attended several graduation parties where alcohol was being served. Maurer said witnesses reported Baron had been drinking heavily.

Baron was at a graduation party on Grant Avenue when he became belligerent and got into a fight with a friend, whom Maurer refused to identify. The chief said the host of the party asked Baron to leave at about 11:30 p.m.

Baron apparently left the party on foot but returned a short time later driving his father's car, which, according to Maurer, he did not have permission to drive. Brilliant Patrolman Cloyd Owens attempted to stop Baron after it was apparent he was intoxicated. However, Baron fled from the officer.

Owens chased Baron south through Brilliant to Riddle's Run Road. Baron then led the officer four miles northwest to the intersection of Riddle's Run and State Route 151, where he turned back east toward Brilliant. As they neared Brilliant, Owens said Baron had stretched a substantial lead on the police cruiser. Owens said he was at least a half-mile away when he saw the taillights of the Chevrolet leave the road. By the time Owens reached the spot where Baron went through the barrier to the park, the vehicle had disappeared over the embankment. Owens said he ran to the edge of the cliff in time to see the vehicle's taillights sink beneath the water.

Chief Maurer speculated that a combination of speed, alcohol, and unfamiliarity with the powerful car led to the tragic conclusion of a promising life.

"You've got to wonder what he was thinking," Maurer said as he watched rescue workers drag the river bottom for the body. "Here's a kid, the class salutatorian, with his entire life ahead of him, and he pulls a stunt like this. Now, everyone's memory of graduation isn't going to be of the good times, but this."

Baron also was a member of Brilliant's cross country and track teams and was a district wrestling champion in the 118-pound weight class. He was the only child of Francis and the late Amanda Baron.

The time frame established for telling this story was simple: I would begin the minute I was sure that Francis "Big Frank" Baron was dead. This plan was potentially flawed by the chance, albeit slight, that Big Frank would outlive me, but I liked my odds. Big Frank was twenty-five years my senior and a health insurer's nightmare. He was a hundred pounds overweight, chain-smoked non-filtered Lucky Strike cigarettes, and could take a twelve-pack out of the fridge and polish it off before the last beer got warm. The possibility that he would outlive me was not a concern. My concern was for my own skin. If I wrote the book while he was still breathing, Big Frank Baron would hunt me down and kill me. Simple as that. Given Big Frank's history, this fear was not unfounded. He was a violent man, and I have retained in my memory the vivid image of the day he backhanded his son for the heinous act of asking for three dollars to go to the movies. After Travis had cleaned the blood from his face and the splatter marks from the refrigerator, we sat on the steps of the back porch as he pressed an ice cube wrapped in a bloody dish towel against a split and swollen upper lip. There were still tears in his reddened eyes when he said, "I wish the bastard would die, but he's so mean he'll probably live forever."

He didn't.

On February 16, 1996, just before nine forty-five in the morning, Francis Martino "Big Frank" Baron dropped dead in a snow-covered parking lot at the Shenandoah Truck Stop along Interstate 70 near Old

Washington, Ohio. He had been heading west to Dayton with a load of cardboard when he stopped at the Shenandoah to buy antacids for what the coroner later speculated was an incorrectly self-diagnosed case of indigestion. Frank was north of three hundred pounds and had the dietary discipline of a hungry alligator, so bouts of heartburn and indigestion were not uncommon. But this was anything but indigestion.

He dropped to his knees in a slush puddle in front of his idling Kenworth, a perplexed look consuming his face. His brows converged and his upper lip hitched. Perhaps he was attempting to analyze the eruption within his chest, or perhaps he pondered the possibility that there were, indeed, powers in the universe stronger than pure meanness. Whatever the thought, it was only momentary, for the screen scrambled and quickly went dark. He was dead before his forehead hit the asphalt, the unopened antacids still wrapped in fingers the girth of summer sausages.

An autopsy would later show that he died of a massive coronary.

When I happened upon his obituary in my paper, the *Ohio Valley Morning Journal*, chills raced up my spine like a million needle pricks. The obit was a sanitized accounting of Big Frank's life, a couple of terse paragraphs stating that he had died suddenly and was survived by a brother, Leonard. He was preceded in death by his parents, Dominic and Esther, a brother, Anthony, and a son, Travis. Visiting hours would be held just before services at William's Funeral Home in Brilliant, with interment at New Alexandria Cemetery.

What the obituary did not state was that Frank Baron was a loathsome human being who had ignored his only son and married at least five times. He had divorced three of his wives, one had died in a suspicious car crash on Dago Ridge, and another drowned in a boating accident on the Ohio River.

Maybe.

Her body was never found, leading to wild speculation that she had actually run off with her lover rather than face a lifetime of waking up next to Big Frank. This was the favorite scenario of most residents of Brilliant, as they were anxious to believe that she had escaped his wrath and was alive, happy and far from the Ohio River Valley. His only son died in the river, too, and like his mother's the boy's body was never found. However, that is usually not the kind of information that ends up in a paid obituary, even for someone as despicable as Frank Baron.

There are many people in my hometown who would tell you that the death of Big Frank Baron at age sixty-seven was long overdue. Upon hearing the news of his passing, a goodly portion of these God-fearing Christians chuckled and said, "About damn time." Even my own mother, as charitable and forgiving a person as I've ever known, said, "Well, the son of a bitch is God's problem now."

I wasn't the least bit sorry to see Frank gone, either, although I had long since moved from Brilliant, and it was only on the occasional visit home that I might catch a glimpse of him, or he of me. The last time I saw Big Frank was in Kennedy's Market less than a year before he died. He was standing at the counter buying Lucky Strikes and didn't recognize me at first. When he did, he snapped his head and frowned, a subtle reminder that, despite the passing years, he hadn't forgotten, or forgiven. But his face was sallow, and the tired eyes were red and rheumy and had lost much of their venom. The arms that I remembered as thick and muscled had turned fleshy and weak. He looked to be exactly what he was—an old man whose best days had been lost to time and alcohol. He was no longer the intimidating figure of my youth. It would have been easy to feel sorry for him, but sometimes the years cannot diminish the bitterness, and that was the case with me and Frank Baron. I cannot sit here today and list one redeeming quality about Big Frank. Not one. Therefore, it was impossible to mark his passing with any sense of loss.

Big Frank was the father of the boy who, for the first eighteen years of my life, was my best friend. I have never had as good a friend since, and I doubt I ever will. Hardly a day goes by that I don't think about Travis. I still miss him and the days when we roamed the hills of eastern Ohio. Travis Baron loved living, and he did it with more spirit than any person I've ever known. The obstacles that were hurled in the path of his short life would have completely discouraged others, but they only made him more determined.

The night after Big Frank's obituary appeared in the paper, I went to my basement office and to a locked wooden trunk that was filled with the treasures of my youth—photo albums, my varsity sweater, trophies, old ball caps, scrapbooks, and the like. Hidden in the bottom was a black, hardcover tablet with the word "JOURNAL" embossed across the front in gold block letters. It had been a graduation gift from my grandmother Malone, and it was nearly full with my reminiscences of growing up in the river town of Brilliant, Ohio. The book's spine crackled when I opened it to the scrawled notes about Travis and our adventures, with newspaper clippings neatly pasted into place. I had written everything I could remember about Travis. I didn't want him to fade from my memory.

I made my first entry in the days after the car he was driving disappeared into the Ohio River. It had been twenty-five years since I made my first entry and five years since the last. The book I planned to write—this book—was contained within the pages of the journal. It included my personal memories, plus extensive interviews with Chase Tornik, Clay Carter, and others, which I had conducted on the sly and tucked away, waiting for the day when Big Frank would be no more. The last interview had been with Tornik while he lay dying of lung cancer at Steubenville Presbyterian Medical Center. We spoke for two hours, while he hacked blood into a hand towel and strained for breath. Despite the pain killers, his memory was resplendent, and I felt bad for the life and reputation he had lost.

The journal contained my memories of growing up in Brilliant, a place where being a varsity letterman or an Eagle Scout was still important. From the time I started first grade until the day I graduated, we began each day with the Pledge to the Flag and the Lord's Prayer, and no one ever made a fuss about whether it was constitutionally or politically correct. It was just something you did.

Graduates of Brilliant High School hung their blue and white graduation tassels on their rearview mirrors and left them dangling until they had faded gray. Most Brilliantites had lived there all their lives, and they supported the town. Everyone bought raffle tickets from the Little Leaguers, chocolate peanut clusters from the Scouts, and light bulbs from the Lions Club. On Saturday afternoons in the fall everyone went to the Blue Devils' football games, which held nearly the same magnitude of importance as a baptism.

I miss my hometown and those simpler times. But the Brilliant I grew up in no longer exists. The steel mills up and down the river have folded, and the once-proud communities that lined the Ohio River have been reduced to decaying shells of grander days. I don't get up the river much anymore. As editor and columnist for the *Morning Journal*, most of my working day is spent in the office in Wheeling. My two young daughters seem to gobble up whatever time is left. My parents moved to the Outer Banks of North Carolina a few years ago and, except for an occasional class reunion, there is no reason to go back. But, when I do go visit, I always take the back road by way of Hunter's Ridge.

At the spot where the car left the road, at the entrance to the park, the adult Bible study class from the Brilliant United Methodist Church placed a white cross made of four-by-fours, with the initials "T.F.B."— Travis Franklin Baron—on the crossbar. I helped Jim Gilmartin haul the cross to the park entrance in the back of his International Harvester pickup truck. We took turns working through the rocky earth with a post hole digger to get below the frost line, and dumped a bag of quick-drying cement into the hole, along with water he brought in empty milk jugs. When he was sure the cement was set and the cross true, he asked me to bow my head, and he said a brief prayer, asking God to give Travis a better life in heaven than he'd had on earth. Two days later, I left for college. As the years passed and Travis Baron grew distant in the memories of many, the letters faded, the cross bleached out, and it was eventually claimed by the hillside.

Like the steel mills, Travis is gone. The loss of the mills and my friend only serves to remind me of the fragile state of life, whether it was a hulking, smoke-belching steel mill or an auburn-haired kid with a crooked smile.

CHAPTER TWO

Saturday, June 12, 1971

The Colerain Coal & Gas Company bought the mineral rights to Tarr's Dome in the early 1950s. Within a year, it was a dome no more. The dozers and power shovels stripped it clean, grading flat the crown of the hill, leaving it cratered and looking like the surface of the moon. Over the years, the grass and foxtail returned to the top of the hill. Wild blackberry and locust bushes and assorted other brambles took root and sprouted, followed by some sickly pines and maples that could never get solid purchase in the scarred earth. The craters left behind filled with water, forming a chain of interconnected ponds that stretched across the top of the hill. For reasons that are unknown to me, they were referred to as the Tea Ponds.

The Tea Ponds were shallow and a heavy rain would send water streaming over their banks and down the east face of the hillside. Over the years, the falling waters had created rutted paths that one minute could look like a dried creek bed and the next be home to a torrent that could dump tens of thousands of gallons of water down the backside of Brilliant, filling the air with the pungent smell of sulfur. After the spring thaw or a late summer downpour, the muddy swill would rush down the streets, washing gravel out of parking lots and driveways on its way to the floodplain. The Brilliant Church of Christ was built in the 1920s, three decades before Tarr's Dome was stripped. Now, however, the old stone church had the misfortune of resting on a small plateau between the steepest part of the hill and the floodplain, square in the middle of the water flows. The heavy spring rains annually flooded the basements of the parsonage and church and made a lake of the parking lot.

Such was the case on the Saturday afternoon of the memorial service for Travis Franklin Baron. The gravel parking lot was under six inches of water. Those attending the memorial service were forced to park down the street or in the Miners and Mechanics Bank lot. As the mourners tiptoed across the squishy turf at the back of the property, or danced from one exposed rock to another in the church driveway, three shoeless, bare-chested boys of about ten frolicked in the temporary sea surrounding the church, throwing mud balls at each other, blithely oblivious to the somber mood of those around them. I wanted desperately to join them. I was consumed by the desire to strip off my shirt and shoes and do a running belly flop in the puddles. What a wonderful diversion it would be compared to the simple, yet painful task to which I was duty-bound—attending the memorial service for my best friend. Sitting on the stone wall that sloped downhill from the parsonage toward the bank parking lot, I stared alternately from the playing boys to the water that flowed through the ditch along Campbell Avenue. My world smelled of dead night crawlers and fetid mud. The humidity being pulled from the earth dampened my shirt and salted my upper lip. Unrelenting static filled my ears, and a headache that pounded with each beat of my heart had settled in behind my right eye. I wanted to vomit, hoping that the violent expulsion of the acid and bile that had settled in my throat would somehow cleanse me of the overwhelming sadness and pain that had engulfed me for seven days.

I sat on the uphill end of the wall, nearest the church, with my friends Snookie McGruder, Urb Keltenecker, and Brad Nantz, and my cousin Nick Ducheski, whom everyone called Duke. He wasn't one of the Brilliant gang. He lived in Mingo Junction, our rival community to the north, but Duke, Travis, and I had spent hours together in our youth, and he came to support me.

None of us wanted to go inside, but as the organ began to play, low and soft, we all stood as though controlled by the same puppeteer and started toward the sanctuary.

After three days, the torrential rains had finally quit the morning of the service, though low, slate-colored clouds stretched across the valley, clinging to the hilltops to the west, as though merely granting us a brief respite, a subtle reminder to the valley below that their work was not yet complete.

The doors to the church were brass and every bit of ten feet high. They had been propped open to allow for some circulation in the muggy church, and Mr. Janowicz was ready to close them when he saw us walking up the steps, our shoes all damp from the dance across the gravel drive. He smiled a faint smile and waited until we had passed to pull the doors shut.

Frank Baron was taking up a generous portion of the second pew, sitting next to his brother, Leonard. Big Frank was hunched forward, his elbows resting on his knees, an ill-fitting olive sports coat stretched tight across his back. His pants were black and too short, revealing a pair of white socks and worn black dress shoes. His face was ashen and drawn, battered by nearly a week of little sleep. My natural cynicism made me feel certain he was more distraught over the loss of his beloved Chevy than that of his son. Between his teeth he rolled a toothpick, while nervously twisting a pinkie ring on his left hand. We walked across the back of the church and slipped into one of the last remaining seats, about halfway up and against the wall. But I could not do so without being seen by Big Frank, who had turned to scan the sanctuary.

"Is that his dad up front?" Duke asked.

"Yeah, that's the fat man," I whispered.

"Why is he staring you down?"

"Because I've been ducking him ever since Travis died."

"Why?"

"Because he's a horse's ass, and he has questions that I can't answer."

"Two good reasons," Duke said.

The day after the accident, Frank told Snookie and Urb to tell me that he wanted to talk.

"About what?" I had asked.

"What else? The fight," Urb said. "He cornered us at the Coffee Pot. He said he wanted to know what you and Travis were fighting about before the crash."

"What'd you tell him?"

"I said I didn't know," Urb said.

"Me, too," Snookie added. "I didn't want Big Frank breathing down my neck."

They both had lied. They had been there and knew perfectly well what we had been fighting about.

"I've already explained it to the police and my parents, and I don't want to talk to Big Frank."

"I figured you didn't, but I wasn't going to tell him that," Snookie said. "That guy scares the ba-jeesus outa me."

I didn't like Big Frank Baron. Never had. He had been a miserable father to Travis, who everyone around Brilliant had referred to as "the orphan" because Frank paid him so little attention. Travis had practically raised himself, and his dad was never there for any of the important events in his life. He was not there when Travis won the conference cross country title, or the district wrestling championship, or the Jefferson County Oration Competition, which he won for a critical analysis of John Steinbeck's *Of Mice and Men*. I don't think Big Frank ever made a single parent-teacher conference. He could not be bothered, and I despised him for the years of abuse—a lifetime, as it turned out—he had heaped on Travis. And, frankly, like most other people in town, I was terrified of him, too. You really didn't want to piss off Big Frank Baron.

As I took my seat, I could feel his eyes on me, but I avoided his glare. I looked at the service bulletin and pretended to mutter to Snookie—anything to avoid looking up.

As the organist finished the last strains of *Amazing Grace*, I saw Big Frank turn around in his seat. I took a breath and looked toward the front of the church as Reverend Horvath stood before the congregation and in his booming voice said, "Lord, make me to know mine end, and the measure of my days, what it is; that I may know how frail I am. Psalms. Thirty-nine: four." He smiled faintly. "Let us pray."

The lower sanctuary and the balcony were full. Nearly all of the Brilliant High School class of 1971 was in attendance. Even Margaret Simcox, who had fought with Travis nearly every day for twelve years of school, sat amid our classmates, sobbing. Travis, I thought, would love this. I half expected to look up in the balcony and see him taking it all in, gleeful, his brows arched, that lopsided grin consuming his face.

Reverend Horvath spoke of how only God could make sense of such a tragic death. I wasn't paying much attention. Nothing Reverend Horvath had to say was going to make me feel any better about losing my friend. Ever since the accident, people kept approaching me like I had lost a member of my family. And, in a way, I had. They offered their condolences, but ultimately they wanted to know if I thought our fight had caused Travis to commit suicide. No, I told them. It had been an accident. That's all. The fight had consisted of Travis popping me once in the nose and the two of us falling into a heap in Mrs. Robinson's peonies. Actually, he also gave me a head butt when we hit the ground, but that was all. I didn't even hit him back. In the six days since then, it had grown to a battle of Biblical proportions. I was tired of the questions and tired of the waiting. I just wanted it all to be over. The organ music was a drone in my ears, and Reverend Horvath's words had no penetration. After the final prayer, several adults went up to offer condolences to Big Frank, and Duke and I slipped out.

But once he had me in his sights, Big Frank was not about to let me go. He hurried past those lined up to speak to him and went out the side door, slogging through water in the parking lot that was over his shoes, his belly jiggling out of his dress shirt, and then running down Campbell Avenue after me. We were almost to Third Street when Duke said, "You've got company." I turned to see Big Frank lumbering down the road, and I stood at the corner of Campbell and Third, waiting.

He was sucking for air by the time he got to me. "You been duckin' me, boy," Big Frank said between breaths. "We need to talk."

CHAPTER THREE

I can't remember a time when Travis wasn't around. In my mind's eye, he was always there, a permanently ingrained part of my youth, with a smudged face, a mop of shaggy auburn hair, and a dirty, oversized T-shirt falling off one shoulder and hanging around his knees. He had a glint in his eye that teamed with a lopsided grin as though they were partners in mischief. Travis was a little guy—"puny" or "scrawny" as my dad called him, though my mother preferred "sickly." Mom was forever shoving food at Travis, trying to fatten him up.

"Travis, would you like a sandwich?" she would ask.

"No, thanks," he would respond.

"Sure you do. You know, you wouldn't have that runny nose all the time if you'd put on a little weight," she would say, pressing a fried bologna and cheese sandwich into his hand. Travis always resisted the offer, claiming he wasn't hungry, but he would wolf down the food like he hadn't eaten in days, which, given his home situation, was entirely possible.

My dad watched in amazement as Travis ate lunch one day and said, "That boy eats like he just got out of a concentration camp."

There were times when I don't think Travis left our house for a week. He had the run of the neighborhood, but he seemed to like our house best. To Travis, my family was a caricature from a Norman Rockwell painting. "You guys are like normal people," he often said. "You eat meals at the table and talk to each other without screaming."

Travis was less than a year old when his mother drowned in the boating accident that was the scandal of the century in Brilliant. Big Frank was out on the road in his tractor-trailer, delivering a load of sheet metal in Arkansas, and, according to the most popular version of what occurred that night, she apparently seized the opportunity to take her lover out on Big Frank's cabin cruiser for a late-night rendez-vous. The couple became so impassioned that they forgot to anchor their boat, and it drifted into the path of a coal barge. The horn and spotlights of the towboat pushing a flotilla of eighteen barges appar-ently forewarned them of the impending disaster, and a naked Amanda Baron and her equally naked partner were seen jumping overboard just before the barge made kindling of Big Frank's boat, *Lady Luck*. Common logic stated that both were killed in the accident, but since neither body was ever found a popular theory among romanticists was that the couple was able to swim to shore and disappear. There had been wild speculation around Brilliant ever since as to the identity of the mystery man, and the rumors ranged from the improbable—Big Frank's brother and the mayor—to the impossible—Clark Gable and Dean Martin. Gable had grown up in nearby Hopedale, and Martin, the former Dino Crocetti, was from the south side of Steubenville, but how they became linked to the case was as much a mystery as Amanda Baron's disappearance. For years after the accident there were reports of Amanda Baron sightings in Chicago, Columbus, Nashville, Myrtle Beach, Richmond, and Las Vegas, where she was purportedly working as a showgirl named Iris Jubilee. Residents of Brilliant argued over whether she was dead or alive, and she became a local folk legend, a kind of Amelia Earhart of Brilliant, Ohio. A day after the memorial service for Amanda Baron, Big Frank dropped Travis off at his parents' house, promising to pick him up "later." "Later" turned out to be nine years. Grandma and Grandpa Baron lived just down the alley from us, where they shared an old frame house with their two youngest sons, Crazy Nick, an established lunatic who once killed the neighbor's cat because "it kept looking at me funny," and Tony and his roughneck wife, Trisha, who once sucker-punched the principal and carried the distinc-tion of being the only girl ever expelled from Brilliant High School. Travis's Uncle Tony was found shot to death in an alley in Pittsburgh in 1959. This fueled speculation in Brilliant that it had been Tony on the boat with Amanda, and Big Frank had him rubbed out for his indiscretion. In reality, Tony had been subsidizing his income as a mechanic at McKinstry's Sunoco by running numbers for Staten's Tobacco & News in Steubenville, which was a front for the Antonelli crime family's gambling operations in the Upper Ohio Valley. Apparently, this wasn't quite lucrative enough for Tony, who developed a plan to skim the bets and help himself to a share of the profits. This ill-conceived plan was discovered almost immediately, much to the chagrin of his Sicilian superiors, including the head of the family, Salvatore "Il Tigre" Antonelli. Tony was found with a single .22-caliber bullet wound behind the left ear. From the stories I heard about Antonelli and his normal punishment for those disloyal to him, Tony got off easy.

Travis's Aunt Trisha remarried and had her new husband and stepdaughter move into the house with Travis, Crazy Nick, and her now-former in-laws. This arrangement lasted about a year, until the newlyweds were sent to prison for their part in an insurance scam that involved stealing cars and selling them to chop shops to be cut down for parts. This coincided with the collapse of their marriage. They divorced about the time they were shipped off to prison, leaving Grandma Baron to raise her former daughter-in-law's former stepdaughter. Trisha moved to Arizona after getting out of prison and was killed in a motorcycle accident a few years later. According to the sketchy reports that got back to Brilliant, she was on the back of her boyfriend's Harley when a pickup truck pulled out in front of them at an intersection and she was launched from the bike and into the grill of an oncoming semi.

Grandma Baron died when Travis was nine. She had a stroke while eating a sardine sandwich. Her sister found her slumped over the kitchen table, an orange tabby straddling her forearm and eating the fish from between the slices of bread she still held in her hand. Finally, Travis went back to live with his dad, who by that time was in the process of divorcing wife number two and was passionately involved with the woman who was to be the third Mrs. Frank Baron. From that point on, Travis raised himself. He was the neighborhood waif. The mothers of all his playmates took turns looking out for Travis, making sure he had the essentials—food, school clothes, a winter coat, and shoes without holes in the soles. Since Big Frank had little time for Travis, he became community property, not unlike Primo, the three-legged mutt who lived in our neighborhood and who everyone took turns feeding. If he wasn't planning a marriage, or the subsequent break-up thereof, Big Frank was either on the road with his semi or tinkering with his 1957 Chevrolet Bel Air, a jet black, two-door sports coupe with red leather interior and a 283-cubic-inch V-8 engine, a Ramjet fuel injection system, and a Turbo 350 transmission, a Holley, four-barrel carburetor, dual exhaust, and chrome that was polished to blinding intensity. Big Frank loved that car more than anything on earth, including his own son and any of his various wives—current or ex. The home Travis shared with his father was a dump—a small frame house in the floodplain that was badly in need of paint and repairs. But the cement-block garage behind the house was spotless. Each door was triple-locked and bars covered the windows. Frank had given the Chevy the nickname "The King" because he believed it to be a vehicle without equal, and he referred to the garage as the palace. He never went to the garage to take the Chevy out for a spin. Rather, he went to the palace to take the King out for a spin.

This gave Travis even more of a reason to hate the car. He hated that car the way a scorned wife hates her husband's mistress. Travis didn't even like Big Frank, but he was still envious of the attention his dad gave the Chevy. On many occasions, Travis said, "I'd love to see him total that car," as though removing the Chevy would somehow cure the dysfunctional relationship he had with his father.

Travis craved attention from his father and hoped for just a sliver of the adulation that was heaped upon the car. When he couldn't win Big Frank's acceptance or approval, he would act out just to get the attention. The attention usually consisted of an ugly encounter with the back of one of Big Frank's massive hands. It was all in futility. Travis was never going to get the attention he craved because Big Frank simply couldn't be bothered.

CHAPTER FOUR

Travis and I loved to go down to the Ohio River to bowhunt for carp.

Just south of the power plant, near the warm-water discharge pipes, the carp swarmed like insects, thousands of them. Carp are the cockroaches of the river. They can live on pollution, mud, and feces, which is a fact, because in the 1960s there wasn't much else in the Ohio River. It was an open sewer. The carp flopped around by the pipes, sucking down the warm water and growing to the size of tunas, and we made sport of shooting them with our bows and arrows. Travis equipped the arrows with hunting tips and drilled tiny holes in the shaft, through which we threaded fourteen-pound test line. After sticking a carp, we would pull it to shore, which wasn't always that easy since they were big, hardy rascals and usually quite unhappy about having been run through with an arrow. We called it sport fishing, although it really wasn't much of a sport because there were so many of them that it was virtually impossible to miss. In twenty minutes we would have a stringer of carp that we could barely carry.

Now, I would never think of eating a carp out of that river. Never! However, Turkeyman Melman, who lived up on the hill a few hundred yards past the water tower, would give us five dollars for a stringer of them, and he didn't particularly mind the arrow holes. Turkeyman had a fifty-five-gallon drum that he had converted into a smoker in which he cooked the carp. He was one of Brilliant's most colorful characters. He was a muttering, squatty little man in constant need of a shave and a bath, and he sported perhaps three brown teeth in his head and an enormous tongue that he was always waggling outside his lips, like an eel poking his head out of his hole inspecting the seascape. His given name was Harold, but he was known only as Turkeyman, or Turk, which was short for Turkey Buzzard, a scavenger in nature as Turk Melman was a scavenger at the township dump.

In the days before regulated landfills, Turk "mined" the township dump, which filled the bottom of an old strip mine gully a mile west of town along New Alexandria Road. He had a beater of an old flatbed truck that he drove daily to the dump, where he walked knee-deep in the garbage, hunting for scrap steel, small electric motors, copper, brass, automobile parts, used appliances, and anything that might bring a couple of bucks from the scrap dealers in Steubenville. You could smell Turk long before you saw him, his jeans sagging so that he walked on his pants legs, a railroader's cap pulled close to the brow. The rumor in Brilliant was that over the years Turk had found a small fortune in gold jewelry, which he had melted down into ingots that were hidden somewhere on his property. Some said he had buried them on the hillside behind his house, where he lived alone. In the mid-fifties, someone looking for the gold, or so it was assumed, nearly beat Turk to death. Turk was found on the basement floor of his home in a coma, his skull fractured in several places. He was in the hospital for weeks and could never identify his assailant. When he regained consciousness he would only mutter nonsense, and no one was ever arrested. The beating had permanently damaged his ability to speak. Around Brilliant, they called his jabbering "Turkey Talk," a nearly unintelligible dialect that was interspersed with facial contortions and growls and laughing. Oddly, Travis and I understood Turk. It took years of talking and listening to him, but eventually we could figure him out.

On a hot, muggy June afternoon in 1967, Travis and I walked down the railroad tracks toward the prime fishing spot. I sensed that something was on Travis's mind. He was much quieter than usual, and, since Travis rarely shut up, silence was a good indicator that something was bothering him. "What's got you stewin'?" I finally asked.

"Nothin'."

"Really, you haven't said ten words since we left the house."

He shrugged as we headed down over the embankment and

through a thicket of milkweed and scrub to the river bank. Tiny waves lapped at the shore and a dead catfish bobbled along in the muddy shoals. The air smelled of oil and sulfur, and the acrid exhaust of the power plant stung our eyes. The rocks along the river were covered with the rainbow sheen of petroleum residue.

Travis took the first shot, drawing a bead on a three-footer who made the fatal mistake of lifting his head out of the water. Travis shot him through the head, a rare kill shot, and started pulling him to shore. As he unscrewed the tip of the hunting arrow, which was sticking out of the back of the carp, he looked up and asked, "What do you know about my mother?"

It was a gut punch, and I was totally unprepared. In all the years I had known Travis, never once had he even mentioned his mother. Of course, I had heard all the stories, but his mother's death due to infidelity was not the kind of topic you discuss with your best friend. And, the truth was, I didn't know all that much. I had picked up dribs and drabs of information, a fact here, an overheard comment there, but nothing substantial. I had asked my parents about her, but got very little in return. As a kid, you learn that adults know everything but pretend to know nothing. I cannot speak for other homes in Brilliant, but in the Malone household such matters were answered with as much ambiguity as possible. I was just six years old and sitting down to eat lunch one day when I told my mother, "Sometimes, Travis smells like pee."

"We don't say 'pee,'" she said. "And perhaps you should consider yourself lucky to have a mother who washes your clothes and makes sure you take a bath."

Finding money was lucky; taking a bath was agony, especially if Dad was washing my ears. "Doesn't Travis have a mom?" I asked.

"No, he doesn't," she said.

"What happened to her?"

"Eat your sandwich," she said, pushing the olive loaf and mustard on white bread toward me. She snatched the wicker laundry basket of clothes from the corner of the table and headed for the living room with the unrealistic expectation that the conversation was over.

I slipped off my chair and followed her into the living room. "Why?" I asked.

"Why, what?" she countered.

"Why doesn't Travis have a mom?"

"She died."

"How?"

"She drowned."

My eyes widened. "In the river?"

"Yes. She drowned in the river a long time ago."

"But, how did she?"

"I don't know, Mitchell, she just did. She drowned. And it was a long time ago."

It might have been a long time ago to her, but it was still new information to me, and I wanted more details. "Okay, but . . ."

"No buts, young man," she said. "She drowned, and it was very sad. Don't ever say anything to Travis about it or you'll make him sad, too. Understand?" I said nothing. She looked at me, her brows creeping down on her eyes. "Promise me that you'll never say anything to Travis about it. He might not even know how his mom died. Then wouldn't you feel just terrible?"

She was good at the whole guilt thing. "Okay, I promise."

"Good. Go eat your sandwich."

I was good to my word. I never brought it up. Not once. Now that Travis had started the conversation, I found my stomach clenching. I pretended to be scouting for our next carp, turning away from him and feigning ignorance. "What do you mean?"

"It's not a real difficult question, Mitch," he said, slipping the stringer through the carp's gill. "What have your parents told you about my mom? What have you heard around town?"

I swallowed. "Nothing."

Travis looked up and smiled. "You're lying."

"Well, I heard she drowned."

"Oh, thank you, Sherlock Holmes. What else?"

"Nothing."

Travis exhaled a breath of exasperation. "Mitch, you're still lying."

"No, I'm not."

"Yes, you are. I can tell when you're lying because your Adam's apple rolls up and down like a yo-yo. You're the worst liar ever. Now, what did they tell you? Come on, you're my best friend. I want to know what you know." I took the bow, said nothing, and edged toward the water, taking quick aim at the nearest carp. "Did they tell you that she was out screwin' her boyfriend on the river when she drowned?"

I missed my quarry by ten feet but ran my arrow through two unfortunate onlookers who slapped and churned the water.

"A deuce," Travis said. "Nice shot."

"God Almighty, Travis! Why would you ask me something like that?"

"Because you're supposed to be my best friend, and I figure maybe you'll tell me the truth. Do you think I don't know people around Brilliant still talk about it? I'm just curious." He took the line from my hands. "I'll do this. You just tell me what your parents said."

"My parents never told me anything, and that's the truth. They told me she drowned and I should never bring it up in front of you."

"Okay, so what have you heard other people say?"

I shrugged. "Nothin' much. She was out on Big Frank's boat in the river and they got hit by a barge. Your mom and the guy she was with drowned, but they never found the bodies."

"So how do you know that she drowned for sure?"

"Educated guess? They saw her jump in the river, and no one ever saw her on the streets of Brilliant after that."

Travis grinned as he dragged the fish over the rocks. "Did you hear that the guy she was with was Clark Gable?"

"Yeah, but I heard it was Dean Martin, too."

"What else did you hear?"

"Why don't you ask Big Frank about this?"

Travis rolled his eyes. "Oh, that would be smart—ask the raging Italian about his wife cheating on him. Hell, I didn't even know that she had drowned until I was ten. Ten! Whenever I asked why I didn't have a mom, all Frank or my grandparents would tell me was that she had died. In my mind, I always saw her lying in a hospital bed with some mysterious illness. I was shoveling snow for old Mrs. McClatchey one day and she said something about how bad she felt the day she heard my mother had drowned, so I went along like I knew it all the time. That's how I found out. I picked up things here and there, but I still don't know many details." Travis shot a midsized carp through the tail and dragged him flipping and flopping over the rocks. "Once I asked Big Frank if it was true that Mom had drowned, and he got all wigged out." Travis looked at me and squinted with his left eye. "I mean, he *really* got upset. He grabbed my hair and pulled me a foot off the ground, screaming about wanting to know who told me that."

"What'd you tell him?"

"I just said I heard it around. If I'd have ratted out Mrs. McClatchey, Big Frank might have thrown *her* in the river."

He put the carp on the stringer and dropped it on the bank. "Do you remember when we were in the first grade and had grandparents' day? Most of the kids had all four grandparents come in. It was the first time I realized that I should have *two* sets of grandparents. I felt like an idiot because I didn't know that."

"Do you ever see your mom's parents?"

"No, they died when I was little. I asked my dad about it once and he said they died of broken hearts after my mother died. I asked where they had lived, and all he would say was 'far away.'"

A half-hour later, I took one end of the stringer and Travis hoisted the other, and we started walking toward Community Park, fourteen carp dangling between us, a few still squirming with their last breaths.

"I want you to help me," Travis said.

"Help you what?"

"Find out about my mom, goddammit," he said, annoyed that I was playing stupid when I knew full well what he was talking about.

"What do you want to know?"

"Everything. I was only five months old when she died, so I don't remember anything. Who was she? Where'd she come from? What was she like? Hell, I'm almost fifteen years old and I've never even seen a picture of my mother. I don't have any idea what she looked like. Big Frank got rid of all the pictures." His eyes were starting to rim with tears, so I looked away. "He acts like she never existed. I'm here, her son, but he won't even show me a picture, if he even has one. I understand that she committed adultery, which to an Italian like Big Frank is a mortal sin, but Christ Almighty, if I was married to Big Frank I'd probably be looking for someone else, too. She probably rolled over in bed one day, got a good look at him, and thought, 'What the hell did I do?'"

I laughed.

He asked, "So, what do you say? You going to help me out?"

I didn't have Travis's stomach for breaking rules and defying authority. I knew I was going to end up helping him in his search, because that's what best friends do. Still, it made my stomach do the churn and burn. "So, what's your plan?" I asked.

"I haven't figured that out, yet."

"There's a first."

Travis laughed, and I knew he was glad I was in. "I'll keep you posted."

I nodded and got a better grip on the stringer. "I don't doubt that for one minute."

CHAPTER FIVE

The Vietnam War had been slow to reach Brilliant. The adults were more aware of the conflict and read the "Military Notes" column that appeared each Monday in the Steubenville *Herald-Star* to keep up with the local boys who were fighting. For my part, I knew the basics. We were fighting a war against the North Vietnamese. The North Vietnamese were communist. The communists were inherently evil. It all seemed simple enough to me.

The bloodshed inextricably linked to all wars made its grand entrance into Brilliant on Saturday, January 14, 1967. That was the day the news about Alex Harmon finally reached home. I was only in the eighth grade, but after that day I knew all I had to know about the war. It had nothing to do with stopping the spread of communism. Simply, it had to do with Alex Harmon and why he could no longer walk.

Alex Harmon was the son that every parent in Brilliant wanted— tall, chiseled good looks, athletic, smart. He lived across the alley from me when I was growing up. He was seven years older than me and my idol. In all the world, there was no one quite like Alex Harmon. All I wanted was to be like him. He had broad shoulders, rippling abdominal muscles, and biceps so big that he would let me swing on them like a chin-up bar. In the summer I would walk across the alley and watch him lift weights in his garage. His dad worked at the foundry and had weights special made for Alex. He lifted so much weight that when he worked out on the bench press the bar sagged on the ends. Whenever he took a break, he would strip the bar down to a few weights and push it across the garage floor with his foot. "Come on, champ, let's see you press it." I would struggle and grunt and groan until he finally helped me get it over my head.

I never left for school in the mornings until I saw him come out his back door; then I would sprint out under our grape arbor so I could walk with him as far as the elementary school. I would walk alongside him, proud, trying to emulate his walk, his looks, the way he carried his books. I pestered my mom until she bought me a school jacket that looked similar to his letterman's jacket. It was royal blue, and in white letters across the back was *Brilliant* arching across the top and *Blue Devils* straight across the bottom, with the evil-eyed devil mascot between the lettering. On days of home football games, I would stand near the tunnel where the team came out. His senior year, Alex was the captain and always the first one out of the locker room. He looked like a warrior, with black grease paint under each eye, his white helmet with the blue stripe pulled snug to his brow, and wearing the home whites. And every week, just before he led the team onto the field—and he never forgot—he would wink and point a finger at me like he was shooting a pistol and say, "Whatta ya say, champ?" His senior year in baseball, he hit a home run that went through the woodshop window. I waited for him after the game, and he gave me the ball, which immediately became my most prized possession.

Alex had dozens of scholarship offers, but his dad insisted that he join the military instead. Many of the old mill hands in Brilliant, Alex's dad included, could not see the benefits of an education beyond high school. "Be a Green Beret," his dad had said. "Now that would be something to be proud of. That will take you further than any old piece of paper from some fancy college."

Alex enlisted in the army and was sent to Vietnam soon after completing basic training. I wrote to him regularly, and he sent back a few replies. In the last letter I received, he wrote:

> *Hey Champ:*
>
> *Great to hear from you again. Glad all is going well with baseball. Work on keeping your hands back. The curve balls won't give you as much trouble.*
>
> *Things are okay over here. Well, as well as they can be in a war.*

Keep your grades up and get to college so you don't have to go someplace like this.

   Go get the weights out of my garage and start using them. I wrote a letter to my mom and told her to let you have them. You're old enough to be lifting them by now. I expect you to be playing for the Blue Devils when I get home.

   Be good.

   Your pal,

   Alex

Mom thought I was asleep the morning she heard the news on the Steubenville radio station. She called up to my dad and tried to talk softly, but I still heard her. "They're talking on the news about Alex Harmon. He stepped on a mine and got hurt real bad. He lost both of his legs."

I knew it wasn't a dream. I wished it had been, and I tried to go back to sleep and make it go away. But, of course, it wouldn't. I thought of how his muscular calves used to extend from his football pants and wondered how someone as invincible as Alex Harmon could be without legs. I got dressed and went downstairs. Mom was frying eggs in bacon grease, and the kitchen smelled of fat and coffee and browning bread. She and Dad exchanged looks, thinking that I didn't see. She set a glass of orange juice in front of me and said, "Mitchell, I've got some bad news."

"I heard you tell Dad," I said. I didn't cry, but I wanted to. It was summer before they could bring Alex home. When they did, the American Legion held a parade in his honor. It was a fine day for a parade. The sun was high and the sky unusually clear for the Ohio Valley. It seemed that nearly everyone in town had lined the parade route to welcome Alex home and salute him for his efforts. I was standing outside our house at the corner of Second Street and Ohio Avenue when the police car and the American Legion honor guard rounded Clark's Corner. I thought my legs would buckle. I was taking short, staccato breaths to keep from crying. My mom stood with Mrs. Winston and Mrs. Jermaine, and I tried to hide behind them. Mom asked me several times why I wasn't acting very excited to see Alex. It was because I was terrified, but for some reason she didn't understand that. She thought that I should be happy he was alive and that I was getting to see him again. She thought the mere fact that Alex had returned home breathing was reason to celebrate. "He's lucky he's alive," she said.

I was betting that Alex didn't think he was so lucky. Here was this magnificent specimen of a man, a standout athlete, who would never again walk on his own legs. Hell, no, he wasn't lucky.

Behind the police car was the high school marching band, which was playing *Stars and Stripes Forever.* After the band, the hood of Myron Baughman's white Cadillac convertible appeared from behind the trunk of the elm on the Clark property. Red, white, and blue crepe paper adorned the car. A cardboard sign on each front door proclaimed:

Alex Harmon
American Hero

I stood behind my mother and saw Alex a full minute before he saw me. I tried unsuccessfully to blink away the tears that rolled down both cheeks, and I swiped them with my shirt sleeves. He looked so thin and pale. He was alone in the back seat, and it looked as though it was taking all his strength just to sit up. I wanted to run. I couldn't. I couldn't even move. When Alex saw me, his face lit up. He told Myron to stop. He smiled and waved me out to the car. "Go on," my mom said, pushing my back. "He wants to see you." I took a couple quick breaths, made a final swipe at my tears, and walked to the car, watching my shoes until I could feel the enamel of the back door with my hand.

"Whatta ya say, champ. Jeez, it's good to see you." He put his left hand down for support, then reached out and shook my hand.

I started crying again and this time made no effort to hide the tears. "Good to see you, too, Alex," I said between sobs and sucks of air. I looked down to where his legs should have been. They were gone below the knees. Whatever was left was covered with the light blue blanket with silk trim. I shouldn't have looked, but I couldn't help myself. It was as if I wouldn't believe it until I saw for myself.

"Thanks for all the letters," he said. "They really helped."

"You're welcome." It was the best I could muster.

There was now some considerable distance between the band and the convertible. "Did you get those weights out of my garage?" I nodded. "Are you lifting them?"

Again, I nodded. "A little." It was a lie, but I didn't want to disappoint him.

"Get on them. As soon as I get used to the artificial legs they got for me, I want to come watch you play. Got it?"

"Sure." I stepped back from the car, realizing Mr. Baughman was getting impatient.

Alex leaned toward me and said, "Don't worry about me, champ. I'm going to be just fine. I promise."

I was still crying as Myron pulled away. When Alex was far enough down the street that he could no longer see me, I went into the house and cried some more.

I slouched on the couch in our TV room, staring at a fishing show that didn't interest me in the least. I couldn't get past thinking how unfair it was. The drapes were pulled and the room was dark except for the dancing light from the screen. I was at peace with my misery, content to allow time to slowly wear away at the memory of a crippled Alex Harmon.

My solitude, however, was short-lived, interrupted by the familiar sound of the feet of Travis Baron across our back porch. Travis had a distinctive pattern of approach, always entering the porch deck by leaping over the stairs, which was followed by two quick footfalls as he slowed before the door. I yelled for him to come in before he could knock. He cut through the kitchen and stopped at the entry of the TV room, giving his eyes a chance to adapt to the darkness. "What's this, Dracula's castle? You all right?" he asked, mostly feeling his way to my dad's recliner.

"Yeah. Fine."

"Pretty rough seeing Alex like that, huh?"

"It just doesn't seem possible."

We sat a few minutes watching the television. It took him that long to get to the point of his visit. "How about riding out to the cemetery with me?" he asked.

"You have an odd way of trying to cheer someone up," I said, keeping my eyes on the television screen.

"I want to go find my mom's grave. I've never seen it."

"There's a reason for that, Travis. They never found her body. She doesn't have a grave."

"Well, right. But they put up some kind of memorial or monument to her at the New Alexandria Cemetery. I want to see if I can find it."

"How do you know that?"

"I found a little newspaper article about it in my Grandma Baron's Bible. It was in a box of stuff down in our basement." He turned on the lamp on the end table and stood, pulling his wallet from his hip pocket. He pried it open with a thumb and carefully removed a yellowing, one-column newspaper clipping.

Baron Memorial to Be Dedicated

A memorial garden in memory of Amanda Baron, the Brilliant woman who was killed in October 1953 during a boating accident, will be dedicated at the New Alexandria Cemetery at 1 p.m. Saturday.

Although her body was never found, Mrs. Baron is believed to have drowned after her boat was rammed by a coal barge.

The garden is being sponsored by the Brilliant Church of Christ, where Mrs. Baron was a member. The service is open to the public.

"No mention of that messy adultery thing," Travis said.

I grinned. I had wanted to sit and sulk away the rest of the day, but the worst of moods should not keep someone from helping their best friend locate a monument to his dead mother. I said, "You know, that place is huge, and there are thousands of graves out there. How do you propose to find it, just walk around until we spot it?"

"There's usually a map of the graves at the caretaker's place. It'll show us where it is."

"How do you know this stuff?"

"Television, man."

I nodded. "Let's go." Travis didn't really need help finding the memorial. He just didn't want to be alone when he got there.

Big Frank was out of town, heading for Fort Wayne with a load of cat food. It was a good time to go, since Travis was keeping his research a secret. We rode our bicycles to the New Alexandria Cemetery, which was six miles beyond Tarr's Dome off of State Route 151 on a hillside that was once the location of a mining town. The caretaker's home was located at the bottom of the hill, just inside the stone pillars that marked the entrance to the graveyard. No one was home when we got there, but a black notebook containing the plot maps was chained to a table on the front porch. It was cross-referenced in the back and contained the names of four members of the Baron family—Travis's grandparents, his Uncle Tony, and Amanda, whose monument was not located anywhere near the other three.

"They didn't put the memorial with the rest of the family," Travis said, noting that the family plot was clear across the cemetery, two hillsides away from his mother's monument. "Section fourteen, row twelve," he said. He took a minute to find the plot location on the map. "Here it is. It's way back in the corner." We followed the rutted gravel road over the most distant hill. Once over the knoll, the road took a precipitous drop, ending at a nameless stream that rimmed the cemetery to the east. In the northeasternmost corner of the cemetery, isolated by the knoll from the rest of the graves, in an area shaded by poplars, oaks, and maple trees, and covered with a thick blanket of grass, was a semi-circle of four granite benches on which was inscribed: GOD, FAMILY, LOVE, and TRUST. In the middle of the benches was a three-by-four-foot slab of polished granite, on which were the words:

IN LOVING MEMORY
OF AMANDA VIRDON BARON
BORN: April 15, 1931
INTO GOD'S HANDS: October 2, 1953
The Voice and the Heart of an Angel
Dedicated August 19, 1955

I stayed several steps behind as Travis knelt at the stone and ran his fingers over the letters of her name. "You didn't know this was here?" I asked.

"No idea."

He sat down in the grass next to the stone, his left leg tucked under his rear, and continued to trace the letters. "I wonder who cuts the grass," he said.

"The caretaker," I said.

"Yeah, but what about around the stone and the benches? This has been trimmed. Those other ones haven't been trimmed."

I looked beyond the knoll to tombstones that had tall grass creeping up around them, some of which was so high it covered the names of the deceased. "Probably members of the church. They do stuff like that."

Travis nodded. "Prob'ly." He got up and looked around, then walked toward the stream to a mound of grass trimmings, weeds, and branches that someone had gathered and piled neatly at the water's edge. "Kind of nice down here, huh? Real peaceful."

I concurred. Travis kicked around at the pile of trimmings, then jerked his head up and scanned the area, like a nervous camper that had just heard a noise in the night. He asked, "This little garden is the only spot in this part of the cemetery that's been maintained, isn't it?"

"Looks like it," I said.

"Then these trimmings had to come from around my mom's monument."

"Yeah. So?"

Travis reached into the pile and pulled out a withered bouquet of daisies and lilies. "Then who left these?"

CHAPTER SIX

In that fall of 1967, I was a freshman and an expendable member of a very poor varsity football team. The days of Alex Harmon, when the Blue Devils had been the class of the Big Valley Athletic Conference, seemed a lifetime past. During summer two-a-day practices, I was relegated to the unit that was fondly referred to by one of two endearing terms, "cannon fodder" or "scrimmage bait," which meant we were draped in gaudy yellow vests, designating us as the opponent, and used as sacrificial lambs against the first string. On this particular day, a torrid August afternoon where the meager breeze served only to lift dust from the practice field to our nostrils, the defensive middle guard on our cannon fodder squad had been taking a tremendous beating and decided to suddenly become ill with a mysterious stomach virus, and I was recruited from my defensive back position to middle guard—all burly 117 pounds of me. Our center was Rex Tate, who wasn't all that good—like most of our team—but he outweighed me by 110 pounds. Thus, I continued to spend the rest of the afternoon in the defensive backfield because that's where he kept knocking me, much to the delight of the coaches. It made for a miserable day.

It had been several hours since practice ended, and I was resting on the back porch swing, nursing an orange juice, a bruised body, and a badly battered ego, when I saw Travis heading down the alley toward the house.

"Jeeesus, what happened to you?" he asked.

"Oh, I spent a couple of hours this afternoon being Rex Tate's personal punching bag."

"Looks like he had a good day."

I turned my head, slowly and painfully, toward Travis and nodded. "I think he rather enjoyed it, yes."

"I've got some good news," Travis said, taking a seat on the porch deck, resting his back against one of the wooden supports. "I've come up with a plan."

"A plan?" I sipped my juice and frowned. "A plan for what?"

Travis's mouth dropped. "My plan, you know, my plan for . . ." Travis twice arched his brows.

It had been several months since our carp shoot and a month since our trip to the cemetery, and I had temporarily forgotten about his latest project, which he had named Operation Amanda. "Sorry, Trav. I forgot. Your plan, what is it?"

Travis leaned forward and motioned for me to do the same, which took no small effort as I was bruised from my shoulders to my kidneys. He whispered, "I remember a long time ago, Big Frank sent me up to the attic to get something. He's gotten so fat he can't get up there anymore. Anyway, I remember that Frank's got all these old boxes full of junk up there. I'll bet there's something in there that would tell me about her."

"That's it? That's your big plan? Sneak up to your own attic?"

"It's not as simple as it sounds," Travis said, annoyed at my response. "The only way to get up there is through an access panel in the closet ceiling in Frank's bedroom, and the attic isn't finished. It's just a bunch of rafters with a couple of boards across them to stand on, and it's like walking in a cave, darker than hell. I'm going to need some help."

"Uh-huh, and you want me to climb up there with you?"

"You said you would help."

"Have you lost your marbles? I said I'd help, but I didn't know that meant sneaking into Big Frank's bedroom! You neglected to tell me that little fact." My blustering made my stomach and chest ache.

"Well, at the time I didn't know that, either. I just thought of this the other day. Come on, man, be a buddy. You said you were going to ask your mom about it for me, and I'll bet you forgot that, too."

"Ask his mother what?" my mom chimed in, having just stepped onto the porch after picking a basket of grapes from the arbor at the back of our house.

"Oh, ah, Travis wants to know if I can go camping with him Saturday night. Is that okay?"

My mother squinted and said, "You know, dear, your Adam's apple jiggles something terrible when you lie." She turned to Travis. "What was he supposed to ask me about, Travis?"

"I wanted him to ask you if you knew anything about how my mom died."

There was a moment of awkward silence, and I could tell by the way her face had puckered up that she was wishing she had just answered the camping question. I smirked.

"Why, she drowned in the river, sweetheart."

"I know that, Mrs. Malone, but how? She was out on a boat with her boyfriend? Do you know who he was?"

As the red flush consumed my mother's neck, she looked away from Travis and started toward the back door. "I think that's something that you'd better just talk to your father about," she said, disappearing into the kitchen.

Travis looked at me and shrugged. "See what I mean? No one wants to talk about it. It's like everyone in this town is trying to keep a big secret from me."

The implication was obvious. "Trav, I don't know anything. Honest. If I did, I'd tell you. And, against my better judgment, I'll help you look through the attic. When do you want to do this bit of exploration?"

"I don't know yet. Soon. The next time Big Frank's out of town."

I snorted a burst of laughter that sent daggers though my chest. "When Big Frank's out of town? Padnah, that's a given if you want my help." I looked over to make sure my mom wasn't listening through the screen door. "Just out of curiosity, what do you think Big Frank would do if he found out you were snooping around in his attic looking for information about your mom?"

Travis shrugged, a sign that he was well aware of the ramifications but preferred not to think about them, or at least discuss them with me. For all his bravado, I knew Travis was terrified of Big Frank. A year earlier, we were watching a war movie at his place when Big Frank was on a road trip. The soldier on the screen was making his way through a mine field, feeling his way through the sandy earth with his toes, trying to get to his injured buddy. It was a very tense scene, and when it was over Travis said, "That's exactly what it's like living here with Big Frank. You creep along, trying to be quiet, trying to be careful, trying to stay hidden because you never know when you're going to trigger one of the mines. Remember when I asked for the money to go to the show and he backhanded me?"

"Vividly," I said.

We were twelve and wanted to take the bus to Steubenville to see the movie *The Dirty Dozen*. I had permission and my three dollars. We needed only to secure three dollars for Travis. Permission was not a problem, as Big Frank wouldn't have cared if Travis hopped on a rocket to the moon. As we stepped onto the back porch, I could see his massive outline through the gray mesh of the screen door. He was sitting at the table, his belly stretching the seams of a sleeveless undershirt, his forearms resting on the table's white baked enamel surface. It was barely one p.m., but standing at attention before him was an amber phalanx of empty Pabst Blue Ribbon longnecks, the bottoms of which were full of soggy ashes and butts.

"Dad, can I have three dollars to go to the show?"

"Three bucks, huh?"

Big Frank turned in his chair and stood, wobbled, and grabbed hold of the table for balance. A smoldering cigarette dangled from the right side of his mouth. The eye above the smoke was closed and his face crinkled. "Three bucks, you want?"

Travis nodded. "Yes, please."

Frank pulled his wallet from his hip pocket and opened it. It was empty. "See any money in there?" Frank asked.

"No, sir," Travis responded.

Never in my short life had I seen anything as fast as the backhand that lashed out and raked Travis across the mouth. It was a cobra strike.

His little head whipped back and blood and spittle flew from his mouth and splattered in a bright, upward spray of little dots on the side of the refrigerator. "You want money? Go fuckin' earn it." Big Frank then turned to me, his eyes dark, malignant. A minute earlier I had been an innocent twelve-year-old excited about going to the movies with my best buddy. In the instant that flesh struck flesh, I became a voyeur in the home of Big Frank Baron and the world in which Travis lived.

"Did your mommy give you money for the movies?" he snarled at me. I nodded. "That figures." And he staggered down the hall.

Travis slipped off the edge of the porch, snapped a bunch a grapes from the vine, and sat down next to me on the swing. "It's like that all the time. Not as bad, usually, but you never know when he's going to explode. If I say the wrong thing, look at him wrong, anything, he goes off. Sometimes he just screams or whacks me up along the back of the head. Sometimes he busts me. You know why?"

I nodded. "Yeah, because he's a mean prick."

"Well, that, too. But you know what I think really gets him? I'm smarter than him, and he resents it. I'll never let him wear me down. Never. I put my grade card on the table every time I get it—straight As. I know he looks at it, but do you think he'd ever say anything? Not a word. Not one word. He'll sign it, but he has never once said, 'Good job.'"

I continued to rock on the swing, pushing against the wooden deck, listening to the ache of the springs and watching the cars pass along Ohio Avenue. "So you don't know when this little expedition is taking place?" I asked.

"I'll let you know," he got up, stretched. "Get ready for Operation Amanda—Phase One. But listen, buddy, you can't tell anyone."

I stood up, having decided to try to soak away some of the soreness in a hot tub. "Oh yeah, I've got this death wish, so I'm going to blab it all over Brilliant that I'm going over to Big Frank Baron's house to sneak through his attic."

The touchdown came in the waning minutes of the fourth quarter. Our fullback slid off tackle, bounced off their third-string outside linebacker, spun, and stumbled two yards into the end zone. The crowd on the Brilliant side of the field erupted.

The touchdown made the score 62–6 in favor of the Warren Consolidated Ramblers. The reason the Brilliant faithful were making such a fuss over a late-game touchdown against the Ramblers' third-team defense was because it was our first score of the year. In the first three games, we had been summarily thrashed by a total score of 142–0. So despite the fact that we were about to go oh-and-four for the third straight season, there was considerable excitement over the fact that we had scored.

The positive aspect to this otherwise pitiable season was that Coach Haines had gotten so disgusted with the team, the upperclassmen specifically, that the freshmen were actually getting some playing time. We were no better at stopping the other teams or scoring than the upperclassmen, but we weren't any worse, and we were young, so at least we had an excuse. The games were miserable and the practices worse, but I was secretly delighted over the fact that I would earn a varsity letter as a freshman.

Because we played Saturday afternoons, my aunts, uncles, and cousins would all come to the games. Afterward, we all met at our house for my mother's Reuben sandwiches and potato salad. My cousins were stellar athletes, and I had never been their equal. Johnny was a running back for the Steubenville Big Red, and Duke was a quarterback for the Mingo Indians, both of which had respectable football programs.

We were sitting on the family room couch with paper plates piled high with food while the adults enjoyed their food and beer in the kitchen. "You guys need some work," Duke said.

"I know," I said.

"You guys suck," Johnny said. "I don't care how hard you work, you suck."

Duke choked back a grin.

"You should try not to sugarcoat everything that comes out of your mouth, Johnny," I said.

"I'm just sayin', you guys are really bad."

"I played in the game, Johnny," I said. "I know how bad we are."

He shrugged and stuffed half a sandwich in his mouth.

The beer flowed, and it was nearly one in the morning before everyone cleared out and I staggered upstairs to bed. The phone rang at eight o'clock Sunday morning. Mom, who had been up for three hours by this point, called up the stairs, "Mitchell, it's Travis." I went downstairs in my underwear and took the phone. "Yeah?"

"All systems are go for Operation Amanda. The Big Bad Wolf is leaving town at noon."

It took several seconds for the message to penetrate my morning fog. "Where's he going?"

"I didn't ask to see his bill of lading, for cryin' out loud. He said he was going on an overnight. Come on down about twelve-thirty."

"Okay, but if . . ."

The phone went dead.

Travis lived two blocks away in a small, two-story house, squeezed hard between the Pennsylvania Railroad tracks and the Ohio River, and across the street from the Tip-Top Bread bakery. When the river flooded, it consumed the first floor of his house. When a freight train passed, the entire house shook. The aroma from the baking bread was the only redeeming quality of the patchwork neighborhood of old homes and house trailers. When I arrived, the tractor-trailer—a red Kenworth cab with Big Frank's CB handle, The Big Bad Wolf, painted on the doors and a sinister cartoon wolf huffing and puffing and blowing a house of sticks onto the fenders—was gone from its gravel pad behind the house. Travis was waiting at the door and pushed it open when I hit the front steps. "Is he gone?" I asked, keeping my voice low.

"Yeah, left about a half-hour ago, thank you Jesus. He was in a swell mood all morning. Come on in."

I stepped over a maze of dirty clothes and newspapers that were strewn across the living room. The only time the Baron house got cleaned, Travis said, was when Frank was on the prowl for a new girl-friend. The house had been neglected for years and was now more in need of a wrecking ball than a coat of paint. The fly ash from the power plant had stripped the paint down to the wood, giving the siding the weathered, gray look of a house that sits along the seashore and is pounded by salt and sand. The wooden pillars on the front porch had rotted at the base, and the roof sagged in the middle. It was one good snowfall from total collapse, and I hurried through the front door, just in case it decided not to wait on winter.

I followed Travis up the narrow staircase and down the short hall to Big Frank's bedroom in the back of the house, where the lone window overlooked his precious garage. A stepladder had been placed in the opening of the closet door, and the plywood hatch at the top of the closet had been slid to one side. "You go up first," Travis said. "I'll give you a boost. Then you help me up."

Simply thinking about climbing up into Big Frank's attic was ter-rifying, but at the same time strangely exciting. It was a bit like trying to get our baseball out of old lady Tallerico's yard while it was being patrolled by her formidable German shepherd, Minnie Fay. One kid would go to the far corner and distract the beast, while another—we took turns—hopped the fence and dashed for the ball. Then it was a dead run-like-your-hair-was-on-fire sprint to the fence, followed by an angry head full of teeth, slobber, and attitude. If Minnie Fay or Big Frank caught us where we should not be, the results were likely to be the same. From the stepladder, I jumped up and grabbed hold of the wooden rim around the hatch and pulled myself up to my elbows, then waited for Travis to put his shoulders under my dangling feet and boost me the rest of the way. Once I had my feet on the rafters, Travis handed up two flashlights, then raised his hands for me to take hold. Straddling the hatch, I squatted down and pulled Travis up through the opening. For extra leverage, he put a foot on the clothes bar and pushed off. It sagged and creaked but blessedly did not break.

The beam of my light scanned the attic. It had a low peak, with several one-by-eight planks lying haphazardly across the rafters to walk on. It smelled musty, and faintly of dust and old newspapers. Cardboard boxes of junk lay scattered around. One box, which had split at the corner, was full of hard-core porno magazines that had spilled into the insulation. I shined my light over the magazines. "Big Frank has quite an extensive library," I said.

"Yeah, he's a connoisseur of fine literature," Travis countered, balancing himself on the rafters and making his way to the furthest stack of boxes. Travis began sorting through the boxes, which mostly contained the accumulated junk of three failed marriages. One entire box was dedicated to legal documents from Big Frank's previous divorces. There were several boxes of Christmas ornaments, old clothes, and the miscellaneous junk that you would find in any attic. Just a few minutes into the venture, sweat was rolling down my cheeks. We picked through the heaps of boxes and dust, none of which contained a single item relating to Travis's mother. We had scavenged nearly the entire attic when he moved a box containing old car magazines and revealed a large clothing box jammed between two rafters and resting atop the insulation. It had a plastic handle, was big enough to hold a woman's coat, and had come from the Hub Department Store in Steubenville. It was yellowed with age and creased in the middle where a piece of twine was cinched tight. Travis dug his hand deep into the insulation and, as though he suspected the box contained the treasure he was seeking, gently lifted it out of its resting place. He worked the knotted twine down the sides of the box, allowing it to breathe for the first time in many years.

Travis pulled the lid from the box and for several moments shined his light on its contents. Lying in the box was a red leather book, the gold embossed word *Diary* barely recognizable across the top. There was a stack of yellowed envelopes bound by a brittle rubber band, three high school yearbooks, two thick scrapbooks, a white letter sweater with three maroon stripes on one sleeve and a maroon, chenille "N" over one pocket, a variety of other papers and treasures of youth, and a cigar-box-sized wooden chest with tarnished brass fittings. Travis lifted the diary from the box and opened it to the middle. The pages were yellowed at the corners and full of a light blue, blotchy script that had been put down with a fountain pen. Photographs and newspaper clippings were scattered throughout the diary like so many bookmarks. "This was my mom's," Travis said. "This was her diary." He flipped back to the front page. There was a black line under the words *Property Of*, on which was written in the same blue ink script, *Amanda Virdon*. He began reading silently, and I felt like a voyeur, as though I was looking into the window of a very private part of his life. When he picked up the envelopes, the rubber band crumbled into the box. He thumbed through the bundle like a young boy with a new pack of baseball cards. He opened one and gently unfolded the two pages inside, cradling it with the care usually reserved for ancient scrolls. "They're all from her father," Travis said.

"How do you know?"

"This one's from him and all the others have the same return address." He read aloud: *"I hope you have truly found happiness. Even a good marriage is sometimes difficult to make work. There will be tough times, but you are my flesh and blood, and strong. You can make it work. I wish you much happiness, my darling daughter."*

He slid the letters back into the box. "Kinda personal. I think I'll read this stuff later," he said, pulling the wooden chest from the box. There was a tiny bar on a brass chain holding the front clasp together. The box was full of trinkets and mementos from Amanda Virdon's adolescence—a class ring, a locket, several medals on faded strands of ribbon, a fountain pen, a graduation tassel, and several wallet-sized, black-and-white photos. There were three identical head-and-shoulder photos of a dark-haired woman in a white graduation gown, her head tilted up slightly and to the side. Soft brown curls dangled against her naked shoulders.

"That's my mom," he said, barely audible. In the faint light I could see tears welling in both eyes. "I never even knew what she looked like 'til just now." He held the flashlight's beam on the photo for several minutes, drinking in the image that was, in part, a large piece of the mystery. "She was pretty, wasn't she?"

"Are you kidding me? She was beautiful."

He shook his head. "Makes you wonder what the hell she was thinking when she married Big Frank."

"My dad always says that there's no accounting for taste."

Travis reached back into the box and pulled out another photo—a curled, black-and-white Polaroid of the same woman standing on the beach, resting her head on the shoulder of a young man with thick black hair, a wide smile, and washboard abdominal muscles that looked like they were chiseled out of stone. "Look at this." Travis said, passing me the photo.

"She was a beauty, Trav. She should have married that guy."

Travis smiled as he took back the photo. "She did."

I reclaimed the photo for a closer examination. The Big Frank Baron I knew rarely smiled. He was balding and had a belly so large that the slightest physical activity caused him to suck for air and gurgle deep in his throat. "That's Big Frank?"

Travis nodded.

"Holy smoke. What the hell happened to him?"

"I don't know. Somewhere along the line he decided that fat and insufferable was preferable to trim and happy."

For several more moments, he squatted on the rafters, the image of his mother disappearing with the fading beam of his light. I was happy for Travis. He had found the first clue in his quest. The letters and the diary would, I hoped, supply some of the answers he sought.

I only wished he could have enjoyed the moment longer; unfortunately, the silence was broken by the unmistakable grind of the downshifting of Big Frank's Kenworth as he pulled it onto the gravel at the back of the property. For a moment we stared at each other, frozen, praying the grind was a figment of our collective imaginations. Then, our collective imaginations heard the air brakes release. "Jesus, Mary, and Joseph. It's Big Frank," Travis yelped, walking a rafter like a tightrope to the opening. "He'll kill me if he catches us up here."

"You said he was going out of town," I yelled in a whisper.

"Well, that's what he said. I don't know why he's back. Quick, help me down."

I snagged Travis's wrists and helped lower him through the opening. I started to follow. "No. Christ, I'm not supposed to have anyone in the house. Stay up there 'til he leaves. He probably just forgot something and will be gone in a minute."

There was no time to argue. I slid the plywood cover over the hatch and listened as Travis shoved the stepladder under the bed and slammed the closet door. With the last of the dwindling light from my flashlight, I maneuvered away from the hatch and stood straddling two rafters. When my light faded, I was left in darkness, with only slivers of faint light filtering through the vent at the rear of the house. The front door slammed and I strained to hear the conversation between Big Frank and Travis. Unfortunately, the conversation was becoming clearer by the second. The steps groaned as Big Frank started upstairs. His shipment hadn't been ready and wouldn't be ready until later in the afternoon.

It is astounding how still and quiet one can be when one thinks that the slightest move might result in immediate death. I could hear them talking and walking into the bedroom, following each creak of the floorboards, when I clearly heard Big Frank say, "I'm going to sack out for a while, so don't be makin' a bunch of goddamn noise."

It had been a good life, I suppose, for someone who had yet to see his fifteenth birthday. Besides never having had sex or gotten drunk, I don't know that I missed all that much, although sex is obviously a big thing to die without, I would think. It was, however, too late to remedy that, as I figured my death was imminent. After all, I was straddling the rafters over the bed of a napping Frank Baron. Big, mean, paranoid, hateful, sleep-with-a-.45-caliber-semiautomatic-pistol-on-his-nightstand Frank Baron.

I did the only thing I could do in such a situation, which was nothing. I straddled the rafters and looked straight ahead, concentrating on breathing through my nose and staring at the ventilation grate on the far wall. I remembered reading about prisoners of war who helped save their sanity and pass the time by building houses, brick-by-brick, in their minds. I tried that, but it failed. I didn't know how to build a house, and I couldn't get past the first few bricks before the mental image of rotund Frank Baron snoring in his boxer shorts crept back into my mind. If sheer fear wasn't bad enough, I was suddenly suffering from sensory overload. Parts of my body that had never itched in my life were screaming to be scratched. My bladder, I was sure, was close to rupture. And I wanted to sneeze, fart, cough, and belch. I was fighting the release of a bodily function cacophony that would literally shake the rafters. Scattered at my feet were Big Frank's porn magazines. I stared at them and became semi-erect, creating additional angst.

Adding to this misery was the fact that it was a hot day for early October, and the sun was heating the attic to a broil. Every pore in my face was leaking, causing little droplets of sweat to boil up on my skin until they began a maddening roll down my face, dropping in succession from my nose and chin, or rolling down my neck in a ticklish torture. Soon my shirt was soaked and flush against my chest. My jeans had a ring of sweat several inches past my waist. What sweat didn't drip off eventually ran down my legs and into my tennis shoes, which I was sure would squish if I ever got the chance to walk again.

My legs began to cramp above the knees. The calves followed suit. I couldn't move to rub them for fear of making the rafters creak and causing Big Frank to send three or four salvos into the ceiling. Eventually, the cramps subsided, but I could no longer control my bladder. It is miserable and humiliating to piss your pants when you are nearly fifteen years old, but it was such a relief that I was willing to ignore the shame. My jeans, shorts, socks and tennis shoes were now soaked, and the stench of urine was added to that of must and dust.

I prayed to God to get me out of Big Frank's house alive. And I made a solemn vow that if he allowed me to escape, to live and again breathe fresh air, I would repay his gracious and divine intervention by strangling my best friend Travis.

Then my mouth and nostrils were dry and my legs were starting to spasm. Below me, Frank was farting in his sleep. I was getting woozy, like you do when you stand up too quick, but I couldn't shake the feeling and I was forced to hold on to the crossbeam, resting my head in the crease of my elbow. I hoped that if I lost consciousness and fell through the ceiling that I'd land directly on Big Frank and render him unconscious just long enough to get out of the house.

I didn't know if I had been in the attic four hours or four days when Big Frank finally awoke. I think I had actually dozed for a while, or possibly passed out. Either that or I was loopy from dehydration. However long it had been, it was apparently longer than Big Frank had wanted to sleep. I heard the bed springs squeak and him say, "Oh, shit." This was followed by both heavy footfalls and profanity. "Why did you let me sleep so long, goddammit," he yelled at Travis as he ran down the steps. I heard the toilet flush and the back door slam. It was another minute before the truck pulled away, and several more before Travis pushed open the attic door and the beam of his light entered the attic.

"I hope you're not going to hold me personally responsible for that," Travis said.

"Just who else would I hold personally responsible?" I yelled. "This was all your idea, remember?"

"Jesus, Mitch, I'm sorry. I didn't know he was coming back. He said he . . ." Travis shined his light over me. "Man, you look awful. Did you piss yourself or something?"

Travis struggled to get up through the hatch but seemed to know better than to ask for my help. I lowered myself to one of the one-by-eights and sat, massaging my thighs and calves while Travis gathered up the box of treasures he had found. "Come on," he said, slapping at my shoulder. "You can jump in the shower, and I'll throw your clothes in the washer. Then we've got to hide this stuff."

"You better leave it up here," I said, struggling to get back to my feet. "If Big Frank catches you with it, you're dead meat."

"He'll never find it. I know the perfect hiding place."

I started to ease myself down the hatch. "Where's that?"

"Your house."

CHAPTER SEVEN

In the months that passed after my near-death experience in Big Frank's attic, my perspective on the entire ordeal changed. Rather than viewing it for what it had actually been—another insane situation into which I had allowed Travis to con me—I began seeing it as the ultimate test of my manhood. And I had indeed passed. I was a gladiator, a fearless warrior whose incredible courage had enabled him to return home after a great battle. I had been tested, and in my mind's eye I was better for the experience. It was amusing that I viewed myself as some kind of stouthearted war hero—Sir Mitchell the Bold—when, of course, I had been scared totally witless.

The collection of literature and baubles that we had mined in the attic were keeping Travis busy, so he was not causing me much discomfort with Operation Amanda. For a while, I assumed that he had learned all that he wanted about his mother. He had located a photo, her diary, and newspaper clippings. This, of course, was not going to settle the mystery of her death, but I believed that was beyond our reach.

Travis made regular trips to the cemetery to visit the memorial garden erected in his mom's memory, dragging me along with him more often than not. At least once a month we would find fresh flowers placed within the semicircle of granite benches or lying on the inscribed stone. During a Saturday morning visit in December we found the snow had been brushed from the stone and a pair of men's boot prints led to and from the grave. It had stopped snowing at eight o'clock the previous night, so whoever had visited the grave had done so under the cover of night. The prints obviously didn't belong to Big

Frank, and Travis found it quite perplexing that someone was making regular visits to what amounted to his mother's grave.

"What if the guy she was out on the boat with lived and swam to shore, but she drowned?" Travis asked during one wintry visit to the memorial.

I nodded. "That's possible. He feels guilty or he's still in love, so he keeps bringing flowers to her memorial? I like that theory."

"But who could it be?"

"I don't know, Trav."

"It's not Big Frank, so who else would care?"

I looked at him and shrugged. "I don't know."

"Is it you? Are you just doing this to screw with me?"

He was serious, and I could feel my left eye start to twitch at the accusation. "You know, every once in a while your train goes completely off the tracks. Be serious, Travis, you know I wouldn't do that. Besides, I'm only a nine-and-a-half. Those boot prints in the snow were at least size thirteens."

Travis squinted and rubbed his chin. "I wonder what size shoe Clark Gable wears?"

"Clark Gable is dead."

"Oh sure, that's what they want us to believe." He laughed. "Look, when the weather breaks, we're going to camp out at the cemetery and try to catch the person putting flowers on the grave."

I had never cared for camping out and cemeteries gave me the willies, so there was nothing about this idea that appealed to me. I never joined the Boy Scouts because I didn't like camping and soggy sleeping bags, and I was deathly afraid of and highly allergic to poison ivy, which I assumed lurked everywhere around the cemetery, along with all the tortured souls whose spirits roamed the hills each night.

In the meantime, I remained the guardian of the attic treasures, making them available to Travis whenever Big Frank was out of town. He would take the diary or a stack of letters back to his house, where he was transcribing them into some kind of notebook. He had asked me not to look at the letters or the diary, which I had no intention of doing. I wanted no part of the information inside that box. I didn't know what intimate thoughts had been written, but I considered them too private for my eyes. It made me nervous just having the stuff tucked deep in my closet behind shoeboxes of baseball cards and my collection of Matchbox cars.

Travis, however, shared bits of the information with me. His mother, the former Amanda Virdon, had met Frank when he was in the Navy and stationed in Norfolk, Virginia. Her father, a career Navy man, was also stationed in Norfolk. She was eighteen and had just graduated from high school and was working at Melba's Taffy & Ice Cream Shoppe on the strip in Virginia Beach. Frank was twenty-one, a few days from his twenty-second birthday, and in the company of a half-dozen of his Navy buddies, drinking away a three-day pass, when he tapped on the window to get Amanda's attention.

She didn't look up. "I can't talk," she said. "I'm working." He tapped again, and this time she looked. He smiled and waved her over to the window. "Do you want something?"

"You're the most beautiful woman I've seen on the strip all night," he said.

"I'm not allowed to give you free ice cream," she said.

He smiled and asked, "Is your phone number free?"

Drunken sailors on leave asked for her phone number at least a dozen times a week, and her response was always the same: "We don't have a phone at the house, but if you'd like to call my dad at work, Vice Admiral Virdon, he can get me a message."

This usually sent them scrambling. Frank said, "If that's what it takes to get a date, I'll call him."

That night, she wrote in her diary that she had met "a man from Ohio named Francis Martino Baron and he was absolutely charming."

"Big Frank? Charming?" I interjected.

Travis said, "Not just charming, but 'absolutely charming.' She must have had some sort of youthful character flaw."

Frank's hitch in the Navy ended the March after he flirted with Amanda in the ice cream shop. They were married in a simple ceremony in Virginia Beach and had a small reception in the backyard of the family home. Her parents liked Frank and were happy for their daughter. She wrote, "Frank bought me the most beautiful ring I have ever seen. It is a marquis-cut diamond with a crescent of rubies around one side of the stone. It is simply gorgeous, and I was mad at him for spending so much money on a ring, but I love it! Frank has promised me that when we have saved enough money we can move to the country and raise horses. My life is a dream come true. Mrs. Francis Martino Baron. I love the sound of it. Frank is going to take care of me forever."

Unfortunately, "forever" turned out to be about eighteen months, the best Travis could tell. By the time they had been married two years, the tone of the diary entries had turned from dreamy to nightmarish. The one true Francis Baron had surfaced, and he was considerably less charming than the version she had met at Melba's Taffy & Ice Cream Shoppe. Travis said he didn't want to reveal everything he had read, which he described as "nauseating," but Frank had apparently knocked her around, punched her several times, and each time apologized and promised that it would never happen again. But it always did. One of the letters from her dad revealed that he knew Frank had hit her, and he volunteered to drive to Brilliant and move her back home.

"I wonder why she didn't go," I said.

"Who knows? She wasn't much older than us, and she was already married. She was probably still living this fairy-tale dream—figured she could change him or something." He flipped through the pages of his spiral notebook. "Listen to this: 'I went to see Dr. Adams this morning. I'm pregnant. I am so excited. I stopped on the way home and bought material so I could start making a baby quilt. I told Frank, and it saddens me to write that he wasn't very happy about my pregnancy.'" Travis looked up from the book, grinned, and said, "And almost fifteen years later, he's still isn't happy about it."

Travis flipped to another page, where I could see he had made a list. He said, "Here are some of the things I learned. She taught first grade Sunday school at the Church of Christ. She volunteered two afternoons a week at the library. She liked oatmeal-raisin cookies and hot apple cider. Her favorite color was blue, but green was a close second. She was a cheerleader and her senior class secretary. She wanted to go to school to become a court stenographer and, according to her diary, Big Frank described this as 'a royal waste of time and money.'"

"Even then, he was such a charmer," I said.

"Yep. That's my dad. Always encouraging people to chase their dreams and better themselves." He rolled his eyes. He looked back down at the notebook. "Oh, yeah, she was five-foot-six, a hundred and fifteen pounds, brown hair and . . . check it out." He put an index finger to the skin below his right eye and pulled down, revealing most of his lower eyeball. "She also had green eyes."

"Did she have grotesque red veins in her lower eye, too?"

He ignored me. "I love going through her stuff," he said. "I love touching the things that she touched. Holding the things she held. I've read that diary cover to . . . well, she never got it filled out cover-to-cover, but I've read it all three times. I wish I knew what she sounded like. I wish I could hear her voice saying the words." He closed his notebook and fought back tears. "I wish I could."

While I was not personally reading the letters or diary, I was getting a pretty good idea of the mental image Travis was creating of his mother. He believed that she had been sweet and caring, the kind of person who smiled and laughed a lot. He was certain that she'd had happy eyes, always bright. And, nothing against Mrs. Malone, he said, but he was sure his mom would have been the best in the world. He was painting the picture of the perfect woman. What he wanted was to believe he was the product of at least one person with some redeeming qualities.

CHAPTER EIGHT

O ur freshman year and following summer passed without
further progress in Operation Amanda. Travis had gotten a
job bagging groceries and stocking shelves at Kennedy's Market. I had a
lawn-mowing business and was playing baseball for the Brilliant American Legion. We had spent three Friday and two Saturday nights that
summer camping at the cemetery. My parents thought we were somewhere on Tarr's Dome. I lied to get out of the house, as I'm sure my
mother would have been apoplectic at the notion of her son hiding
behind tombstones trying to catch the mystery bouquet deliverer. Fortunately, I had no encounters with poison ivy or apparitions. Unfortunately, we had no encounters with the mystery man, either.

While we had been unsuccessful in catching the mystery man,
the flowers continued to show up periodically at the memorial. I got
my driver's license that October, which helped considerably with our
ability to keep surveillance on the cemetery. While we didn't know
what time of day the flowers were being placed on the grave, they most
frequently appeared between Thursday morning and Friday evening.
During the first week of November, we found no flowers at the site on
Thursday night but discovered a bouquet of six yellow roses when we
returned Friday evening. "That's it," Travis said. "All we need to do is
camp out on a Thursday and we'll find out who it is."

I said, "Okay, first of all, the flowers don't show up *every* Friday.
Secondly, it's probably just someone from the church. And, thirdly, I
am not camping out in the cemetery in November on a Thursday night.
It's a school night and my parents will have none of that, and friendship
has its limits."

"Fair enough. Can we keep doing the drive-bys—keep trying to see which nights are his favorites?"

"No problem. It's virtually impossible to get frostbite in a Buick."

While this seemed to suit Travis, he had little else to do in regard to Operation Amanda. He had pored through the contents of the box retrieved from the attic several times. Consequently, he had a lot of time to speculate on the identity of the mystery man, which he did continually throughout our first-period American Government class. This was bad for me because I actually had to listen to absorb information, which was difficult with Travis's continual bantering about the mystery man, who interested him far more than any lecture on the Bill of Rights.

One of the things you should know about Travis is that he was smart. I mean, *really* smart. Off-the-charts smart. His intelligence was intimidating. There wasn't a mathematical concept that he couldn't grasp in seconds. He would do crossword puzzles in English class, read the paper during biology lectures, pester me about Operation Amanda in American Government, never take home a book, and ace every test. We were studying the human anatomy in biology class and Travis was reading the sports page, making no attempt to hide it, when Mrs. Fristick said, "Travis, would you identify this organ, please?" She whacked at a spot on the human diagram on the pull-down screen.

Travis looked up and said, "It's not an organ. It's an adrenal gland."

He went back to his paper and she smirked. "Wrong. It's the pancreas."

Travis jerked his head up, squinted, and said, "No ma'am, the pancreas is down and to your right a smidge. That's an adrenal gland."

That was another thing about Travis. Even if he was wrong, he made statements with such conviction that you started questioning yourself. In this case, however, he was right. It was an adrenal gland, which Mrs. Fristick was forced to concede after further inspection. However, it so infuriated her that she made a show of walking to the back of the room and snatching away the newspaper.

There was a certain danger in being close friends with Travis.

Teachers can be vindictive, and I couldn't afford to lose guilt-by-association points simply for being his friend. In American Government, however, I was safe, as Mr. Hamrock had grown to appreciate Travis's knowledge of national and world affairs. Most of us never read anything in the paper except the sports section and the comics. But Travis read the newspaper front to back. This allowed him to engage Mr. Hamrock in lively debate, which they both relished.

We were in Mr. Hamrock's class the winter of our sophomore year when Travis decided to expand Operation Amanda beyond his attic and the cemetery. Mr. Hamrock paced the front of the class, shaking a piece of chalk between cupped hands, and said, "Today, we're going to discuss the importance of public documentation, open meetings, and Ohio's open-records law. Most citizens would be astonished to learn that information they believe to be private is actually quite public. Anyone can go look at them: tax records, voter registration, police and fire reports, land records, birth certificates, death certificates, and autopsy reports, just to name a few."

I could feel Travis's eyes boring in on me.

"How about that?" he whispered. "I'll bet there's some kind of police report about my mom's drowning."

I shrugged, and whispered, "So, what's the big deal? If there is a report, it isn't going to tell you anything about your mother. The only thing in that report will be about the accident."

"Let's find out."

CHAPTER NINE

Although my bedroom was infinitely safer than Travis's as the headquarters for Operation Amanda, it could still be a dangerous location, as my mother never knocked before entering. I was sprawled across my bed, propping up my head on my left palm; Travis sat at my desk chair, sideways from the desk, with Mr. Hamrock's book on public records on his lap. My mom had already made one trip into the room with a load of clean clothes, but Travis paid her little mind. When she asked what we were doing, he told my mother that we were working on a project for American Government. Actually, the question had been directed at me, but Travis answered before I lied and my Adam's apple started its frantic dance.

After she set the basket on the floor with instructions for me to put away the contents and left, Travis licked his fingers and flipped through the book to a page he had earlier dog-eared. "Okay, listen to this: *In accordance with Ohio law, the county coroner has jurisdiction in the investigation of all deaths, suspicious or natural. This includes, but is not limited to, murders, traffic accidents, suicides, household and industrial deaths. In most death cases, the coroner relinquishes his jurisdiction to the county sheriff or the local police department. In most, but not all, cases, the coroner acts at the behest of law enforcement. All law enforcement incident reports are public information, as are autopsy results. Information concerning evidence about an ongoing investigation, however, is generally protected information.*

"*Coroners may, and frequently do, conduct investigations into unusual or suspicious deaths. These are called coroner's inquests. All documents relating to a coroner's inquest, unless part of a continuing investigation, also are public record.*"

I faked a yawn. "So."

Travis was clearly perturbed at my lack of interest. "So? You don't call the possible drowning of two people who had been fornicating moments before their untimely deaths suspicious? Christ, I'll bet the cops were fighting over who got to investigate this one."

"The whole affair got a lot of attention, but what was the coroner going to investigate?" I asked. "There were no bodies. The coroner's primary function is to perform autopsies. You can't perform an autopsy if you don't have a body."

"There still might be some kind of incident report with the coroner or the sheriff."

"Well, let's say you find the report. So what? What light could that possibly shed on your mother? It's not going to help you understand any better who she was, and isn't that your ultimate goal?"

"Granted, but I still want to see it. It's a piece of the puzzle, and I want all the information I can get."

"Okay, so how do we find these reports? It's been a long time since she died. Would they still be around?"

He held up the book. "According to this, they have to keep all public documents indefinitely and make them available to anyone who wants to see them."

Central Records was located on the third floor of the county courthouse. Jefferson County had merged its record-keeping sections years earlier in an attempt to save money. Rather than have the auditor, clerk of courts, and sheriff's department maintain old records, they were shipped to Central Records for storage. Actual paper records were kept for all documents less than twenty years old. Anything older was microfilmed.

We were off school for Easter break beginning the Thursday before Good Friday, and Mom let me use the Buick to drive to Steubenville. We arrived at a door with a frosted glass window, on which was painted in gold letters with black trim, "Central Records." A brass bell attached to the top of the door jingled as we entered. The attendant had her back to us. She was a skinny thing, hunched over a mound of papers at her desk, a yellow pencil pushing through gray hair that was pulled away from her face and wrapped in a tight bun. She turned slowly in her chair and looked up at us over a pair of reading glasses. "May I help you?" she asked.

"Yes, I'm looking for a copy of a report," Travis said.

"We have lots and lots of reports, young man. Did you have any *particular* report in mind?"

"My mother died in a boating accident in 1953. Her name was Amanda Baron. I want to see if there might be a sheriff's department report on the accident."

"I see. 1953, is it? That was quite a while ago. Any report that old would be in storage in the basement annex. I feel certain that will take some time to locate."

"How long will it take?"

"Oh, that's hard to say." She stood, walked to the counter and slid a Public Records Request Form and a pencil in front of Travis. "Fill this out to the best of your knowledge and we'll see what we can do. Check back in a couple of days."

Travis called the following Monday and Wednesday. On Friday, I drove him up after baseball practice. Each time we were told the search was continuing but no report had been found. I made the next trip with Travis the following Friday, more than two weeks after our initial visit. This time, however, it was there. When she saw us walk in, the woman stood and pulled a set of stapled pages from a folder. "Five pages," she said. "That will be twenty-five cents. I can only give you the sheriff's incident report, which essentially is an accounting of the events the night your mother died. I can't release the detective bureau report."

His brow furrowed. "Excuse me?"

"I said, you can have the incident report, but not the investigative report by the homicide detectives. The investigative report is considered the sheriff's department work product. As long as it's an active case, the work product is not public record."

Travis slid a dollar bill across the counter. "But it was an accidental drowning. Why would there be a homicide investigation?"

"I'm quite sure I don't know." She fished through a coin drawer below the counter and pushed three quarters back across the counter.

"Can I just look at it?" Travis asked. "I mean, it's what, sixteen years old? Why is it still active? Who would care about it now?"

She shook her head. "That is a question you'll need to ask the sheriff. The reason we had such trouble finding the incident report was because we were looking in the archives. It wasn't there because it remains an active case. The sheriff gave me the file, but with explicit orders not to copy or release anything but the incident report, which you now have. If you have additional questions you need to take it up with him."

"Okay, but I'm still confused. Why is it an active case? Does that mean they thought someone killed my mom?"

"Again, you will have to ask someone at the sheriff's office." She turned and went back to her desk of orderly piles. "Good day to you, young sir, and good luck."

As Travis walked to the door, he watched as she put the file folder in a wire basket at the edge of her desk. As we stepped outside the office, I turned to Travis before he had a chance to speak, and put an index finger near his nose. "Understand me, Travis. I've seen that look in your eyes before, and I know what you're thinking. Sneaking into your attic was one thing, but under no circumstances—none, zero, nada—am I going to break into that office, or the annex, or anywhere to steal that report."

He waved me off, dismissing me. "I'm not going to ask you to break into anything. God, you're such a namby-pamby."

"The mere fact that you're calling me that tells me that's exactly what you had in mind."

He stopped on the landing. "There has to be another way to get it, but why does it even exist? What the hell were they investigating?"

Travis had borrowed two books from the Brilliant Public Library to help him in his search for his mother's past. One was written by a private detective who specialized in tracking down missing persons, and the other explained how to trace your family history. Both suggested checking the public library for back issues of the local newspaper as a good source of information. I told my mom that I needed to go to the library in Steubenville to research back issues of the Steubenville *Herald-Star* for an American Government project. This was entirely plausible, and she didn't question it when I asked for the car keys.

The back issues of the *Herald-Star* were on microfilm, tucked neatly in file drawers in the research section on the second floor. The reels of film were wrapped around blue spools. Each spool contained three months' worth of newspapers. After placing one end of the spool on a spindle and threading the film under the lens and onto an empty spool, Travis turned a knob and the October 1953 editions of the *Herald-Star* began running across the screen. The stories were not hard to find. This had been big news in the Upper Ohio River Valley, and the stories stretched across the top of the front page under bold, banner headlines.

"Jesus Christ, look at this story. This must have been some big deal," Travis said.

October 2, 1953:

BRILLIANT WOMAN, MALE COMPANION
BELIEVED DEAD IN BOATING MISHAP

A 22-year-old Brilliant woman and her yet unidentified companion were believed to have drowned early today when a barge laden with iron ore rammed their drifting pleasure craft on the Ohio River, about two miles north of the LaGrange Locks.

At press time today, authorities were continuing to search the river for the bodies of Amanda Baron and the man, both of whom are missing and presumed dead.

Jefferson County Sheriff Stuart DiChassi said Mrs. Baron, of 232 Shaft Row, and the male were seen jumping from a 20-foot cabin cruiser about 1 a.m., shortly before the barge reduced it to kindling. The captain of the tug pushing the barge said the couple appeared to jump clear of the wreckage, but may have been pulled under the barge, or drowned in the strong current.

The craft was owned by Mrs. Baron's husband, Francis M. Baron, who authorities were attempting to contact at press time. Mr. Baron is a long-haul trucker and left yesterday afternoon for a trip to Arkansas, according to relatives.

"There are a number of unanswered questions, but I'm not sure we'll ever get them answered unless we identify the gentleman who was on the boat with Mrs. Baron and find him alive, which seems highly unlikely at this point," the sheriff said. "We've received no reports of a missing man anywhere in the area, so I guess it's possible that he swam to shore."

Asked if Mrs. Baron could have swum to shore, too, DiChassi said, "Anything is possible, but I don't find it likely."

According to DiChassi, the *Belle of the Ohio*, a tug owned by the Monongahela Iron and Coal Company of Pittsburgh, was transporting an 18-barge train of iron ore to the Wheeling-Pittsburgh Steel Plant in Martins Ferry when the accident occurred. Captain Jess Kull, 52, said he was aligning the barge for passage through the LaGrange Locks when he saw the small craft.

According to the incident report, Kull said he had no time to reverse his engines or steer clear of Baron's boat. Kull told authorities that he blasted his horn, and a naked man and woman ran out of the cabin and leaped from the side of the craft. Kull said the tug and barge continued downstream another quarter-mile before coming to a stop.

DiChassi said Mrs. Baron was the mother of an infant son. He said the boy was apparently left alone at the Baron home, but is now with his grandparents.

"She left me alone in the house, for God's sake!" Travis yelped, turning heads our way throughout the second floor.

"That doesn't sound like something she would do, based on everything you've told me about her," I whispered.

He said nothing, but turned the advancement knob and scrolled to the next day's edition of the *Herald-Star*. Again, the headline stretched across the top of the front page.

October 3, 1953:

SEARCH CONTINUES FOR MISSING BRILLIANT WOMAN, COMPANION

Authorities entered their second day of searching the Ohio River near the LaGrange Locks for the bodies of Amanda Baron of Brilliant and a male companion.

Jefferson County Sheriff Stuart DiChassi said rescue workers expanded the search to an area south of the locks, some two miles from where Mrs. Baron's pleasure craft was rammed by an iron ore barge early yesterday. Members of the Brilliant Volunteer Fire Department walked the river's Ohio and West Virginia banks for five miles yesterday, but failed to find the missing woman or her yet-unidentified companion.

DiChassi said the search will continue until he is certain the bodies cannot be located within his jurisdiction. "If the bodies went over the dam, then God only knows where they could end up," DiChassi said. "This is such a tragedy, and it's taking a heck of a toll on these men."

Mrs. Baron and the unidentified man were seen jumping from a cabin cruiser shortly before it was rammed by the barge.

Mrs. Baron was married and her husband, Francis, was out of town at the time of the accident. She is the mother of an infant son, Travis, who is with relatives. Mr. Baron, an independent truck driver, returned from a trip to Arkansas early today. DiChassi said Mr. Baron could offer no explanation as to why Mrs. Baron would be out on the river, with another man, after dark. Relatives said Mr. Baron was too distraught to speak to the *Herald-Star*.

DiChassi said deputies are attempting to retrace Mrs. Baron's steps Thursday night in hopes of learning more of the events leading to her death. DiChassi said it was "very critical" to learn the identity of the mystery man who was on the boat with Mrs. Baron.

The following Monday's paper carried a terse story on the front page, below the fold.

October 5, 1953:

OFFICIALS HALT SEARCH FOR
AMANDA BARON, MYSTERY MAN

Authorities have called off the search for a missing Brilliant woman and her male companion, who disappeared after their pleasure craft was crushed by a barge early Friday.

"It breaks our hearts to quit, but it just seems fruitless to continue searching" said Brilliant Fire Chief Dick Schultz. "We'll just wait and see if the river gives something up."

Killed in the accident were Amanda Baron, 22, and an unidentified male companion. The couple was seen jumping from the 20-foot boat just seconds before it was hit by the barge.

Travis began rolling through the microfilm, trying to locate the front page of each edition, spinning it, stopping it, backing it up, stopping it, moving it forward, stopping it, backing it up. It had a hypnotic effect; I stood behind him and watched until I found myself listing to the left with a case of motion sickness. "We'll be forever trying to find stories this way," he complained.

I was already walking away from the microfilm machine, reaching for a seat at an oak table in the middle of the research area. That's when I remembered "Fast Freddie" Doucette.

When we were in Florence Braatz's sixth-grade class and given an English assignment to write a five-hundred-word essay about a living hero, my immediate choice was "Fast Freddie" Doucette, who was a flanker and kick returner for the Wheeling Ironmen of the United Football League and my favorite player. A patient librarian in the research section showed me how to use the microfilm machine, then showed me a book that had the name of anyone mentioned in the Steubenville *Herald-Star* and the dates their name appeared. As I sat down at the table to regain my equilibrium, I looked across the room and on a shelf opposite the microfilm machines spotted a row of books bound in black leather. On the spine of each was printed, *Steubenville Herald-Star News Index*.

I wobbled over, snatched the 1953 and 1954 editions and sat down next to Travis as he whirled through the reel.

November 21 had been the last story filed about Amanda Baron in 1953. It was another follow-up on the futility of the search. I also found her name in the 1954 directory.

Baron, Amanda—Jan. 14

"Get the microfilm for January 1954," I said.

He slipped the microfilm into the reader and rolled to the date. Again, the story consumed the top of page one.

DEATH OF BRILLIANT WOMAN
BEING PROBED AS HOMICIDE

The homicide squad of the Jefferson County Sheriff's Department has launched an investigation into the reported drowning of Brilliant housewife Amanda Baron in October.

Sources told the *Herald-Star* that Homicide Detective Chase Tornik began investigating the case late last week. Questioned by the *Herald-Star*, Tornik confirmed that he was investigating Baron's death, but refused to give details of the investigation. "Obviously, we believe foul play may have been involved or we wouldn't be looking into the case," Tornik said. "Let's just say that some evidence has surfaced that warrants a closer look."

Asked how he could conduct a homicide investigation when no proof exists that Mrs. Baron is dead, since her body was never recovered, Tornik said he was unable to reveal any particulars. However, he added, "Just because you can't find the body doesn't mean she wasn't murdered."

Baron was believed to have drowned after her pleasure craft drifted into the path of a barge carrying iron ore. The captain of the barge claimed he saw Mrs. Baron and a male companion jump from the boat just seconds before it was rammed by the barge.

The remainder of the article was a recap of earlier stories.

Oddly, it was the only story about Amanda Baron to appear in the Steubenville *Herald-Star* the entire year. There was no one-year anniversary story and never a follow-up on the progress of Tornik's investigation. "That's bizarre, don't you think?" Travis asked. "This was a big deal. How can you write a story about a homicide investigation, then never have a single follow-up?"

As with most of Travis's questions about his mother, I didn't have an answer. "Maybe they investigated it and found out there was nothing to it."

"Okay, but shouldn't there have been a story that said so? And that still doesn't answer the big question, which was why did this detective think she might have been murdered?"

"Don't make too much out of it," I suggested. "Maybe the guy was just grandstanding, trying to get an article for his scrapbook."

Travis adjusted the story on the screen, pointed at the critical passage and read, "'*We believe foul play may have been involved or we wouldn't be looking into the case,' Tornik said.*"

Throughout our work on Project Amanda, I continually reminded myself that this was Travis's mother. He had many unanswered questions, and this article had just added to it. I pondered this for a minute, then suggested, "We're three blocks from the sheriff's office. Let's walk over there. Maybe that Tornik guy is still a detective. If he is, I'll bet he'd tell you."

Travis nodded. "That's a good idea."

"I have those once in a while," I said.

There was no acknowledgement from Travis, who simply started rewinding the microfilm reel.

The sheriff's office was in the courthouse annex, just north of the main structure. It was a two-story building that housed the county jail in the basement, the sheriff's office on the first floor, and juvenile court on the second floor. The lobby of the sheriff's office looked like the inside of a bank, with a single window opening covered with chrome bars. The door to the left led back to the sheriff's department; the one to the right into a stairwell. Both had magnetic locks that could only be opened by a worn-out looking platinum blonde with thick hips sitting at a desk behind the grated opening. We stood at the opening for several moments before she raised her eyes from the paperback she was reading. "Yes?" she asked, cracking her chewing gum.

"Uh, does Detective Chase Tornik still work here?" Travis asked. "We wanted to talk to him about a murder investigation."

Without any sign of emotion, she picked up the phone and punched in a number. "There are two kids up here who are asking for Chase Tornik.... No, I'm not kidding.... They said it's about a murder investigation.... I don't know.... I don't know." She took an exasperated breath. "I still don't know. Why don't you come up here and ask them?" She hung up her phone and went back to her paperback. "Someone will be up in a minute."

Sheriff Beaumont T. Bonecutter could block out the sun. He stood an imposing six-foot-four and had shoulders like a bear, which caused the light blue, polyester shirt to strain across his chest. A pair of thick, muscular forearms extended from the short sleeves, revealing a mat of curly, gray hair the same shade as those projecting from his nostrils and ears. His black tie was a clip-on and he smelled of Vitalis and bay rum. He had two of the biggest hands I had ever seen on a human being, and when he set the paws on the counter I noticed a wedding ring being suffocated behind a mound of flesh. His arms were spread wide, and through the bars he asked, "What do you boys want?"

"We wanted to talk to Chase Tornik," Travis said.

There was a moment of silence. "Chase Tornik?"

"Yes, sir."

Bonecutter snorted—part laughter, part disgust. He looked at Travis, then me, then Travis again. "What do you want with him?"

"We wanted to ask him some questions."

"I don't have time to play twenty questions with you, junior; what's this about?"

"My mom. My mom was Amanda Baron. She drowned . . ."

"I know who your mom was. Were you the one looking for that report?"

"Yes, sir."

He nodded. "Okay, so what's that have to do with Tornik?"

"We found an article in the newspaper that said he was investigating her death as a homicide, but there was only one story. I want to find out why he thought it was a homicide and what happened."

Bonecutter chewed on his upper lip, frowned, then said, "Let 'em in, Sally."

The electronic latch on the door to our left released and I followed Travis, who followed Bonecutter, into the inner sanctum of the sheriff's office. "Is Mr. Tornik in?" I asked.

The sheriff never broke stride as he led us toward his office. "He doesn't work here anymore."

"When did he quit?"

"He didn't. We fired him when he went to prison." Bonecutter pushed open the door to his office and motioned us in with his head. "Have a seat." As I walked by I could smell the cigar smoke that clung to him. He walked around a mahogany desk that was as big as my bed, sat in a leather-padded chair that exhaled under his weight, and asked, "What are you trying to find out?"

"I'm just trying to track down information about my mom," Travis said. "We were looking up articles at the library. That's where I found the one about Detective Tornik investigating her death as a homicide. That's why we wanted to talk to him."

"You're not familiar with Tornik?"

"Not at all," Travis said.

He nodded slowly for several seconds, twirling a bent paper clip in his fingers. "Best goddamn detective I'd ever seen," Bonecutter said. "I was his patrol sergeant when he cracked the DiCarolis case, but I don't suppose you know about that, either?" We both shook our heads. He pulled a Marsh-Wheeling Stogie from a package, fired it up, took several puffs, and slid the silver lighter across his desk blotter. "The DiCarolis family was a very powerful crime family out of Youngstown. In December 1948, there was a triple homicide at the Little Napoli Restaurante . . ." He pointed over his shoulder. "It's not there anymore, but

it was a little hole-in-the-wall place north of town on Jewett Road by
the Pottery Addition. We got a call about a shooting, and Tornik was
the first officer on the scene. He goes in, finds the restaurant's owner,
Eddie LaBaudica, they called him Sweet Fingers, and his brother-in-
law, Santino Potenzini, dead in the dining room. It had dropped well
below zero, and the power had gone out in a storm. There was frozen
blood everywhere. Sweet Fingers was facedown, his face frozen solid in
a plate of angel hair pasta and marinara—I'll never forget that—and he
had a pair of .22-caliber slug holes behind his left ear. The cook, I can't
remember his name, died the same way. Potenzini, however, had apparently put up a struggle, and he was lying on the floor, his gun still in his
hand, blood everywhere.

"Potenzini was a lieutenant in the Antonelli crime family of Pittsburgh. The Antonellis controlled gambling in the Upper Ohio River Valley.
The don was Salvatore Antonelli—Il Tigre. You've heard of him, right?"

We both nodded. Everyone in the Ohio Valley knew of Il Tigre.
He had a reputation as the most ruthless mob boss in the country. My
dad played the numbers and bet on pro football games at Carmine's
Lounge in Mingo Junction, and he once saw El Tigre there. He said the
don had a complexion like a gravel parking lot and such girth that he
gulped down air in bursts and gurgled when he exhaled. Dad also said
he had the dark, depthless eyes of a predator and he was happy to place
his bets and get out of the lounge.

Beaumont T. Bonecutter continued, "The Antonellis used the
Little Napoli Restaurante as their base in the Valley. The DiCarolis
family had been trying to move in on the action, and this was meant as
a wake-up call for the Antonellis.

"Since Tornik was the first one on the scene, the detectives asked
him to help out with the investigation. We're a small department, and
we all pitch in. Tornik is looking around and he finds a butter dish lying
upside down, frozen. He picks it up and it has a perfect imprint of three
fat fingers—a deep scar running the length of the middle one—and
a man's ring—a square face with a large, centered rock, chipped, surrounded by the initials 'JS.'

"He puts the butter dish in the freezer and gets the art teacher at the high school to make a plaster cast of it. She used that to make a latex mold, which we used to make several plaster casts." He pointed to one of the casts on the shelf behind his desk. "'JS,' we figured, stood for Joey Sirgusiano, who was this slob of a numbers runner and enforcer who worked for DiCarolis. Tornik brings Sirgusiano in for questioning. He shows up with an attorney who is wearing a suit that cost more than I make in a year. I'm watching from behind a two-way mirror. Sirgusiano's attorney says, 'The only reason I'm agreeing to this interview was because of the ludicrous suggestion that Mr. Sirgusiano is somehow involved in the tragic murders at the Little Napoli.'

"Sirgusiano and the attorney are looking at each other and smirking. Sirgusiano says, 'Hey, sonny boy, are you old enough to carry a real gun?' Tornik was only about twenty-three and looked sixteen. Then Sirgusiano points at the two-way mirror, which I'm behind with the county prosecutor and two detectives, and says, 'Hey, guys, how come you're sending a boy to do a man's job?'

"Tornik starts asking questions, acting timid. Sirgusiano's answering them exactly as the attorney had scripted them. He had never in his life been in the Little Napoli Restaurante, although he heard the eggplant parmesan and risotto were the best in the Ohio Valley. Which, by the way, was true. Eddie 'Sweet Fingers' LaBaudica? Never heard of him. Never in his life. Santino Potenzini? Him neither. Were those two of the men who died? They were? How tragic. No, he didn't know nothin' about nothin'.

"Finally, the lawyer asks, 'Officer, my client is a very busy man. How much longer is this charade going to take?'

"This is where it got really good. Tornik says, 'Oh, not long at all, actually.' He points toward the ring finger on Sirgusiano's right hand and says, 'That's a beautiful ring, Mr. Sirgusiano. May I see it?'

"The lawyer says, 'What? Absolutely not. Keep it on your finger.'

"Tornik reaches into his jacket pocket and pulls out a search warrant. He says, 'Do you see this, counselor? This is a search warrant. The location of the search is the person of one Joseph Dominic Sirgusiano.' He winks at Sirgusiano and says, 'That's you, dipstick. The object in question is a ring—flat face, chipped center stone, initials JS.' I swear to Jesus, every bit of color drained from Sirgusiano's face. He didn't know whether to shit or go blind. He couldn't even work up a spit. The attorney reads the warrant, then shrugs and says, 'Give him the ring. We'll get it back.'

"Sirgusiano tugs it off his fat finger and slams it down on the middle of the table. Tornik held the ring up close for several minutes before reaching back into his jacket pocket and pulling out a plaster replica of the ring and the three chubby fingers. He says, 'You know, your ring bears a striking resemblance to the one in this cast. And wouldn't you say the scar on the middle finger of this mold matches the one on your middle finger, Mr. Sirgusiano?'

"Now, there's sweat rolling down Sirgusiano's forehead. Tornik says, 'You probably have already figured out where we got this, but for my personal enjoyment, let me tell you. On the day of the murders, I found this lovely specimen pressed into a frozen butter dish at the Little Napoli Restaurante—the very same restaurant that just a few minutes ago you said you'd never in your life set foot inside.'

"The lawyer tells Sirgusiano to clam up.

"Tornik says, 'We don't think you killed the boys at the restaurant, Mr. Sirgusiano, but we're betting you know who did. And the first guy to the door is the one who gets the deal.' The lawyer says, 'Don't say a word. Mr. DiCarolis will take care of you.'

"Tornik knows he's in charge, so he leans back in his chair and says, 'Sure, listen to your counsel, Joey. Go on back to Youngstown. I'm sure Mr. DiCarolis will take care of you, just like your lawyer said. What is it that all his friends in the mob call Mr. DiCarolis? Let me think. Oh, yeah, I remember—Donny Death. I'm sure Donny Death will be very understanding and loyal to a second-rate thug who leaves behind evidence that implicates the family in the slaughter of three people, two of whom are known associates of the Antonelli family. So, go ahead. There's the door. You can leave now, if you like. But, I'll tell you this, even if Mr. DiCarolis forgives you, I'm not so certain that Il Tigre is going to be so understanding. He probably doesn't care about you shooting the cook, but he's not going to be too happy that you dusted one of his top lieutenants and the owner of the Little Napoli.' Tornik smiled and said, 'I understand Il Tigre was very fond of the eggplant parmesan.'

"Sirgusiano blurts out, 'I'll talk, I'll talk, I'll talk. Just get me a real lawyer and you've gotta promise me protection.' Before morning, Joey Sirgusiano was tucked away in a cottage in the Allegheny National Forest near the Pennsylvania-New York line with Tornik and the county prosecutor. He was the star witness against the DiCarolis crime family. The top six members of the DiCarolis family went to prison, as did seven of their lieutenants."

We had been mesmerized by the tale and sat slack-jawed as the sheriff relit his cigar. Finally, I asked, "Why'd Tornik go to prison?"

Bonecutter sent a stream of blue smoke over his desk. "He started believing his own press clippings," Bonecutter said. "There was a big feature story in one of those national news magazines about him—talked about the boy cop who brought down the DiCarolis crime family. He started writing first-person stories for those true crime rags. Pretty soon, he thought he had to solve every crime in the county. He started to phony-up evidence to solve cases and protect his reputation. He was planting evidence, forcing confessions, and paying witnesses for bogus testimony."

"Like what?" Travis asked.

"The one that brought him down involved a guy here in Steubenville named Leon Jefferson—a black guy, everyone called him Stony— who got charged with a string of burglaries. After Stony got popped for the burglaries, he was looking for something to bargain with in exchange for a lighter sentence. He tells the prosecutor that Tornik had paid him two hundred dollars to testify against Willie Potts in a murder trial the year before. Stony said he witnessed Potts stab Luther Bigelow to death. Potts got convicted and was sent to Death Row. Turns out, Stony wasn't within ten miles of Luther Bigelow the night he got popped. That opened up the floodgates. The prosecutor started going back through Tornik's cases and found three or four other instances of misconduct. Those were just the ones he could prove. There were probably more, but that was enough to send Tornik to prison."

Travis asked, "Do you know why he was investigating my mom's death as a homicide?"

Bonecutter shook his head. "No idea, son. Hell, it was probably just more of his grandstanding. Like I said, the guy was a hell of an investigator, but he had an ego as big as all outdoors. When he started to phony up evidence, he made us all look bad. Most guys around here think he's lower than whale shit. They can't say his name without getting a bad taste in their mouths. But he paid the price. He got convicted and did hard time, and former cops don't have a real easy time of it in prison."

"Is he out of prison?" I asked.

"Yeah, he got out a while back."

"Do you know where we can find him?" Travis asked.

"Nope. I haven't seen him in years. Frankly, if I did know, I'd do my best to stay away from him." The sheriff winked. "It's not good for an elected officer of the law to be seen chumming around with a convicted felon."

As we left the sheriff's office, I said, "Well, based on that story, maybe there was no reason for a homicide investigation. Sounds like he had a giant ego and was just trying to make a mountain out of a molehill."

"I'd still like to talk to him," Travis said.

"Of course you would."

The next day, Travis telephoned the offices of the state parole board. A lady who didn't want to be bothered with our inquiry said that privacy laws forbade the release of any information. Travis also wrote to the Ohio Department of Rehabilitation and Corrections in Columbus, and they responded with a terse, standardized note that stated that Chase Tornik, Inmate No. A-12-0778, had been incarcerated in the Ohio penitentiary system from June 1955 until November 1963, when he was released from the Mansfield Reformatory and paroled to a halfway house in Toledo. He was released from parole in November 1966.

CHAPTER TEN

Travis slouched back into the corner booth of the Coffee Pot, mindlessly stirring his RC Cola with a straw. "At least we know why Tornik didn't finish the investigation," I said. Bea Cranston slid two cheeseburgers and fries across the table, then tore a couple of grease-stained checks from her pad and dropped them without comment.

"We know why Tornik didn't keep investigating, but why didn't someone else pick up the case?" Travis asked.

"Probably because Tornik was poison and no one wanted to be associated with anything he touched." I covered my burger with mustard. Avoiding eye contact, I said, "I have an idea why he might have been investigating your mom's death."

"Let's hear it."

"I heard something once—a long time ago. Now, before I begin, understand this is only a rumor, okay?"

Travis nodded. "Go on."

"Well, this mystery man that was on the boat with your mom—there's always been this speculation that it was someone prominent here in town, and he knew that his reputation would be ruined if they got caught, so after the boat got hit, he swam to shore and let your mom drown. Or . . ." I took a breath. "Or he might have helped her drown."

Travis looked at me with that familiar look of disbelief. "When we started this, you told me you didn't know anything about my mom."

"I just remembered that today. I don't even know where I heard it, I swear. And it never seemed that important. You know, it was just one of the rumors I heard, and who could ever prove it one way or the other? I remembered it when we were talking to Sheriff Bonecutter.

Suddenly, it made sense that Tornik was investigating it as a homicide if he thought that your mom's boyfriend . . ."

"Killed her?" he said, finishing my stammer.

"Yeah. It seems possible that Tornik knew who was with your mom that night and was going after him."

"Why would he drown her if he was in love with her?" Travis asked.

"Maybe he wasn't in love with her. Maybe . . ." I swallowed. "This isn't a visual you want about your mother, but maybe it was just a romp in the hay and he didn't want to explain things to his wife and family."

Travis ran a french fry though a puddle of ketchup. "That's interesting, and suppose it's true. It still doesn't answer the question of why they didn't keep investigating."

"Maybe they did. Maybe there just weren't any more stories in the paper. They could have been investigating this for years, for all we know."

"Who was the guy she was with?"

"I don't know."

"Who did you hear it was?"

"I never heard a name."

He leaned across the table at me. "Say, 'Swear to God.'"

"I swear to God, Trav. I don't know."

"Do you think it's the same person who's been putting flowers on her grave?"

I shrugged. "You think someone has a guilty conscience?"

"If we find out who's been visiting the grave, maybe we'll know."

CHAPTER ELEVEN

"**M**ake sure there's no poison ivy down there," I said, standing on the bank overlooking the makeshift bunker, scanning the rim of our fortification with my flashlight.

I heard Travis drop his sleeping bag and a small ice chest of supplies on the dirt floor of the bunker. Although faint moonlight filtered across the hillside, the bunker was shrouded by the low-hanging limbs of an enormous willow tree. I couldn't see his face through the shadows, but I knew he was rolling his eyes and giving me a look of exasperation. You know certain things about your friends. "I told you, Mitchell, there's no poison ivy here. I've already checked it out. Man, sometimes you are such a wimp."

I started down over the embankment. "I'm not a wimp, I just happen to be terrified of poison ivy. I would rather have a broken leg than poison ivy."

"That's ridiculous."

I shrugged. "It's not logical and it's not a choice; it's just the way it is."

I had suffered through a couple of cases of poison ivy in which it had blanketed me thoroughly. Just recalling those awful bouts made me start clawing at imaginary outbreaks on my arms and legs, a fact that had made my mother especially curious as to why I wanted to go camping with Travis. In reality, of course, I didn't. I told her that it was a chance to celebrate the end of the school year, and Travis had his heart set on it. It was a harmless venture, and she seemed to buy it. If I had told her the real reason, that Travis had conned me into setting up a stake-out operation to catch the mystery man who continued to visit his mother's memorial, she would have locked me in my room. If I'd had half a brain, I'd have done it myself.

But I hadn't and therefore found myself crouching in a bunker that Travis had devised behind the brush and locust trees that divided the northeastern corner of New Alexandria Cemetery from the west pasture of McConnell's dairy farm. Travis had dug out what resembled a shallow grave, which was somewhat appropriate, and piled sticks and twigs at its front, giving it the look of a large beaver dam while providing us with a clear view of the memorial garden for Amanda Baron. "Why didn't we just go up on the hill and hunker down behind one of the bigger tombstones?" I asked.

"You know nothing about military strategy," he said.

"Sorry for questioning you, General."

It was ten o'clock, and a sliver of gray moon was perched over the West Virginia hills. It was cool for early June, and the night was silent except for the ache of the crickets and the soft wash of the nearby stream as it wandered over the shallows on its way to the pond in McConnell's meadow. Mist was forming over the moving water, creeping out between the trees that rimmed the cemetery, slowly consuming the tombstones on the hillside that led down to the small memorial.

Travis had temporarily lost interest in pursuing the homicide angle. Once the weather turned nice, he returned to his previous obsession—finding out who had been putting flowers on his mother's memorial. That spring, Travis had won the two-mile run at the Big Valley Athletic Conference track and field championships. I speculated that this feat was due largely to the number of times that winter and spring that he had made the five-mile run to the cemetery and back. If I couldn't secure a car for the trip, he would get up early and run under the guise of needing additional training. Big Frank thought he was crazy and said so on several occasions.

Travis decided that a stakeout was the only way to catch the mystery man. Thus, on the first Thursday of my summer vacation following my sophomore year, I was hunkered in the bunker, cattle snoozing across the stream, the mist rolling in, poison ivy preparing to attack from all sides, anticipating the arrival of the mystery man.

"Here," Travis said, opening the cooler he had brought along. It was packed with twelve-ounce bottles of RC Cola, peanut M&M's, and pretzels. All my favorites.

"Nicely done," I said. "You even remembered a bottle opener."

He smiled. "Well, I figure it's the least I can do. You deserve some kind of reward for all the hell I've put you through."

"You mean, like causing me to piss myself in your attic?"

"Yeah, that and all the other crap, like you hauling my ass all over the place." Travis actually choked up for a minute, struggling to find the right words. "I just really appreciate you being such a buddy, that's all."

I was touched, and a little choked up myself. "Not a problem, Trav." I gave his shoulders a squeeze. "I'm glad to do it. Hell, you'd do it for me."

We sat in silence, sipping our RCs, enjoying the quiet of the night. Despite the tribulations involved in playing the role of Watson to Travis's Sherlock Holmes, our sophomore year had been a good one. It marked the second consecutive year that Travis had earned straight As, which was creating a particularly amusing situation. Travis Baron was not one to normally concern himself with grades or honors. In fact, his grades through elementary and junior high were only marginal, not because he wasn't brilliant, but because he handed in only about half of his assignments. He couldn't be bothered. Education was not a priority in the Baron household.

His commitment to education began at the end of our eighth grade year, when Margaret Simcox, who since the first grade was considered the brains of our class, made the tactical error of predicting within earshot of Travis that she would ultimately be the class valedictorian and win the Ohio Valley Steel Scholarship, an annual five-thousand-dollar award granted to the Brilliant High School valedictorian. Having heard this bold prediction, Travis decided that winning the scholarship was a goal he wanted for himself. Travis, of course, told Margaret of his intentions, and she laughed in his face. "Not in a million, billion, trillion, zillion years," she sneered.

"Watch me," he countered.

Margaret considered his challenge a joke, and said so to anyone who would listen. Meanwhile, Travis loaded his schedule. Our freshman year, he took algebra, Spanish, biology, English, American history, elements of government, health, and physical education. This was the most difficult schedule a freshman could take. In the first grading period, he got eight As, and promptly caught Margaret in the gym as she was getting ready for cheerleading practice. He held the report card in front of her face and said, "Laugh now, funny girl."

By the end of our sophomore year, the visual of Travis Baron in her academic rearview mirror was clearly getting to Margaret. She was still getting all As, but she was beginning to crack under the pressure. Before the geometry final exam, she broke out in giant hives. Making all this worse was that Travis said if he won the scholarship he was going to use it to attend welding school in Pittsburgh. Two students locked in mortal combat for a scholarship—one wanted to study pre-med at Columbia, the other wanted to be an ironworker.

The conflict didn't begin with Margaret's eighth grade pronounce-ment. That was simply the latest battle in a war that had been raging since the second grade. Margaret hated Travis. Despised him. Loathed him. Travis, meanwhile, was amused that Margaret spent so much time and energy hating him. To Travis, Margaret was not an enemy but simply a target for his humor. He only tormented her because it was so much damn fun. Never once did she disappoint him by failing to come to a boiling rage, little white bubbles of scalded saliva churning at the corners of her mouth, her face turning crimson and her teeth grinding like the wheels of a giant locomotive coming to a halt. The war had its genesis at our second-grade Christmas party. Margaret, under the direc-tion of her mother, had everyone in the class bring in fifty cents to buy a Christmas present for our teacher, the lovely Miss Carter, upon whom Travis had an enormous crush. On the day of the party, Margaret placed a neatly wrapped package beneath the glistening silver branches of our aluminum tree. When it was time to give Miss Carter the gift, Margaret thought it was her right, seeing how she had collected the money and her mother had bought and wrapped the gift. Travis, however, thought it should be his job, since he was seated closest to the gift and, more important, because no one was more in love with Miss Carter than he. As Margaret reached for the package, Travis snatched it from the table and started toward Miss Carter's desk. Margaret squealed and lunged for Travis. An ever-so-brief tug-of-war ensued. The gift was some kind of glass vase, or something else very fragile. We never knew for sure because it got busted into a pile of shards that its own mother couldn't have identified. Margaret raked her fingernails across his face. Travis responded by ripping the silver leash off her poodle skirt. They went for each other's eyes and fell into a screaming heap, rolling around on the floor, kicking and punching one another. Miss Carter had to pry them apart, but not before they rolled into Snookie McGruder's desk and a glass of orangeade fell into Margaret's hair, which her mother had fixed so nicely with red and green bows. Miss Carter was crying; Margaret was crying; Travis went back to his chair on the verge of tears, fearing that because of that goddamn Margaret he would never again be the love of Miss Carter's life.

The hatred festered from that point. Now, Travis had perfect grades halfway through high school, and Margaret was starting to crack. Her young life would be ruined if her nemesis were to be awarded the Ohio Valley Steel Scholarship, which was all so delicious to Travis.

About midnight, maybe a little after, I draped my sleeping bag over my shoulders and slouched back in the bunker. The fog had filled the hillside and lapped at the granite benches surrounding Amanda Baron's marker, and in the coolness of the night, I drifted off. I don't know how long I had been asleep, but I was awakened when Travis cupped his hand over my mouth, leaned close to my ear, and whispered, "Someone's coming."

A jolt of adrenaline surged out of my chest, and thousands of icy pinpricks raced through my arms and legs. I shed the sleeping bag and peeked through the brush. In the darkness beyond the closest hill, I could hear the steady footfalls in gravel creating a methodic, eerie scuffling in the mist. My spine tingled with fear and excitement, but mostly fear. We watched in silence until from the blackness appeared an even darker figure striding toward the monument.

He was tall, with a broad chest and shoulders producing a silhouette that looked ominous in the night. A bouquet of flowers extended from his right hand, hanging softly at his knees. We remained silent, peering as he emerged from the mist, cutting an angle from the gravel path toward the memorial. For several minutes he stood at the side of the garden, behind the granite benches, and appeared to pray. Then, he walked slowly toward the memorial bearing the name of Amanda Baron and knelt, placing the flowers at the base of the stone.

Travis looked at me; I shrugged and shook my head, silently answering his look. It was too dark; I didn't recognize the figure. We watched for a moment longer, stealth sentries hoping for a clue. When the man stood and started back up the knoll, Travis feared that an opportunity was about to elude his grasp. He stepped out of the bunker and, still under the cover of the willow limbs, said, "Hey, mister, I want to talk to you."

Travis's mother would have been thirty-nine-years-old. So, for the sake of argument, let's say that the mystery man was thirty-nine, also, which is well past the age when ghosts and goblins should be a concern. Still, I expect that when the silence of a dark, apparently empty cemetery is broken by the words, "Hey, mister, I want to talk to you," it would be enough to put the adrenal glands of the bravest amongst us into overdrive. The mystery man jumped and started sprinting back up the gravel road. Travis took off after him. I ran up the hillside along the edge of the cemetery, behind the last row of tombstones and under the darkened canopy of elms and maples. I stumbled twice on roots extending out of the ground. Despite the darkness, I could see the mystery man struggling to get up the hill, gravel sliding under his feet as he ran parallel to me, about a hundred feet to my left. Every few steps he turned and looked back for Travis; he didn't sense my presence to his right. I continued to sprint to the top of the hill before turning to my left and starting down the southern face of the cemetery. As I made the turn, the jagged edge of a tombstone slashed my calf; I leaped several limestone headstones. Even in my heightened state of excitement, I realized that sprinting diagonally through a garden of granite and limestone obelisks on a near-moonless night was not the smartest thing to do, but my adrenaline was surging, too. Darting to the right of the arch designating the final resting place of former school superintendent Joseph Grodin, I found a path between plots that led straight downhill to the gravel road. I beat the mystery man to the peak of the hill by three full steps.

He was breathing hard and had turned to look for Travis, who was nowhere in sight, when I stepped onto the gravel and from behind his back snagged a thick bicep. "Hey, mister, relax. All we want is . . ."

In a single motion he jumped, jerked his arm free of my grip, and slashed his elbow across my mouth. I rocked back two steps before I lost my balance and sprawled on my back in the gravel. Blood squirted from my ruptured lip, and the taste of warm copper filled my mouth. His shoe landed next to my ear as he passed me; I reached but grabbed nothing but air. "You sonofabitch," I yelled, on my feet in an instant. The race was on. The gravel road was one of two that dissected the southern face of the hill. The first was about one-third of the way up the hill; the second, on which I had just been dropped, was two-thirds of the way up. The mystery man was sprinting downhill between the two gravel roads, which was the steepest part of the hillside. I was surprised at how fast he was moving, but fear can be a great motivator. He was heading at an angle toward the caretaker's house. I cut across a corner of the cemetery to the asphalt road that ran from Route 151 to the ridge, bisecting the old and new sections. The mystery man was ahead of me and moving quite gracefully through the minefield of granite impediments. Beyond the lower gravel road, the ground began to level out. I jumped off the asphalt road, danced between several headstones, and found another corridor between plots. I was going to catch him; I had the angle and was blocked from his view. He had broken clear of the headstones and was in the grassy area between the first row of headstones and the parking lot when he finally saw me, but it was too late. In my head I could hear the squeaky voice of our defensive coordinator, Rudy Palmer, screaming, "Head up, drive your shoulder into him, wrap him up, Jesus Christ, Malone, you hit like my grandmother." It was a textbook tackle. My head slid in front of his chest and I drove my shoulder into his ribs. It was my best shot, but he was thick and solid and it was like hitting a moving headstone. I grunted and the air rushed from my lungs, but he went down. He sprawled on his chest, me on my side, and as he scrambled to get away I grabbed his right ankle and pulled his calf to my face. He started dragging me across the grass, stepping with his left and dragging his right, and fell again. I couldn't get a breath of air. It felt like daggers were stabbing at my lungs, but I wasn't letting go of that leg—at least not until his left heel smashed into my balls. I released one hand to cover the jewels, and he jerked his right leg free. I made a last, desperate lunge as he stood, grabbing his heel and cleanly stripping his shoe from his foot. I rolled over on the shoe like a linebacker covering a fumble. Even in my temporary delirium, seized with pain from lungs and testicles, I sensed its value.

The mystery man apparently saw no such value in the shoe. I heard him run through the gravel and a moment later, from somewhere beyond the caretaker's house, a car door slammed and tires squealed. He drove without headlights until he crested the hill two hundred yards down the road.

It was ten minutes before I fully caught my breath, at which point I threw up twice—cleansing my system of the RC Cola, a package of peanut M&M's, and several pretzel rods—and started walking back toward the bunker, cradling the shoe like a prized trophy. Blood continued to ooze from the inside of my mouth where the mystery man's elbow had hit me. My lower lip drooped; it was already twice its normal size and swelling at about the same pace as my testicles. When I got back to our encampment, there was no sign of Travis.

"Trav?"

"Over here," he called from somewhere in the darkness and the mist. I walked, slowly and bowlegged, in the general direction of the voice. During the early stages of his pursuit, Travis had been rudely introduced to Mildred (1893–1961) and Edmond (1888–1950) Figler when he ran headlong into the extended left wing of the guardian angel that stood atop their tombstone. It had lanced a fishhook-shaped gash at his hairline and a razor blade–thin cut just above his right brow. The collision had knocked him loopy, and when he came to he was prone across the Figlers' graves. By the time I found him, Travis was sitting on the edge of the tombstone, his hand cupped over the cuts, which was doing little to staunch the bleeding. The right side of his face was covered in blood and his right eye was already swollen nearly shut. "Christ Almighty, Travis, you're going to bleed to death."

He looked up and squinted with his good eye. "Oh, Mildred, Ed, this is my friend Mitchell that I was telling you so much about. Say hello to the Figlers, Mitch."

"We've got to get that looked at."

Travis laughed. "I'm sure Big Frank would be happy to get a call from the emergency room at three a.m. 'What the hell were you doin' in the cemetery?' Oh, not much, just trying to catch the guy who's been leaving flowers at the memorial to your ex-wife. You know, the memorial you never even told me existed. Now, *that* would go over big, wouldn't it?"

I dropped the shoe, peeled off my T-shirt and handed it to him. "Press this up against it. Maybe it'll stop the bleeding."

"Couldn't catch him, huh?"

"Oh, I caught him. Twice, in fact. I just couldn't hold him."

Travis looked up, for a moment excited. "Did you get a look at him?"

"Not his face. But I got a dandy close-up of his elbow and he introduced my balls to the heel of his shoe." I fingered my still-swelling lip with one hand while I picked up the black shoe with the other. "Here. I did get you this." I dropped the black wingtip in front of him.

"He lost his shoe?"

"No, he didn't lose it, goddammit. I took it off of him, and I'm probably never going to sire children because of it."

He picked up the shoe and gave it a closer inspection. "Good God. It's a gunboat. Who has feet this big?"

"Figure that out and maybe you'll find your man."

"How did the prince find Cinderella?"

"I gave him a pretty good shot to the ribs. Why don't you just look around for someone wearing one shoe and walking doubled over?"

Travis held out his free hand and I gave him a lift up and we started back toward the bunker. "G'night, Mildred, g'night, Ed. Nice meeting you folks." Travis draped his free arm around my neck. "Look at this," he said, pulling my ruined shirt away from his eye, "You gave me the shirt off your back. I'm telling you, man, you are one great friend."

"After tonight I'm starting to wonder if that's such a good thing."

And we limped into the night.

CHAPTER TWELVE

We sat in the bunker for a long while. I fished in the cooler for a couple handfuls of ice and stuffed them into my bloody T-shirt, then twisted the cloth around the ice like a tourniquet and applied it to Travis's cuts. "You're the best mom ever," he said, forcing a short laugh. I held an unopened bottle of RC Cola against my lip as I sat with legs splayed on a rock, trying to provide relief to my aching privates.

When Travis appeared to have regained his equilibrium enough to walk, we packed up the gear and started the trek home over Tarr's Dome, which was no small task in the dark of night. By the time we reached my house, the faintest crease of morning light was creeping over the West Virginia hills to the east. The ice had melted in the T-shirt, but Travis was still holding the soggy cloth to his head. He looked like a soldier straggling home after a battle. We stripped down to our undershorts behind the grape arbor and turned on the garden hose, holding it over our heads to remove the blood, grime, and cinders. The swelling and split flesh remained.

In the glow of the streetlight, I got a better look at Travis's cuts. The gash at his hairline was deep and wide, and I could see his skull when I put my thumbs on either side of the wound and gently moved it apart. The one above the brow was deep but was a cleaner cut. "Good God, Trav, we've got to get you to a doctor. Those are some nasty cuts."

"Mitch, just get that out of your head. I'm not going to the doctor. Get me some butterfly bandages. I'll be fine."

"You might have a concussion."

"Yeah, you know what they give you for a concussion? A couple of aspirin and tell you to take it easy. So grab me some aspirin, the butterflies, and I'll take it easy."

The bathroom light was on upstairs. Dad was up and getting ready for work. I waited for the kitchen light to go on, the sign that Mom was up and making coffee and packing Dad's lunch. It startled her when the back door opened. "You scared me half to death," she said. "What are you doing home so early?"

"Oh, the place where we usually camp was all flooded and the mosquitoes were eatin' us alive, so we just came back here and slept in the yard." I was lisping around the swollen lip, and she stopped me at the sink.

"What happened to your lip?"

"Fell. Coming down Tarr's Dome. It would be funny if it didn't hurt so bad."

She held her hand to my face and winced. "That looks horrible."

"It hurt when it happened, but it doesn't feel so bad now."

Her eyes narrowed. "Where's your shirt?"

"Outside. It was hot in the sleeping bag." Independently, both statements were true, though not the least bit interrelated. However, it seemed to pacify her and I went to the medicine cabinet in the utility room and shoved a handful of butterfly bandages into my pocket, then opened the aspirin bottle and tapped three tablets into my hand. "I've got to get Travis a couple of aspirin; he's got a thumper of a headache."

Travis washed down the aspirin with a tepid RC Cola and gnawed on a pretzel rod while I applied the bandages to the cuts. I pulled the skin tight and applied one side of the bandage, then pushed the wound together before pressing the bandage down on the other side. The brow injury was a little tricky, as I had to adhere the bandage to his nose and the corner of his swollen eye. I stepped back and admired my handiwork. I said, "Everything considered, it's a fine job of doctoring by a sixteen-year-old without any formal medical training."

"Thank you, doc."

The aroma of bacon was wafting through the backyard as Travis gathered up his camping gear and headed for home. I'm sure he wanted breakfast, but he didn't want my mom to see the swollen side of his face. "I've got to book. I'll call you later," he said. I watched him as he walked down the alley, his sleeping bag tucked under his right arm, his left hand fingering the tender wounds.

"Where's Travis?" Mom asked when I walked back into the house.

"He said he had to get home. Big Frank has some work for him to do around the house today."

"He couldn't stay ten minutes for breakfast?" I shrugged. "Where's that shirt?"

I looked around like I was trying to find it in the kitchen. "I don't know. Travis must have accidentally put it in with his stuff."

Sensing that something wasn't quite right, she stared at my Adam's apple the entire time I spoke.

Travis called that night. He said his eye was swollen shut and it looked like someone had shoved a tennis ball under his eyelid. When he showed up at my house two days later, the eye was infected and looked like a spoiled cauliflower, a grotesque shade of black, blue, green, and yellow. Pus was dribbling from the outside corner, and it smelled like roadkill. "Travis, you've *got* to get that looked at," I said.

Apparently he realized a needle and Big Frank's wrath were better than losing an eye. "Okay," he said.

"Mom, would you come here for a minute, please?"

My mom walked into the upstairs bathroom and immediately both hands flew up and covered her mouth. "Oh, dear God! Travis, what have you done?"

"I cut it a little," he said.

"A little!"

Big Frank was somewhere on the road, so Mom loaded us into the car and drove to Doc Puncheon's at the north end of town. He had been an army physician in Korea, but the sight of Travis's eye made him wince. "Marabelle, you know I need his father's permission to treat him."

"His father is God-only-knows-where. If there are any problems, I'll take responsibility and pay the bill. Clean him up before he loses that eye."

Doc cleaned it with a cotton swab and rinsed it with a solution that he dispensed from a device that looked like a turkey baster. He gave Mom a prescription for some antibiotics. "When was the last time you had a tetanus shot?" he asked Travis.

"I don't want a . . ."

Marabelle Malone slapped Travis across his back. She was in no mood. "Give him the shot," she told Doc, never taking her eyes off Travis. "For someone who gets straight As, you act like you don't have a nickel's worth of common sense."

As he prepared the needle, Doc Puncheon asked, "You know, if you'd have come in right after you did that, you wouldn't be left with such a nasty scar there at the top of your forehead. How did you say you did this?"

"Mitchell and I were out camping. I fell on our camping lantern."

The needle on Marabelle Malone's bullshit meter flew deep into the red zone. The needle extending from the syringe in Doc Puncheon's hand sank into the meaty pad below Travis's shoulder. Travis was grateful for the injection, which hurt so bad that it gave him an excuse to avert his eyes from my mother's glare. She looked at me and frowned. I had tried to dismiss my swollen lip and bowlegged walk as the result of a fall, too. She sensed lies of titanic proportions and questioned me for several days before finally dropping the subject, unconvinced that we were telling the truth but without tangible evidence to the contrary. After a couple of days, the swelling subsided to where you could see a sliver of his eyeball. That weekend, Travis systematically walked the streets of Brilliant, taking into account the age and physical dimensions of the men living in each house. He came up with a list of five possible suspects for the mystery man. Then, on the following Wednesday night—trash collection eve in Brilliant—he rifled the trash cans of the suspects for a single black wingtip. He was chased off by a dog at one house and an irate owner of the trash at another. I thought this was a first-rate piece of detective work. But amid all the trash he found not a single shoe—black wingtip or otherwise.

As the weeks of summer passed and his eye returned to something that resembled human, the near miss in the cemetery became even more disheartening for Travis. He replayed the botched mission over and over in his mind. Long before our night in the cemetery, Travis had convinced himself that the mystery man was, indeed, his mother's companion on the boat. Who else, he reasoned, but a secret lover with a guilty conscience would continue to make clandestine visits to a graveyard fifteen years after her death? Now, the opportunity was lost forever, since the mystery man certainly would never return.

Looking back, it was easy to find flaws with our plan. The frontal assault had been a disaster. Why, we reasoned later, hadn't we simply hidden amid the tombstones, then doubled behind him? We could have been sitting on the hood of his car when he returned. It was such a simple plan. We could have let the air out of his tires and demanded an explanation. Even if we didn't recognize the mystery man, we could have gotten the license plate number and it would have been easy enough to track him down.

If Travis Baron was anything, he was resilient, and after two weeks of flogging himself for the failed mission, he turned his attention back to Chase Tornik. We returned to the library and searched for follow-up stories on the homicide investigation that we might have missed during the first visit. There were none.

"It's a dead end," Travis said.

"Not necessarily," I said. "Let's track down this Tornik guy and find out what he knows."

CHAPTER THIRTEEN

I n late July, Travis was ramping up his training for that fall's cross
country season. He hated running cross country, which he called
a sport for the brain-dead, but did it to keep himself in shape for wrestling, which was his favorite sport. Unfortunately, on many days he
insisted that I run with him. He said it would get me in shape for football and provide him with company.

I hated running. In part, because I wasn't any good at it. I ran with
all the grace of an albatross on take-off—arms and legs flying in every
direction. I was slow and, according to Travis, "clunky." Travis was a
smooth runner and he glided, each step effortless. Travis would stop
by my house by seven a.m. and pick me up. We ran a three-and-a-half-
mile route that wrapped up at the intersection at Main and Labelle
streets. The danger in running this particular circuit was that at the
corner of Main and Labelle was the neat—very, very neat—red brick
home of Captain Troy Mathews, head of the United States Marine
Corps recruiting office in Steubenville. The country was still at war in
Vietnam, and Brilliant males approaching draft age avoided Captain
Mathews like he was . . . well, like he was the head of the local Marine
recruiting office. Nothing cleared the halls at Brilliant High School like
the crew-cut sight of Captain Troy Mathews, USMC.

You couldn't ask Mr. Mathews for the time without him launching
into a sermon extolling the virtues of a career in the Marine Corps.
At skit day at the high school two years earlier, the seniors did a skit
in which a student portraying Captain Mathews was approached by a
panic-stricken teenage boy seeking help because he and his girlfriend
had just been involved in a terrible automobile accident. The boy,

dazed and bleeding profusely from the head, stood before "Captain Mathews" and pleaded for help for his girlfriend, who was seriously injured and still in the car. To this, "Captain Mathews" responded, "I'm sure the medics will do a fine job trying to save her life, Billy, but if she doesn't survive and you become overwhelmed with guilt and loneliness, perhaps you should consider an exciting career in today's Marine Corps."

We were finishing a run on a muggy July morning when Travis made an unprecedented move for a Brilliant male, stopping at the Mathews's home while the captain was edging the grass along his sidewalk.

Captain Mathews had half-inch-long graying hair that stood at attention like a landing strip on the top of his head. He was dressed in olive work pants—never, ever shorts—and a pressed white T-shirt that stretched across a pair of solid shoulders, which remained erect even while he was doing yard work. I was bent at the waist, sucking for air.

Captain Mathews looked at Travis and said, "You seem to be in a lot better shape than your friend."

"Yes, sir. I am. He's not much of a runner."

He flicked Travis's abs twice with the back of his fingers. "Boot camp would be a breeze for someone in your kind of shape."

Travis smiled. It had taken Captain Mathews all of five seconds to put on his recruiting cap. "I can't imagine that Marine boot camp would be a breeze for anyone, sir, no matter how good of shape they're in." Sweat rolled down Travis's face and dripped off his nose. His T-shirt was dark gray with perspiration and tacked to his skin.

"The Marines make men out of boys," Captain Mathews said, bending back down to his chore. "What's on your mind, son?"

"What makes you think there's something on my mind, sir?"

The captain looked up, the thinnest of smiles across his lips. "I'm not the sharpest knife in the drawer, Travis, but I know this isn't a social call. Most boys your age avoid me like the plague. So you either want to join the Corps, or you've got something on your mind. Which is it?"

Travis said, "I was wondering if you're still a sheriff's deputy."

"Yes, I'm still in the auxiliary."

"Do you remember a detective at the sheriff's department named Chase Tornik?"

The captain looked up from his work. It was, I imagined, the same icy stare that some North Korean saw before getting a belly full of bayonet. "I knew Tornik," he said. "Once upon a time he was a terrific detective."

"That's what I've been told. Whatever happened to him?"

"I don't know, and I couldn't care less. As far as I was concerned, they should have taken the guy out behind the courthouse and shot him—saved the taxpayers some money." Captain Troy Mathews's steely gray eyes turned to little slits and his jaw tensed, sending little ripples of vibrations back toward his ears. "Where did this come from? Why do you want to know about Chase Tornik?"

Although Travis should have been prepared for the question, he wasn't, and it caused him to stammer. "Oh, uh, no reason, really."

"No reason, huh? Out of the clear blue Ohio sky, and for no apparent reason, you stop by and ask the local Marine recruiter about a crooked cop who went to prison, what, fifteen years ago?" Travis just shrugged. He was afraid to tell the captain the real reason for fear it would get back to Big Frank. Fortunately, like most residents of Brilliant, Captain Mathews was no fan of Frank Baron. "I don't know where Tornik went after he got out of prison. I know he got out quite a while ago; I remember seeing it in the paper. Regardless, he's trouble and you ought to stay away from him." He stood up with his trimmers and stretched his back. "I've got a pretty good idea what you want to talk to him about, but I'd advise you to be very careful. Sometimes, it's best just to leave the past in the past."

"Did you know your mother, Captain Mathews?" Travis asked. The captain swiped at beads of sweat on his upper lip but said nothing. "If it had been your mother, would you be able to keep it in the past?"

I walked up alongside Travis. Captain Mathews looked away and started cleaning the blades of his trimmers with his fingers. "A couple months after your mother died, Tornik asked me about your dad. You know, the usual stuff—what did he do for a living, where'd he work, what kind of a guy was he. If a wife dies under mysterious circumstances, checking out the husband is standard procedure. The husband is always a suspect. Tornik told me there was something hinky about your mother's death, so he was trying to get some background on your dad. I told him what I knew about your dad, which wasn't much. They checked out his alibi and could account for his whereabouts the day before the accident. As I recall, it all checked out—gas and food receipts and things of that nature—all the way to wherever he was going—Mississippi or Arkansas, somewhere down south, I think."

"If he thought it was a murder, who did Tornik think killed her?"

Mathews shook his head. "He didn't say, and I didn't ask. If someone tells you something like that and it leaks out, all of a sudden your ass is in a sling. I just told him if there was anything I could do to let me know. Seems to me that Tornik went down in smoke not long after that."

Travis nodded, wiped his sweaty palm on his shorts and extended it to Captain Mathews. "Thanks. I appreciate it."

We had walked just a few steps up Labelle Street when Captain Mathews said, "Travis!" We stopped. "There is one thing I should tell you," the Marine said, taking a few steps toward us. "I'm no fan of Chase Tornik, but I'll tell you this, he was a hell of an investigator. A *hell* of an investigator. He had this uncanny sixth sense for knowing who had committed a crime and how it went down. He just knew. It was incredible to watch. He could survey a crime scene, talk to a couple of neighbors, and say, 'Okay, here's what happened,' and he'd start ticking it off, step by step. And by the time we got done with the investigation, I'll be damned if he wasn't right ninety-nine percent of the time. Chase Tornik had his faults, and they proved to be significant. However, if he thought your mother's death was a homicide, I'd bet my bottom dollar that there was something to it."

CHAPTER FOURTEEN

Travis got a job that summer working at the bakery across the street from his house. He gassed up the trucks each afternoon when they came back from their routes, then unloaded the stale loaves of bread and cupcakes that were returned. He was saving his money to buy a car, which he planned to use to drive as far from Brilliant, Ohio, and Big Frank Baron as possible, the day after he graduated high school. The recent focus of Project Amanda had been to track down Chase Tornik. Travis had no idea how to do this. Since those who had worked with Tornik spat out his name like a mouthful of soured milk, Travis reasoned that Tornik was living the life of a recluse, forever shamed by his deeds.

We sat in the back room of the Coffee Pot one late summer evening, Creedence Clearwater Revival playing on the jukebox, the rain falling in waves and flooding the gutters along Third Street. "I've got a plan for finding Tornik," he said.

I said, "I'm all ears, so long as it doesn't involve climbing into your attic or camping out at the cemetery."

"It doesn't. I'm going to take the money I've been saving for a car and hire a private investigator to track him down."

"Really? Good plan. How much is that going to cost?"

"I don't know. I really don't want to spend the dough, but I figured a private investigator could find him quicker than the two of us."

"How much money do you have?"

"I've saved about eighty bucks, so far."

"I don't know much about private investigators, Trav, but I'll bet they charge a lot more than eighty bucks to track someone down. Why can't we look for him?"

"Like how?"

"I don't know. Did you try the phone book?"

He rolled his eyes. "The phone book? After what he went through, I doubt very much he's going to be in the phone book."

"How do you know?"

"Everyone we talked to would rather cuddle up with a leper than Chase Tornik."

"Lepers are still allowed to have a telephone."

"He probably doesn't even live around here. How could you possibly live in a town where you screwed up so bad that everyone hates you?"

I shrugged. "You never know." I went to the pay phone on the back wall and retrieved the Steubenville Area phone book from the shelf below the coin return. And there he was, snug between Torak, R. L. and Toronado, Thuman H.

Tornik, C. W. 844 E. Wheeling Ave. . . . 883-3323

"Dammit. Why didn't you suggest that to begin with?" he asked.

"I knew it would somehow be my fault." I shoved the phone book across the table to him. "You're the brains of the outfit. I assumed that would have been your first move."

He was sitting on the porch steps of a duplex, extremely neat by the standards of the neighborhood, with aluminum siding, new windows, and a porch so recently built that it had yet to be painted. On one side of the duplex was an abandoned house with waist-high weeds and gutters sagging under their own weight, and on the other was a one-story brick ranch with the screen door hanging from one hinge and dirty, shirtless kids playing on a beaten patch of ground.

It was our third trip to the south Steubenville neighborhood in search of Tornik. The first night he wasn't home, so we parked down the street and waited for him. One of the little brats from the brick ranch pedaled his bicycle up to the driver's-side door and asked, "What are you doin'?"

"None of your business," I said.

"Got any money?"

"Yeah, I've got money, but you're not getting any of it."

The little turd called me an ass wipe and spit on my windshield as he pedaled off.

We waited an hour, but Tornik never showed up.

We returned two days later. Again he wasn't home, and again we staked out the house. The same kid came pedaling straight at my car. "You spit on my car again and I swear I'll beat the livin' . . ."

Again, he hawked on the windshield and yelled "bite me, ass wipe," while he pedaled away. Travis laughed. As we waited, a black kid no older than ten started chucking rocks through the windows of the abandoned two-story house on the other side of Tornik's. This lasted until mamma came out of a house across the street, picked up a two-by-four from the yard, and started after him. He easily outran her, but the last thing I heard her say was, "Thas awright, you have to sleep sometime."

Again, Tornik didn't show.

He was on the porch when we drove past on this Saturday shortly before noon. The neighborhood was full of the sound of kids yelling and crying, but if this bothered Chase Tornik you couldn't tell. He sat on the top step of his porch sipping an amber liquid from a clear glass tumbler. The morning paper lay neatly folded beside him, and his knees served as rests for a pair of sinewy forearms. A cigarette burned between the cupped fingers of his left hand, and he held the tumbler in his right. They both looked natural in his hands, as though years of constant use had made them permanent appendages. He was neatly attired in a white, short-sleeved dress shirt, pressed slacks, and polished black dress shoes. Not a hair was out of place on a coif that was slicked down and a mix of dirty blond and gray. His face was scrubbed white and pockmarked across his cheeks and neck, his nose crimson and rocky, a monument to the fluid in the tumbler. We parked just down the street and walked back. He must have thought we were either Jehovah's Witnesses or Mormons hoping to save his soul because when we neared his porch he said, "Boys, if you're trying to keep me from spending eternity in hell, I'm afraid that train's already left the station."

Travis frowned at me. He didn't get it. "We're not out saving souls today," I said.

"Are you Chase Tornik?" Travis asked.

The man lifted the hand that held his cigarette and shielded his eyes from the morning sun, squinting first into the youthful face of Travis Baron, then at me. One eye squinted in the glare. "I might be. Who wants to know?"

"I do."

The man dropped his hand and took a short hit from his cigarette. "That seems somewhat obvious. How about him?" He nodded at me. "Does he want to know, too?"

"Yeah."

"Okay, then just who might you be?"

Travis swallowed. "This is my friend, Mitchell Malone. My name is Travis Baron."

Slowly, the man nodded his head, the slightest of smiles pursing his lips. "Travis Baron, is it?" He had a rattling voice—dry and rough—that came from deep in his chest and sounded as if every syllable was uttered with great effort. He took a last hit from the cigarette and flicked the burning nub past my ear and into the street. "Yeah, I'm Tornik."

"Do you know who I am?" Travis asked.

Tornik's nod was nearly imperceptible. "I've got a pretty good idea." He pulled a hard pack of Winstons from his breast pocket and used his lips to cull another smoke from the herd, never taking his eyes off Travis. He worked his jaw and, I thought, was searching for a name that hadn't crossed his mind in years. In a tone almost as imperceptible as the nod, he said, "Amanda Baron?" Travis nodded. Tornik lit the cigarette, and a plume of blue smoke escaped from his mouth and curled around his face. "You're Amanda Baron's son?"

"I'm surprised that you remembered," Travis replied.

"Remembering a name is no great feat. What can I do for you?"

"I want to talk to you about my mother."

Tornik nodded for Travis to sit next to him on the top step. I stood by the bottom step, leaning against the handrail. "I don't know that I can be much help. It's been a long time. How old are you, anyway?"

"Sixteen."

"Sixteen!" Tornik repeated. "Christ Almighty." He sipped his drink. "It's been that long, huh? Hard to believe. So, what is it that you want to know about her?"

Tornik had a calm demeanor and no edge to his tone. I got the impression that he didn't rile very easily, and I imagined that surviving seven years in prison as a former cop would make other problems seem somewhat insignificant. "I'd like to know anything that you can tell me about her, anything that you can remember."

"You sure I'm the right person to do that? Is your dad still alive?"

"Yeah, but it's not one of his favorite subjects. In fact, he won't talk about it at all. He's old-style Italian with a nasty temper, and his wife got killed while cheating on him, so it doesn't sit very well."

"I suspect not," Tornik said.

"Mostly, I want to know why you thought she was murdered. I saw an article in the *Herald-Star* that said you were investigating her death as a homicide."

Again, he sipped his whiskey. "That was a long, long time ago, son. I don't remember the article. But, yeah, I was looking into her death as a possible homicide. I recall that much . . ." His voice trailed off. He looked at Travis and slowly shook his head. "I guess, now that I think about it, I don't really remember too much about the case."

He was lying, I thought. He was debating why he should tell her son what he knew. I could sense that he was uncomfortable with the situation. "You remembered her name without any trouble," I said.

Tornik nodded. "Yeah, but I just don't remember much else. I don't think I can be much help to you boys." He picked up his newspaper and started to stand.

"I can refresh your memory, if you like," Travis said, standing up from the porch. I knew Travis, and I knew that tone. The conversation was about to take an ugly turn. "You were doing an investigation into my mom's death when you got sent to prison for being a crooked cop. Does that jog your memory at all?"

The words flew out of Travis's mouth, and for a moment I expected Tornik to rake a backhand across his face. Tornik just frowned, bit his lower lip, and said, "You're a bold little shit, aren't you?" Travis just stared. "You talk to me like that again, boy, and you're in for an ass whippin'. I don't care how old you are."

"Do you think that scares me? My dad is Big Frank Baron. Ass whippin's aren't anything new to me."

"With a mouth like that I can understand why." Slowly, as if to show Travis that any further conversation would be done on his terms, Tornik tilted his head and dragged hard on the cigarette, inhaling deep and exhaling slow. "Why are you so interested in your mother's death?"

"If someone thought your mother had been murdered, wouldn't you be interested?"

Tornik looked at Travis and nodded, blowing a plume of smoke over his head. "I suppose I would, at that." He rolled the newspaper in his hands. "Why did I think your mom was murdered? As I recall, there were some things that just didn't add up. Everyone thought it was an open-and-shut case. She drowned and the river never gave up her body. End of story. But your dad was out of town, so why would she go out on a boat to have a fling? She could have just had someone over to the house."

I recalled what Captain Mathews had told us about Tornik. *He had this uncanny sixth sense for knowing who had committed a crime and how it went down. He just knew.* "That was it?" I asked. "You started a homicide investigation on a hunch?"

"Nothing wrong with a hunch," he said. "And, as I recall, we got some information that all wasn't as it appeared. I started talking to people who knew your mom, people from the church and . . ." Tornik squinted. "Where did she work? The library?"

"She was a volunteer at the library," Travis said.

"That's right. I remember that now. I talked to some people there and they all said it would have been *highly* unlike her to be out on a boat in the middle of the night with a lover—very out of character. I'm not saying your mother was a saint, and I'm not saying she didn't have a lover, but based on the information I got from people who knew her, I think she would have had better sense than to be out in that boat in the Ohio River in the middle of the night."

"So she had a boyfriend?" Travis asked.

Tornik shrugged. "Maybe. But if she did, he wasn't on that boat with her."

"You're talking in riddles. If it wasn't her boyfriend, who was it?"

"That's the million-dollar question, isn't it? I don't know. I was never convinced that it was her on the boat."

"But the barge captain saw them jump off the boat and into the water. I read that in the paper." Tornik said nothing, taking another long hit on his smoke. "If you're trying to confuse me, you're doing a great job. If all these mysterious things were going on, how come no one investigated the case after you went to prison?"

He finished the liquor in one eye-watering gulp, the ice cubes pressing against his lip as he drained every drop. "No one else was interested, I guess. Actually, I think there were some other detectives who had suspicions, but I bet the real reason is that no one wanted to touch anything I had been associated with."

"Maybe they just thought you were wrong," Travis said. "Maybe they looked at the case and decided it was just an accident."

He shrugged. "That's possible. I don't believe it for one second, and I don't think you believe it, either. You think your mother was murdered."

"You don't know that."

"Sure I do. That's why you're here. You're looking for someone to confirm your suspicions. You may not know much about your mother, but you just can't convince yourself that it was an accident. You can't convince yourself that she would leave you at home, alone, while she went out for a rendezvous with her boyfriend. That's why you're talking to me." Tornik took a breath, looked at Travis for a long moment, then dropped the bomb. "You want to know the real reason why I started looking into her death?"

Travis said, "Of course. That's why I'm here."

"I was asked to do it."

"By who?"

"Your grandfather—he thought she had been murdered, too. That's why he called me."

"My grandfather Baron?"

Tornik winced. "What? Hell no, not your grandfather Baron. The other one. Her dad. I can't remember his name."

"Virdon."

"That was it. Virdon. He was a military man. I remember that. He called me and said he didn't believe it had been an accident. He thought your mom had been murdered and then dumped off the boat to make it look like an accident."

"When was this?"

"I don't remember, exactly. It wasn't too awful long after she disappeared, a couple of weeks, maybe a month. I remember that your grandfather didn't think too highly of your dad. He said your mom was planning to leave your old man. I guess things weren't going very well. Your grandfather believed with all his heart that she had been murdered. Frankly, I'm half surprised that he didn't come up here looking for your dad."

"So it was that simple, huh? He had a bad feeling and you started looking into it?"

"Pretty much. Have you talked to your grandfather?"

"He's dead, he and my grandmother Virdon." Travis's eyes bored in on Tornik. I could see the flush in his cheeks. "So now we'll never know."

Tornik shook his head. "It's been too long."

Travis stood, appearing to fight back tears. "Maybe that's what you tell yourself, that it's been too long. But if . . ."

"If!" Tornik said, his voice climbing for the first time as he cut off Travis's attack. "If what? If I hadn't screwed up and gone to prison I might have solved the case? It's water over the dam, son. I'm sorry, but there's nothing I can do about it now." Chase Tornik grabbed his newspaper and stood. "If you want me to admit I screwed up? That ain't happening. People can believe what they want about your mother, and they can believe what they want to believe about me. I don't give a shit anymore."

CHAPTER FIFTEEN

The chink in Margaret Simcox's academic armor was exposed that summer.

She could not parallel park.

Margaret had taken driver's education through the school that summer. She botched nearly every attempt to parallel park, and though she earned her driver's license, she also earned a "B" in the course. A half-credit "B" in driver's education put her behind Travis in their competition to be our class valedictorian. Travis took full advantage of this and began calling her "Crash" every time they passed, and it nearly brought her to tears.

Our first football scrimmage of the year was against Harrison Local, a team made up of the sons of thick-necked Eastern European immigrants with such names as Waskiewicz, Mroczkowski, Zelkowski, Andreichuk, and Orizczak. We played them to a 12–12 tie, a moral victory for Brilliant.

I limped home from the game and found Travis sitting on the glider on my back porch, slowly rocking in the dark. "How'd it go?" he asked.

"Pretty good. We tied 'em, 12–12." I set my equipment bag on the porch and eased onto the glider to Travis's left.

"How'd you do?"

"Not bad. Caught three balls—one was a nifty little over-the-shoulder grab with one of their safeties hanging all over me. Unfortunately, I followed that up by letting one go right through my hands on a buttonhook. It hit me in the facemask and went about twenty feet straight up in the air and they intercepted it. So that quick..." I snapped my fingers. "... the over-the-shoulder grab was forgotten and the muff remembered. It's going to look really bad on the films."

"Coach Oblak will be so excited about tying Harrison Local that he won't even remember that drop."

"It happened on our last drive on their seven-yard line."

Through the darkness I could see him choking back laughter. "Okay, forget what I said, the coaches might remember that one."

"What are you up to?"

"Well, I thought you'd like to know that I had a little chat with Big Frank tonight."

"About?"

"My mom."

"Ka-ching. That's interesting. What prompted you to do that?"

"Actually, I blundered into it. I got home from the bakery, made a sandwich, and turned on the TV, and the afternoon movie was *Titanic*, with Clifton Webb and Barbara Stanwyck. So I'm watching it and Big Frank comes in and sits down, and it's right at the end of the movie where the ship's going down and people are drowning all over the place, and Big Frank says, 'God, drowning would be an awful way to go.' It was out of his mouth before he realized what he had said. I told him, 'You know, Mom drowned, and you've never really talked to me about that. I'd really like to know more about her.'"

"Nice transition. What did he say?"

"He said, 'Your mother was a *baldracca*.' He said it with this guttural Italian accent, just like my Grandpa Baron used to talk when he got pissed off about something."

"So what's a baldracca?"

"I don't know, but since he spat it out like a fly had flown into his mouth, it certainly can't be good. I asked him what it meant and he just looked away. If I had to bet, it's probably Italian for whore. But he didn't leave. He just got this look of resignation on his face, like he was tired, and said, 'What do you want to know?'"

"That opened the door."

"Yes and no. You've got to know how to work Big Frank. You've got to pick your shots. Ask him one question, be very specific, and hope you don't cross that line in the sand that will cause Mount Baron to blow sky high."

"How do you know where the line is?"

"That's always the challenge with Big Frank. The line changes from day to day, depending on his mood."

"What did you ask him?"

"I said I wanted to know what she was like. What was her favorite food? What did she smell like? How did they decide to name me Travis? Did she want me to be a doctor or join the Navy, or what? What kind of movies did she like? I wanted to know anything like that."

"And?"

"Nothing. I don't think he was trying to be evasive, or that he didn't remember. I don't think he ever knew. He said, 'Hell, boy, I don't know,'" Travis said, dropping his voice several octaves to imitate Big Frank. "'It's been a long goddamn time. Movies. She liked movies. Don't everybody?' I think it was probably a little embarrassing that he didn't know anything. I said, 'Dad, what color were her eyes?' He thought about it for a moment and finally said, 'Beats the hell outta me.'"

"Green," I said.

"Right, but he had no clue. He was telling me about getting discharged from the Navy and moving back to Brilliant. Now, mind you, he remembers driving his 1947 Mercury convertible back to Brilliant . . ." He reverted to his Big Frank voice: "'The Merc, what a helluva car, I bought it off a guy in my unit who couldn't keep up with the payments. That was one sweetheart of a ride, I'll tell you that; had a three-fifty in it, damn, it was so sweet. I wish I still had that puppy.' And he can tell you that *How High the Moon* and *The World Is Waiting for the Sunshine* by Les Paul and Mary Ford were the big songs on the radio during the trip. He probably remembers the odometer reading from every oil change he's ever had, but he can't remember the color of my mom's eyes. Doesn't that strike you as weird?"

"To be real honest with you, Trav, a lot of things about Big Frank strike me as weird."

A coal train rolled past, making the windows behind us vibrate in their panes. Its horn blasted as it neared the Penn Street crossing, echoing off the hills.

I asked, "What did he remember about the night she died?"

"He said he left Brilliant on a Thursday morning for Arkansas to take some coiled steel to a processing plant near Fayetteville. When he got there, there was a message for him to call home. When he does, my grandma Baron tells him that my mother was out on the river in the boat and drove it into a barge and they couldn't find her. He said he was thinking there's no way, because she hated the boat and she hated the water. He said he thought maybe someone kidnapped her and made her go out on the river. He drove all the way back. That's when he found out that she and some guy were seen jumping off the boat. He said the boat didn't have any running lights on and it drifted into a barge full of iron ore. It was like a bulldozer hitting a storage shed and the boat ended up in a million pieces."

"Did you ask him if he knew who the guy was?"

"Yeah. He said he didn't know and didn't care. He called the guy a coward who saved himself and let my mom drown so their affair wouldn't be known."

"Did you ask him about the homicide investigation?"

Travis nodded. "He said there was nothing to it. He said it was just Tornik trying to add to his scrapbook. 'Tornik being Tornik,' is how he described it."

"Did you tell him that we talked to Tornik and he said your grandfather Virdon had called because he suspected Big Frank of murdering your mother?"

"No, I do place some value on my life."

I smiled. "He was pretty forthcoming."

"Yeah, I know, he was actually pretty congenial." Travis looked at me and frowned. "You know, I almost hate it when that happens. Big Frank's more suited to acting like a complete bastard. When he acts like a human being it makes me think there's something wrong in the cosmos. You know, like the world's spinning off its axis." I laughed. "Okay," Travis continued, "here's the best part. I asked him if he thought Mom drowned because she got pulled down in the undertow of the barge. And, he said, it wouldn't have mattered because she couldn't swim. He told me that twice, like he was really trying to emphasize it. He said, 'Your mom couldn't swim a lick.'"

I nodded. "So, consequently, once she hit the water that night, she didn't have a chance."

"According to Big Frank."

"That makes sense to me," I said. "They couldn't get the boat away from the barge and she panicked and jumped, even though she couldn't swim. So why is that the best part?"

"Turn on the porch light for a second; I want to show you something." I got up, my lower back aching from the pounding I had taken earlier in the evening, opened the screen door, and reached around the corner, flipping on the overhead light. Travis had a folded piece of paper in his hand, which was covering a metallic object. "This was in that cardboard box we found in the attic. I thought it was neat to have, but I never realized its true significance until this afternoon." He handed it to me. The metallic object was a gold medal hanging from a faded blue ribbon. The front was a tarnished relief of Lady Victory. On the back was inscribed:

First Place
1946
Princess Anne County
Swimming & Diving Championships
200-yard freestyle

"It's a medal she won from a swimming competition when she was fifteen years old."

I inspected it for several seconds and passed it back. "Maybe it's not even hers."

"It's hers. Inside that box was a purple velvet bag with a drawstring, like the kind whiskey bottles come in, and it was completely full of swimming medals—dozens of 'em. The scrapbook had a couple of newspaper articles about her and swimming. Look at the paper."

I carefully unfolded the paper, which was yellow at the corners and along the creases. It was a Red Cross Senior Life Saving Certificate. Written in fountain pen on the line below the words *Presented To* was the name, *Amanda Virdon*.

"So not only could she swim, but she was a hell of a swimmer," I said.

"Exactly," Travis said. "She was a lifeguard and a champion swimmer. So why did Big Frank make a point to tell me she couldn't swim?"

CHAPTER SIXTEEN

"**H**ey, mister," Travis yelled.

The man slowed his run across the rain-pelted gravel lot. "What?" the man called back, never stopping his movement toward the protection of the cement block building in the corner of the lot.

"Is Chase Tornik inside?"

"What do you want?"

"I want to talk to Chase Tornik."

"Why?"

Loud enough for me to hear, Travis said, "None of your business, asshole." Then he yelled, "It's personal."

Through the rain and the only window in the front of the cement block building on the far side of the lot, we watched as the man walked across the illuminated lobby and pointed toward us with a thumb. Chase Tornik walked out of an office and appeared to squint into the night. Slowly, he pulled on a raincoat and a ball cap, lit a cigarette, and exited the building. Tornik hunched against the wind and rain as he crossed the gravel lot of the Ohio Valley Cement and Masonry Company. Through the darkness and rain, Tornik strained to see the outline of Travis and me standing beyond the seven-foot chain-link fence with barbed wire that ran along Smithfield Street. As he neared the fence, Tornik said, "Harvey said some smart-ass kid wanted to see me. I figured it had to be you."

"You don't know any other smart-ass kids?" Travis asked.

"I don't know any other kids, period," he said.

Travis was wearing a thin windbreaker. His hair was plastered to his head and he was shivering in rain the size of shooting marbles that were hitting like BBs. The wind blew across Travis's face, sending droplets cascading in rapid succession from his chin and nose. I had grabbed my hooded football raincoat out of the trunk of my car, which was insulated and covered me from my head to below my knees. I felt sorry for Travis, but not so sorry that I would consider giving up my comfort. After all, he was the one dragging me up here for another go-around with Tornik. We had gone to his house and found it empty. The older woman who lived in the other half of the duplex told us that we would find him at the cement factory, where he worked as a security guard.

"I thought you'd be back sooner," Tornik said.

"I've been busy. I need to know some things."

"You picked a beautiful night." Tornik motioned us to the main gate, which he opened by pushing a button near an empty guard booth. We followed him into the block building and back to an office in the far corner. Tornik pulled off his raincoat and ground out the nub of the cigarette, adding to the growing mound in the ashtray on his desk. A rim of cold ash encircled the ashtray, the residue of Tornik's misdirected flicks. He lit up another and extended a hand holding the pack. "Smoke?" We both shook our heads. "Don't start. My voice didn't always sound like a cement mixer."

"Why don't you quit?" I asked.

He looked at me, inhaled deep, and began talking as the smoke escaped from his mouth. "After I got out of prison, I met this woman, Lucy Bannister, who was a social worker at the halfway house. Nice girl, good Christian. She'd been divorced twice. She had a severe character flaw; she was attracted to men she thought she could cure of a lifetime of bad habits, which probably explains why she was attracted to me. We had been going out a couple of weeks when she started badgering me to quit smoking. I wouldn't quit. Finally, I said, 'Lucy, on the day I got to prison, just after I got out of the van and into the indoctrination area, this big, black bubba walked up to me, leaned up in my face and said, "I've always wanted to fuck me a cop." And that night, he did. And the next night, and the next night, and the next night. So do you think I'm concerned about a little thing like lung cancer?'" I felt myself shake as a wave of cold chills started in my spine and exploded through my entire body. "Don't smoke and don't go to prison. That's my advice."

He turned his attention to Travis. "Now, what do you want to talk about?"

"You said my mother's death was suspicious. You said some things just didn't add up, remember?"

"I remember."

Travis looked hard into Tornik's eyes. "Who killed her?"

"I don't know. If I knew I . . ."

"Who do you think killed her?" Travis asked, cutting Tornik off in mid-sentence.

He dragged hard on his cigarette and for a brief moment looked away. "Look, kid, just because someone starts a murder investigation doesn't mean you automatically have a suspect. I know your grandfather suspected your father, but that doesn't mean he did it. Like I said, it's been a long time and I don't really remember if I had someone in mind."

"Mr. Tornik, I may be only sixteen, but I'm no idiot. I know if you had a suspect, you'd remember who it was. I want to know. I'm desperate to know. Was it my dad? If so, the least you could do . . ." I put a hand on Travis's arm, cutting him off as his voice began to climb. His left forearm felt like knotted steel, and his right foot went into overdrive, the heel bouncing off the floor in rapid succession. A wave of crimson was racing up his neck.

I said, "Mr. Tornik, when we started poking around we were just trying to find out about his mom, you know, what kind of person was she, stuff like that. But now, we've got more questions than we do answers, and that's mostly because of the story we found that says you were investigating her death as a homicide. We know someone still visits her . . ." I stopped, not sure if Travis wanted that bit of information revealed.

He nodded. "Someone still visits the memorial they have to her at the cemetery—to this day still puts flowers on her grave. Who does that after all these years? Somebody with a guilty conscience? We don't know. We're just looking for some answers."

Tornik took a final hit off the cigarette and this time dropped the stub in a Styrofoam cup half-filled with coffee. It fizzled out. "Who do you think is putting the flowers on the memorial?" he asked.

"Like Mitchell said, someone who is having trouble living with their guilt," Travis offered.

He shook his head. "Not a chance. People's consciences don't bother them for that long. A guilty conscience lasts about forty-eight hours, not sixteen years. It's someone who cared about her."

"Who?" Travis asked.

"Guys, like I told you the last time, it's been a long damn time. I don't remember all the details. And if I told you who I thought it was, you'd go out and do something stupid."

"We wouldn't. I swear," Travis said.

"Uh-huh. You'd be on his front porch tonight."

Of course, Tornik was right. Travis looked at Tornik, anger and frustration building on his face, blotches of red consuming his cheeks and ears. "You don't know who it might be, or you're just not going to tell me?"

"Both. I'm not sure, and for that reason, I'm not going to tell you. I won't speculate so you can disrupt someone's life."

"My dad said whoever she was with let her drown so everybody wouldn't find out that they were having an affair."

"Your dad is guessing. Besides, if that is what happened, there's no law against letting someone die. It's cowardly, but not illegal."

"Goddammit, tell me what you know," Travis said, his torso leaning toward Tornik. "She's on a boat, she jumps off, and the guy lets her drown. You say that's not a crime, but still you start a homicide investigation! Jesus Christ, what kind of mind game are you playing with me? Just tell me what you know, what you suspect. Anything. Don't you see that nothing here makes sense to me?"

"There's nothing to tell."

Travis squeezed the arm rests until his knuckles went white and looked like a miniature ridge of snow-capped mountains. "My dad was right. You were in it for your own glory."

Tornik's brows arched. "Really? That's what your old man told you, huh?"

"He said it was an accident, plain and simple. My mom was a tramp. She was out screwin' her boyfriend and got herself killed. He said it wasn't murder; it was just stupidity."

"You believe what you want to believe, son, but your mom was not a tramp."

"Oh, you remember that much, huh? You were trying to set my dad up to take a fall, weren't you? This was getting a lot of attention in the papers and you wanted a piece of it, didn't you? Wasn't that the plan, to send him to prison like those other guys you tried to railroad?"

Tornik stood, came out from behind his desk, took a calming breath, and said, "It's time for you to leave."

I stood. Travis crossed his arms and remained seated. "You sonofabitch," Travis said.

Tornik snatched him up by the collar of his windbreaker and in one surprisingly quick move, twisted him out of the chair and threw him toward the door. I was moving behind Travis and herded him out of the building.

"Why didn't you just tell me that in the first place, huh, superstar?" Travis yelled back as we left the block building. "Why didn't you just tell me that you were standing on my mom's body so the spotlight would shine on you a little brighter?"

CHAPTER SEVENTEEN

The remainder of our junior year passed without further progress on Project Amanda. Tornik wouldn't talk. The mystery man was no longer putting flowers on the memorial. Travis had again systematically covered the town trying unsuccessfully to find a match for the lone shoe. There seemed to be little else we could do.

In early June of 1970, we hosted Steubenville in an American Legion doubleheader. I pitched the first game and got clobbered 9–2. If that wasn't bad enough, my cousin, Johnny Earl, hit two home runs and a double off of me. He chuckled as he rounded the bases after the first home run, and I tried to hit him in the ribs with the first pitch the next time he came up. He just stepped back, let it pass, then hit the next pitch into the elementary school playground. It scalded me that we shared the same DNA, and I hadn't hit two home runs all summer. Johnny could be a knucklehead, but he could crush a baseball.

We came back and won the nightcap 4–3, which brought me some measure of satisfaction. After the game, Johnny left with his sweaty arm draped over the shoulder of Dena Marie Conchek, one of the most beautiful girls I had ever seen. He winked as he passed by our dugout. There was no justice in the world, I thought. Travis couldn't find out what happened to his mother, and my cousin Johnny was dating Dena Marie Conchek.

Travis sat in the bleachers and watched both games. Afterward, I changed out of my cleats and back into my tennis shoes for the walk home. "Your cousin is really good," Travis said.

"You think?" I said. I took my handkerchief from my hip pocket and blew eighteen innings of dust and the usual Ohio Valley pollution out of my sinuses.

"That one he hit in the playground would have gone out of Forbes Field."

"Yeah, Travis, I know. I stood on the mound and watched it, remember?"

He was silent as we headed down Second Street, and I could tell there was something on his mind. "Out with it," I said.

"I want to track down my mom's relatives," he said.

"That works for me," I said. "Any idea on how we get started?"

"I have a plan."

"You always do."

He grinned. "We start by tracking down some information on her father. I know both her parents are dead, but I think he will be the easiest to find because he was in the military."

"That's a start," I said.

"Not much of one. If we could figure out where they're buried, maybe we could work backward from there. You know, maybe find an aunt or uncle."

"Maybe," I said. We took a few silent steps before I looked at Travis and squinted. "Refresh my memory. How did you find out that her parents were dead?"

"Big Frank."

I stopped in the sidewalk, amazed. "Big Frank told you that your grandmother and grandfather Virdon were both dead?"

"Yeah. So?"

"Isn't he the same guy who told you that your mom couldn't swim?"

Travis went back to working in the bakery, loading and unloading bread trucks. He worked a split shift, four to eight a.m. loading the trucks for that day's deliveries, then again from three to five p.m., unloading the returns that were sold at half-price at the discount store in the front of the warehouse. Consequently, there was always a box of day-old cupcakes or cinnamon rolls in the Baron kitchen, which was the only thing Travis did on a regular basis that seemed to make Big Frank happy.

The second week of June, Travis got excused from his afternoon shift at the bakery and we headed for Pittsburgh. The Pirates were in town against the Giants and, ostensibly, we were going to the game to celebrate the arrival of summer and officially becoming high school seniors. This caused my mother's eyebrows to arch, and she said, "I hope this trip isn't as painful as your last celebration of summer," a snide reminder that she still didn't believe our stories of how we came to be injured the night we encountered the mystery man. The Pirates game offered a good cover for the next stage of Project Amanda, which was our real reason for going to Pittsburgh. Pittsburgh is a traffic engineer's nightmare. Located at the confluence of the Allegheny and Monongahela rivers, the city was built around water and hills. The streets were narrow and crowded by trolleys, which rumbled and squeaked and clanged, zipping by pedestrians who seemed oblivious to the steel monsters. There was no semblance of order in the traffic patterns, and you could become hopelessly lost in an instant. Still, there is no more magnificent view than emerging from the Fort Pitt Tunnels to see the city burst to life in gleaming steel and glass. As we came down off the bridge, we pulled into a nearby parking lot, just off the Boulevard of the Allies. I loved the city. It was a gritty steel town, still full of many first-generation immigrants. The banter on the streets could be heard in any number of languages, and the air was full of the smell of smoke, sulfur, and cheap cigars. We walked the narrow streets, heading south in the direction of the Lafayette Building. We had hours to spare before the game, and the freedom of walking the streets of the city was invigorating. There was, however, a fire down deep in my belly, a nervous churning not unlike the feeling I got just before game time.

We passed through Market Square, where street vendors were selling flowers and fresh vegetables and newspapers were held down under a stone and you paid your dime on the honor system, and past Trinity Episcopal Cathedral, a monster of a stone building that had been stained black by decades of steel mill smoke. The sun was shining and hot. We bought Cokes from a vendor and continued to weave our way across town. The jitters were getting worse as we neared the Lafayette Building at the corner of William Penn Place and Seventh Avenue. It was an old building, sixteen stories of dirt-stained red brick. It housed several low-budget law firms—ambulance chasers; a sheet music sales company; several insurance agencies; Teamsters Local 203, which marked each of its windows with "UNION YES" bumper stickers; and the Western Pennsylvania office of the Veterans Administration, which occupied the middle six floors.

A security guard in the lobby sat behind a steel desk working a crossword puzzle, barely raising his head as we passed. A glass-encased building directory was on the far wall, where I found my target. "You know, you don't have to do this if you don't want to," Travis said.

"I know. I'm okay."

"Scared?"

"Not scared. A little nervous, though," I admitted.

"Great, that means you're ready. You're going in alone, soldier."

"What? Why? I thought this was a team project."

"It is. But I'd just be baggage."

He was right, and when I turned after stepping onto the elevator, he had disappeared into the newsstand on the far side of the lobby. The elevator was small and slow, groaning its way to the fifth floor. My throat tightened as I stepped out and started down the hall in search of room 518. Like the others on the floor, the door was solid oak with a frosted glass window. Painted on the glass was:

518

Counseling Services

I tapped lightly on the glass and a woman's voice answered, "It's open." I stepped into the small outer lobby where a receptionist sat. She was a stout, middle-aged woman with a friendly smile and several large moles on her neck. Next to her, standing stiff-legged and leaning over the side of the desk, was a man in his mid-twenties, handsome, with chiseled features and broad shoulders. He glanced up, "How ya doin'?" he asked.

"Good," I said.

The man gave the woman a few more directions, tapping a paper on her desk with the eraser of a pencil, then turned and walked with an unsteady gait toward his office.

"Can I help you, young man?" the receptionist asked, just about the time that the image of my face began to faintly register deep in the brain of Alex Harmon. He took hold of the door jamb and turned slowly, his artificial legs moving in halted, jerky steps.

He stared for a long moment, the gears continuing to churn. Finally, he asked, "Mitchell?"

I picked up where I had left off three summers earlier and tears welled in my eyes. "Good to see you, Alex."

"My God, I don't believe it." He took a couple of steps and extended his right hand, gripped and pulled me close, hugging me with his muscular left arm. "What the hell are you doing here, boy?"

I returned the hug and took a step back, taking a quick swipe at my eyes with the back of my right hand. "I was in Pittsburgh for the Pirates game and thought I'd stop by and see you."

"Damn. I can't believe it." He gripped my shoulders. "My God, look at you. You're a man." He slid his hands down to my biceps and squeezed. "Been hitting the weights, huh?"

"A little, sure."

"I guess. You've got some nice shoulders there." He turned toward the receptionist. "Rose, this is Mitchell Malone, my across-the-alley neighbor back in Brilliant. Mitchell, this is Rosemary O'Hara, my secretary."

The chubby lady smiled. "Nice to meet you, Mr. Malone."

"Man, I just can't believe this," Alex continued. "I haven't seen you since . . ."

"The parade."

"Yeah, the parade. Jesus, it's been that long, huh?"

I nodded.

Alex slapped my shoulder. "Come on in," he said, pushing me toward his office. "I've probably wondered how you were doing a million times. Whenever I talk to my cousin I always ask about you, but he never seems to know anything. You're going to be a senior this year, aren't you?"

"Yep. Can't wait."

"Great. What do the Blue Devils look like this year?"

"Not bad. We're a little light on the line, as usual. But we've got good skilled people."

"Are you one of them?"

I showed him my hands. "Split end, maybe a little tight end, and I'll do all the kicking."

"Man, that's great, Mitch, just great."

And so our reunion began. He was, it seemed, the Alex Harmon of old. Laughing. Talking about football and Brilliant. "So, it's been since the parade, huh? Well, let's see, what have I been up to in the meantime? I finished up my rehabilitation at the VA Hospital in Chillicothe, before they sent me to another veterans' hospital up here for a mental evaluation. The doctors in Chillicothe said I seemed to be adjusting too quickly and too easily to my injuries."

"Is that true?"

He shook his head. "Nope. It was harder than hell, but no amount of bitterness or complaining or wishing was going to bring my legs back, so I needed to make the best of the situation. Fortunately, I hooked up with a therapist up here who believed me when I told her that I wasn't going to commit suicide or end up in a bell tower with a high-powered rifle."

"Good thing you got assigned to her," I said.

He smiled and pointed to a photo on the credenza of a gorgeous brunette with perfect teeth. "I ended up marrying her. She's the one who got me interested in counseling. I didn't harbor the bitterness that a lot of injured vets have when they return, and she thought that would make me a good counselor. I'm about two courses away from a bachelor's in psychology at the University of Pittsburgh. I'd like to be carrying a football for the gold and blue, but I just can't cut back against the grain with these things." He smiled and knocked twice on his artificial right leg.

On the shelf behind his desk were Alex's Brilliant football helmet, his all-Ohio certificate, and a trophy denoting him as Brilliant High's football MVP his senior year. He saw me looking at the mementos and said, "I'm not on a big ego trip. I figured I need to show the guys who come in here that I lost something besides my legs. I lost the plans I had for my future. I was hoping those legs were going to carry me to a football scholarship when I got back from the war. I tell them, this isn't going to be easy, but you can still live a full life." He smiled. "You might even meet a beautiful woman who is completely out of your league and convince her to marry you." He winked.

We had visited for an hour and I was a little ashamed that I had waited until I needed something to make the contact. Alex suspected the call wasn't purely social. "So, what's on your mind, champ?" he finally asked, grinning. "What's the other reason you stopped by?"

"Nothing. I just wanted to see you." I was such a coward.

"Is that a fact?" Alex persisted, now smiling broadly, enjoying watching me squirm.

"That's a fact," I said.

"So there's no other reason," he continued. "You just wanted to look up your old buddy."

"That's it." I forced a smile.

Alex Harmon put his palms on the surface of his desk and used his muscular arms to push himself up. He took a few steps and eased himself onto the corner of his desk. "My friend, you are such a terrible liar. How do you get away with anything at home?"

I took a breath and looked away. "I don't get away with much there, either."

"Probably not. You know, your Adam's apple rolls like the tide when you lie."

"Yeah, so I've been told." I rubbed that cursed Adam's apple—my lie beacon.

"Okay, out with it, champ. What's up?"

"I need a favor."

He nodded. "Shoot."

"Do you remember Travis Baron?"

"Vaguely. I remember seeing him horsing around in the alley with you. Frank Baron's kid, right?"

"Yeah. That's the one. His mom drowned when he was real little."

"Sure. The big mystery of Brilliant. She was out on Frank's boat when it got rammed by a barge. They never found her or her mystery lover. So, what about it?"

"Well, for the past three years I've been helping Travis try to find out about his mom and her family. I'll spare you all the gory details, but Big Frank doesn't like to talk about it, so Travis was forced to do the investigative work on his own."

"And he hired you as his trusted assistant?"

"The pay's lousy and the hours are worse, but it's been a lot of fun." Alex smiled. "Anyway, in the process of this search, we found out that Travis's grandfather was a career Navy man. Travis asked his dad about the grandfather, and he said the grandfather died not long after Travis's mom drowned in 1953."

"And you want to find out when he died?"

"We want to find out if he died at all. Travis has asked his dad some questions and he's been pretty liberal with his versions of the truth."

Alex's eyebrows arched. "Interesting. So, you want me to find out if the old man is still alive."

"Yeah. And, if he is still alive, where is he? If he was career military and retired, he's got to be drawing a pension, doesn't he?"

Alex folded his arms and exhaled, long and slow. "You know, those records are private. I get caught doing that and they'll put my balls in a sling."

"I know. But we don't know where else to turn."

For several moments, Alex stared out the window. Finally, he smiled and squinted. "Did I ever tell you about the time Frank Baron switched my ass raw?"

"No, I don't think so."

"We were just kids, me and Jimmy Kidwell—about six, I guess. Big Frank lived in an old place up at the end of Shaft Row."

"That's where they were living when Travis was born."

"Jimmy lived just a few doors down from Big Frank. He and I had been down in the creek catching crawdads and minnows to sell to the bait store. We were coming back, cutting across Big Frank's backyard, and we saw that he had poured some fresh concrete over the cistern . . ."

"The what?"

"The cistern. Before we got city water in Brilliant, everyone had cisterns. They were like wells to catch rainwater. People used that water for their gardens so they didn't drain their wells. Once we got city water, they didn't need the cisterns, so people capped them."

"Why?"

"So little kids out catching crawdads and minnows didn't fall in them and drown, I guess."

"Okay. Go on."

"We saw that they had just poured this cap over the cistern, so we found a couple of sticks and started writing our names in the wet cement. Well, we didn't see Big Frank behind us. He grabbed a switch off a mulberry tree, sneaked up behind us, and beat our butts royal— called us some names that I had never heard before, or since, and I was in the army," Alex laughed. "Needless to say, that was the last time we went adventuring up to Big Frank's."

"He's a bastard," I said.

"Yes, on a good day he's a bastard."

There was a light tapping at the door and Rose poked her head in the door. "You've got a one-thirty with Mr. Lambert."

"Would you give him a call and tell him I'm running about ten minutes late?" She nodded and pulled the door closed. "Who else knows you were coming up here to make this request?"

"Just Travis. He's waiting downstairs."

"Okay. You tell Travis to keep his mouth shut, and I'll see what I can do. No promises, mind you. If it looks like there're going to be problems, I'm going to drop it."

"Fair enough."

"What's his name?"

"Ronald Virdon."

"Navy?"

I nodded. "Do you want me to call you back?"

"No. I'll get word to you. It may take a while, but I'll see what I can do."

CHAPTER EIGHTEEN

On the Fourth of July, the city blocked off the village's two-block business strip, and the Brilliant Polish-American Club held its annual festival. Even as a young boy, I somehow knew the celebration was special, a slice of Americana and one of the memories of growing up in Brilliant that would remain with me long after I left. The carnies descended on the town several days prior to the festival to set up the Tilt-A-Whirl; Scrambler; Ferris wheel; my favorite, the Octopus; the mini roller coaster that occupied the alley space behind the funeral home; the Rock-O-Plane, on which I rode just once and vowed to never again set foot in; and the deadly spinning tubs, in which, when I was twelve, Snookie spun me until I slumped to the floor and centrifugal force pinned me against the wall of the car, making me so sick that I sprinted past the mini roller coaster and hurled on the hood of a 1959 Chevy in the used car lot owned by Urb Keltenecker's dad. The tubs then went on the list with the Rock-O-Plane. The carnies also set up games of chance, and it took me years of trying to knock down milk bottles and throwing softballs into tilted peach baskets and trying to climb a rope ladder to realize they were all fixed.

The civic groups set up booths for food—the Brilliant Volunteer Fire Department had its fish fry; the Junior Women's Club sold cream puffs; the Kiwanis Club sold caramel apples; the Lions Club roasted corn in its husks; the Merchants baseball team sold barbecued chicken, which was cooked on spits over charcoal pits in front of Myron Feldman's house; and the Polish-American Club sold spicy sausage sandwiches with fried green peppers and onions, the memory of which still makes my mouth water.

Each year, a Brilliant senior-to-be would be named Polish Festival Queen, an honor as coveted as homecoming or prom queen. She and her attendants would ride on a float in the Fourth of July parade that had a plywood cutout of Poland propped up in the back and signs that stated "Free Poland of Communist Rule" running the length of the float, covering the sides the way a duster covers the sides of a bed.

At dusk on the Fourth, Ohio Valley Steel sponsored a huge fireworks display at the football field that could be seen for miles up and down the valley. I liked to watch the fireworks from Fifth Street, which was a tarred and gravel road that ran parallel to the river across the western hills over Brilliant. From the front lawns on Fifth, the fireworks seemed to explode right in front of your eyes, and you could watch the streams of fire reflecting in the dark waters of the Ohio River. Travis and I were sitting in the Denzels' front lawn, a sloping bed of thick sod that was perfect for lying back and watching fireworks, when Mrs. Denzel offered us a burger off the grill and a Coke.

"No thanks," I said. I had always been taught to be gracious but not to accept such offers in case they were only doing so to be polite.

"Oh, please," she insisted. "We have more than enough."

We accepted the second offer and sat on the grass with a bottle of Coke and a paper plate holding a well-done cheeseburger, potato salad, and baked beans. I was sitting next to the youngest Denzel girl, Laura, who was two years my junior. I had played basketball in high school and during the summer league for Kennedy's Market with Laura's brother, Phil, who was two years older than me. Laura and her parents always went to the games, but I had never paid her much attention. Then, she was just an eighth-grader and Phil's little sister. However, sometime between the last summer league basketball game and the moment when I sat down next to her as the first rocket of the night exploded against the backdrop of the West Virginia hills, Laura had matured—greatly, magnificently, stupendously, in fact. Her sandy hair was trimmed neatly above the shoulders so that it fell back in a feathered wave. She had on pink shorts, a blue, midriff blouse exposing a tight belly, and the scent of her perfume—a hint of citrus—drifted my way. She gave me an occasional glance, sensing my interest, and I fell in love with her that moment. The booms and bangs and crackles of the fireworks echoed off the Ohio and West Virginia hills as the colored embers fell toward the river. It was on this perfect night that I began to realize that, my narrow escapes with Travis aside, the security of my youth and the cocoon that was Brilliant, Ohio, were about to slip into history. When school began, I would start planning for college and Brilliant would become simply the place where I had grown up. There were times when I wished time would stand still, and this night was one of them.

The big news on this July Fourth was the passing of a Brilliant legend. Earlier that morning, death had claimed the life of our best carp customer, Harold "Turkeyman" Melman. A lifetime of stomping around the dump had finally caught up with Turk. He had stepped on a nail, or something that caused a puncture wound in his right foot. He didn't tell anyone, having a terrible fear of doctors since he had been hospitalized for the fierce beating he had taken some twenty years earlier. The foot had gotten infected and one of the bank tellers, Pammy Yates, noticed that his body odor was becoming particularly fetid, like that of rotten meat, and the Turk was looking pale and weak. She told her husband, who visited him and found that nearly his entire left leg was eaten up with gangrene. It was amputated the next day, but the infection had spread and went to his heart. Antibiotics could not stem the tide. He spent his last days in the hospital, out of his head with fever, muttering and crying.

As he lay dying, Turk's sister-in-law, Van, the wife of Turk's only brother, Luther, a self-ordained minister and laborer at Ohio Valley Steel, sat at his bedside, kindly dabbing his face with a cold sponge, combing his hair, spoon-feeding him what broth he could swallow, plumping his pillow, and trying in vain with all her breath to extract the location of the hidden cache of gold. But Turk was loopy with fever. He rolled his head back and forth on the pillow and repeatedly muttered, "Nomo teemo nomo. Nomo teemo nomo. Nomo teemo nomo."

These were simply the dying cries of an old man, a result of the taunting and traumatic memories that would not allow him to go in peace. Van, however, interpreted them as a garbled code, some type of hidden message directing her to the treasure. She called her husband at work and said, "He told me, 'nomo teemo nomo.' What's that mean?"

"I don't know, Van. It sounds like gibberish," Luther said.

Van slammed down the phone and as soon as Turk breathed his last, she bolted from the room and began scavenging the hill behind his house. Late that afternoon, after news of Turk's death hit Brilliant, Cloyd Owens stretched yellow crime-scene tape around Turk's property in an effort to keep people from digging up the entire hillside.

As the last of the finale faded to wafting smoke, the Brilliant High Marching Blue Devils struck up the beginning of their annual show, *A Salute to Old Glory*, down the block in front of the post office. Travis reached over and slapped my calf. "Let's walk down to the post office. There're some cute girls from Toronto in town—friends of Gretchen Mercer."

They had been cruising through town in Gretchen's dad's Mustang convertible earlier in the afternoon. They were cute, but I wasn't as interested in them as I was Laura Denzel, and she was listening to every word. I shrugged and turned away from Travis. "Laura, do you, uh, you want to walk down to the post office and listen to the band?"

"Sure," she said without hesitation. "Let me ask."

She ran back to the porch where the neighbors had gathered to enjoy the fireworks. "Why'd you do that?" Travis asked. I didn't say anything, and after several seconds a wide grin spread across his face. "Nahhhhh? Get out? Laura Denzel?"

"Don't start, Travis."

He rolled back on his side and smirked. "She's cute, man. Good luck." He twisted his head toward the porch to be sure she was out of earshot. "She smells good, too."

"Yeah, I noticed."

She came back down the hill. "My dad said no, but my mom said it was okay, as long as I'm back in an hour."

I could feel Walter Denzel's eyes on me, but I didn't look back. In my dating career, I had found that mothers seemed to like me; fathers did not. Period. So I tended to avoid contact with the dads. I assumed that this wasn't personal. Rather, it was simply the fact that I was a hormone-laden, male teenager with a fully functional penis, who happened to be in the presence of their daughters.

We walked down Ohio Avenue toward the biggest annual social event in Brilliant. It was a beautiful night and I was suddenly quite smitten with Laura, and Travis was thoroughly enjoying the moment. The air smelled of cotton candy and fried dough. The amusement rides that extended down Third Street rattled and clanged, drowned out only by the calls from the bingo table. The post office sat at the corner of Ohio and Third, across from the Coffee Pot. We were slipping through the yellow shop-horse-style barriers that served as street blocks as the band began the first bars of "You're a Grand Old Flag." It was a nice concert, though I had a hard time enjoying it because I couldn't quit staring at my watch, fearing that if I got too wrapped up in the patriotic fervor, I would be late returning Laura home.

I walked her back up the hill, asked her to go out Friday night, and met Travis back at the volunteer fire department's stud poker booth. "Did you kiss her?" he asked.

"You are such a tool," I said.

He grinned. "I'm up four bucks. Ready to call it a night?"

"Let me get a sausage sandwich first," I said.

"A hot sausage sandwich at eleven-thirty at night? That'll sit well in your gut."

I bought the sandwich and began eating it as we walked down Ohio Avenue toward my house. As we passed under the last string of lights near the bingo stand and into the canopy of maple trees that formed a foliage tunnel over Second Street, a male voice called out, "Hey, boys." We both jumped. "What's the deal with you two? You queer for each other or joined at the hip?" All that was visible inside the Pontiac was the glowing ember of a cigarette. He turned on the dome light. It was Chase Tornik.

"What are you doing down here?" Travis asked.

"Looking for you."

"How'd you know where we'd be?" I asked.

"I used to be a detective, remember?" He pitched his cigarette out the window and it skidded across the brick road. He looked at me and said, "That was a cute little girl you were with." I nodded. He waved Travis in with his fingers. "Come here."

"Think he wants to beat my ass?" Travis whispered.

"He might, but I don't think he'd drive down to the Polish-American Festival to do it," I whispered back.

Travis walked up to the car, placing his hands on the roof above the driver's door. "I didn't expect I'd ever see you again," Travis said.

"That little dust-up at the cement factory?" Tornik waved his right hand at Travis. "I've been treated a lot worse. You didn't hurt my feelings if that's what you're worried about. You boys got a couple of minutes?"

"Yeah. Why?" Travis asked.

"Hop in. Let's take a little ride."

"A ride? Why?" I asked.

"Jesus, man, relax. I've got something to show you, and I can't do it here."

Travis looked at me; I shrugged. Travis walked around and got into the front seat. I slipped into the back, situating myself behind Tornik.

Tornik pulled away from the curb and drove down Second Street, sliding around the festival blockade, hopped on Third Street, and headed south out of town. The detective remained quiet until he hit the southern boundary of Brilliant. "I didn't know if your old man would be at the festival or not," Tornik finally said, breaking the silence. "I doubt that I enjoy favored-nation status with him, and I really wanted to avoid any possible contact."

"The Polish Festival isn't the kind of social event my dad usually attends," Travis said. "He'd rather go up to Welch's Bar and drink himself blind."

"I've got a little present for you," Tornik said. "Look under your seat."

Travis reached down between his feet and pulled out a manila envelope. "What's this?"

"That," Tornik said, taking control of the car with his left knee as he slipped a cigarette into his mouth and fumbled with his lighter, "is probably more than you'll ever want to know about the investigation into the death of Amanda Virdon Baron. It's a copy of the investigative file—most of it anyway."

"Most of it?"

Tornik nodded. "I'm holding a little bit back. You digest all that and maybe I'll give you the rest."

Tornik pulled off at the Georges Run exit and drove to the parking lot at Patty's Diner, a popular, twenty-four-hour stop for truckers running the Ohio River route. "You want a coffee or anything?" Tornik offered.

"Nah. I'm good," Travis said.

He looked back at me. "I could use an RC," I said. The sausage felt like it was burning a hole in my stomach lining.

Travis and I got out of the car. He leaned against the right front fender of the Pontiac, unclasped the envelope, and flipped through fifty-one pages of handwritten notes and a more formal, single-spaced report. "Wow, it's like a book; there's a lot of stuff here," he said, scanning the report by the lights trimming the soffit of the diner.

When Tornik re-emerged from the diner a few minutes later, he was carrying a steaming cup of coffee in his right hand and a twelve-ounce RC in the other. He handed me the soda, then set his coffee on a concrete parking barrier and lit yet another cigarette.

"How did you get this?" I asked.

Tornik's brows arched. "Now, you don't really expect me to answer that, do you?"

"I guess not," I said.

"Let's just say there are some folks at the sheriff's office who don't despise me quite as much as the others. And at least one of them owed me a favor."

Travis never looked up from the report. "Jesus, this is a lot of information. Did you do all this?"

"Yeah, most of it. Before you get too far into that report, understand this: I did not start the investigation to set up your dad to take a fall. Okay? I didn't have to. He didn't need my help. He did a fine job all by himself. Your dad says that I was trying to set him up? Well, see what you think after you're done reading. Do whatever you want with that copy, but for the love of Christ, don't let your dad find it. And if he does . . ."

"I'll never tell him where I got it."

"That's the right answer."

"So, this will explain everything?" Travis asked. "I'll read this and I'll be convinced that my dad was involved in the death of my mother?"

"Maybe, maybe not. You read that first, and this," he said, patting the business-sized envelope that was protruding from his breast pocket. "This is the dessert I was telling you about." Tornik pulled a small piece of notebook paper from his pants pocket—a cheat sheet. "Look on page nineteen." He waited until Travis found the page. "Your dad was going to lose that boat." He pointed to a copy of a letter from the Steelworkers Federal Bank to Frank Baron, dated two weeks before Amanda's death. "He'd had the boat a little over a year—bought it from Ohio Valley Boat Sales—and he was six months behind on his loan. This was a perfect way to lose the boat without having it repossessed. The insurance paid it off, and it provided a perfect cover for your mother's death." Travis read the letter aloud.

Dear Mr. Baron:

We have made repeated attempts to contact you concerning payment on Loan No. 53-0041717, which you received from Steelworkers Federal Bank of Steubenville for the purchase of a Speedcraft Pleasure Boat, Serial No. 1317.

Your loan is now six months overdue. This note must be brought up to date immediately or we will be forced to begin repossession measures. You have three days to respond to this letter, a copy of which has been sent to the Jefferson County Sheriff's Department.

Thank you for your immediate attention to this matter.

Sincerely yours,

Alfred Lawyer

Vice President, Loans

"He was in hock up to his ass for that boat," Tornik said.

Travis shrugged. "That doesn't mean he killed my mom. He didn't take the boat out on the river. He was on the road."

"No, that alone does not mean he did it. As you're looking at this, pretend you're putting together a puzzle, a puzzle of that instant in time when your mother died. It's the big picture we're looking at. In a perfect world, it would show you how she died, where, and who was responsible. But you and I both know that isn't possible. You're always going to be missing a couple of the pieces, so you're putting together a puzzle where you'll never get a complete picture. You with me?" Travis nodded. "What we do is look at all the pieces that are available, and we try to put those together. Now, when we're done, maybe we don't have a complete picture with every piece of evidence that we'd like, but we've put together enough of the picture that we can imagine what the missing pieces look like. That's what we're doing here. In itself, that letter doesn't mean your dad did anything, but it's a piece of the puzzle. So you put it on the table and go look for the next piece."

"Okay, what's next?"

Tornik looked back down at his cheat sheet. "Page twenty-four. We found some of the instruments from the boat's console. The switch to the boat's running lights was turned off, but the ignition switch was turned on."

"I don't understand the significance," Travis said.

"If you're out on the river at night, it's common sense to keep your running lights on."

"So? My mom probably didn't know much about the boat. Or, maybe they didn't want to be seen."

"Maybe they didn't want everyone in Brilliant to know they were out on the river, but they would certainly have wanted a barge to see them. After your mom's death, I went for a nighttime ride on that towboat—the same one that was pushing the barge that crushed your mother's boat. That spotlight is strong enough to see a small boat drifting in the river a mile away, maybe further. I think the lights were killed on the boat because it was stashed in the brush near the bank—probably on the West Virginia side. When the barge got close, someone drove the boat out of the brush and toward the front of the barge, but under the spotlight. By the time the captain saw the boat, it was too late to do anything. And here's the important fact: It wasn't drifting, as was first reported. It was driven into the barge. That's why the ignition switch was on: because it wasn't adrift, it was a kamikaze mission."

"Kind of a wild-ass theory, isn't it? They drove the boat in front of the barge and then tried to swim to shore? I don't get it."

I watched Tornik roll his teeth over his lip, and his left eye twitched like a turn signal. Once again, Travis had lit his fuse. "There are two theories to the mystery, and one is that she faked her death and ran away. Since her body wasn't found, no one can prove that she isn't alive. Now, if your mother is still alive, which I seriously doubt, then what better way to fake her own death? Witnesses see you jump in the river and you're never heard from again. The clothes and getaway car are parked near the river bank. Bye-bye, Brilliant. However, if someone wanted to make it look like she was killed on the boat, it's just as perfect."

Travis winced. "Okay, let's assume for a minute that you are right and she was murdered. Do you think she volunteered to be part of her own murder? What did she do, agree to be seen jumping off the boat before she let someone kill her?"

It was, I sensed, the point Tornik had been waiting all night to make. He grinned. "Maybe that wasn't her jumping off the boat," he suggested. "Maybe she was already dead—maybe in the water or in the hull of the boat. The accident was just part of the cover-up."

Travis looked at Tornik for a long moment and let his words sink in. "I think you're reaching," he finally said. "You know what I think? I think she and her boyfriend were screwing and weren't paying any attention to what was happening to the boat and it drifted in front of the barge. End of story."

"Let me tell you something, pally boy, I tagged a lot of tail in my day, but I have yet to meet the piece of ass that would make me ignore a barge full of iron ore rolling down the river shining a spotlight and blasting his foghorn." Tornik's voice was climbing with each syllable. "You've heard those foghorns. They rattle windows for miles away."

"The newspaper story said the barge captain saw the boat drifting in front of him."

Tornik pinched his temples. "First of all, in a moment of panic he probably couldn't tell if it was drifting or moving under its own power. And, if it was drifting, why didn't he see it before then? Someone drove that boat into the path of the barge. The boat fairy didn't just zap it there."

I suspected that Tornik had gone to great lengths to get the investigative report. He had stuck his neck out for Travis, who was refusing to look at the evidence. It seemed obvious to me that Tornik had reread the case and the old investigative juices were again flowing. He knew his instincts had been right. Had he not screwed up his career and his life, he would have solved the mystery of Amanda Baron's death. I had no doubt. Now, for whatever reason, Travis was in denial of every piece of incriminating evidence.

Tornik rubbed his right hand over his jaw, massaging a dark shadow as he tensed. "So tell me, kid, if you're going to ignore all this, why in the hell did you ever come to me in the first place? Just tell me that and I'll get out of your hair, because it's obvious that you aren't interested in the truth. For whatever reason, you're being protective of your old man, when you should be being protective of your dead mother."

Tornik threw the Styrofoam cup and the remainder of his coffee into the gravel parking lot. "Look at the copy of the bill of lading. Do you know when your dad scheduled his load? An hour before he left Steubenville. Pretty damn quick turnaround, wouldn't you say? Read the interviews with the boat club members. Your dad's boat wasn't at its dock the day of the accident. Your dad was on the road, the boat's not at its dock, yet the family automobile is in the driveway all day."

"Now, there's a revelation," Travis said. "The boat's out on the water and the car's in the driveway. Congratulations. That's some dynamite detective work."

"How did she get to the boat that night?" Tornik whispered,

barely controlling his rage. "It was a mile from where they lived to the boat club. She couldn't drive the car or get to the boat because she was already dead."

"Maybe her lover gave her a ride?" Travis countered.

"They found you in the crib. You've been investigating your mother. Do you think she's the kind of woman who would have gone out with her lover and left a newborn at home? Think, junior, think! Your dad was involved."

Travis pushed himself away from the car and faced Tornik. "You never proved that."

Tornik stepped backed and laughed. "I've proved it to myself, kid. Let's remember something—you came to me for help, and I'm telling you what happened. You can believe what you want to believe, but I'm done helping you." He took two steps and slid behind the wheel of the car. He looked one more time toward Travis, shook his head, then sped out of the lot, throwing gravel and leaving us in a haze of dust.

CHAPTER NINETEEN

I watched until Tornik's taillights disappeared on Commercial Avenue and dust from his tires settled over the parking lot and my RC Cola. I turned to Travis, stared for a long moment, and asked, "Seriously, what the hell is wrong with you?" He looked down and kicked at some gravel. "Now, I'm going to be late getting home because we have a three-mile hike in pitch darkness. We can either walk along the berm of Route 7 or on the railroad tracks. No chance of anything bad happening with either of those options, is there?"

We walked south along Commercial Avenue until it deadened into the Penn-Central railroad yard, then followed the main line south toward Brilliant. Railroad tracks are ridiculously scary at night when the tracks begin to vibrate and the single light of the engine can be seen in the distance. We ducked off into the brush twice to let northbound trains pass. It was, in my imagination, not unlike hiding from some prehistoric beast that lumbers along, shaking the ground, only a few feet away.

As we trudged south, I was doing a slow burn, upset about the trek home and the way Travis had treated Tornik. He stumbled over the ties a half-dozen times while he tried to read the report by moonlight. Following another stumble, I said, "You're going to trip and break your neck," I said. "Why is that so fascinating now?"

"What do you mean?" he asked.

"Are you kidding me? Why in God's name did you have to bust Tornik's chops like that? The guy was trying to do you a favor."

"If he hadn't been such a jerk and left, we'd be home by now."

"If you hadn't been such a horse's ass to him, he wouldn't have driven off." I could feel the heat creeping up my neck like a rash. "There aren't many times I feel like this, Travis, but right now, I'd like to punch you square in the teeth. All I've heard for the past two years is how you want to learn the truth about your mother. Then, when the one guy on this earth who knows the most about the case offers to help you, you bite his hand. I don't get it. All of a sudden you're protective of Big Frank. Why? You asked me a long time ago what I knew about your mother's death, and I played dumb because I didn't want to hurt your feelings. You know what I heard? I heard that everyone in town thought your dad had something to do with her death. And you did, too, until Tornik put the evidence right in front of your nose. What's the deal?"

He glared at me, but did not respond. We were just north of Brilliant when we hopped off the tracks by the water filtration plant, just before a third freight train barreled past. We walked in silence the rest of the way home. When he cut across Labelle Street to LaGrange Avenue, he said, "See ya around."

While he claimed to doubt the veracity of its contents, Travis was captivated by the document Tornik had given him, but it caused him to struggle with an internal problem. Even though Travis hated Big Frank, in his heart he didn't want to believe the old man had been involved in the murder of his wife and mother of his only son. Who would? But, as the circumstantial evidence against Big Frank continued to mount, Travis became extremely defensive. Any evidence showing Big Frank was somehow involved in the death of his wife only further squelched Travis's fantasy of someday miraculously finding her alive. Travis didn't talk much about this, but I knew he harbored that dream.

Me? I believed she was dead. Certainly, being married to Big Frank Baron was an excellent reason to run, but I didn't believe for a minute she would leave behind her infant son.

Travis grew more moody as the summer wore on. His mixed emotions over the information in the report were further agitated by the fact that we had yet to hear back from Alex Harmon on the status of his search for his maternal grandfather. Travis spent hours reading and rereading the packet of information Tornik had given him. In the course of his own investigation, Travis gained a grudging respect for Tornik's investigative skills. Even Travis had to admit that Tornik had been methodical and meticulous in his efforts. What Travis couldn't understand is why Tornik spent so much time investigating Big Frank instead of tracking down other leads. Tornik, Travis speculated, had tunnel vision for Frank Baron, and that zeal caused him to overlook any other possibilities.

Whenever Big Frank was on the road, Travis sat at the desk in his bedroom, poring over the pages of Tornik's report. He had punched holes in them and slipped them into a loose-leaf binder, hiding it in plain sight in the bookcase of his bedroom, which was the last place on earth that the nearly illiterate Big Frank would ever look for anything. It was not unlike the size-fourteen dress shoe from the cemetery that Travis was still hiding. It was on the floor of his closet, mixed with other shoes and hidden amid the clutter.

A month after our July Fourth meeting with Tornik, Travis stopped by the house after his shift at the bakery. I was in my room getting dressed for an American Legion baseball game against Bridgeport. "What's going on?" I asked.

"I'm kicking myself now for being such a jerk to Tornik," he said.

"There's a rare confession," I said.

"I still don't think Tornik's interest in going after Big Frank was purely in the name of justice. I think he was going after him strictly for personal reasons."

"To make his star shine even brighter?"

"Something like that. He seems like the kind of guy who always wanted to be in the spotlight."

"Maybe he just didn't like Big Frank."

"That's not hard to believe, but you don't try to pin someone with murder just because you don't like them."

"I wondered about that. What if Tornik didn't like Frank and suspected he was involved in your mom's disappearance? Would he try harder to pin it on him?"

Travis shrugged. "Probably." He sat down on the edge of my bed. "What do you think he was talking about when he tapped that paper in his pocket and called it 'dessert'?"

I tucked my jersey into my baseball pants. "And there it is," I said.

"There what is?"

"The reason you're mad at yourself for showing your ass to Tornik. You want to know what else he has."

He shook his head and said, "Goddamn Baron temper. What irritates me most is that it's this constant reminder that I am, without question, the son of Francis Martino Baron."

"Want to go to the game?"

Travis shook his head. "No, thanks. Big Frank's on his way to Demopolis, Alabama, wherever the hell that is, and I'm going to start back through the report."

"Why don't you give it a rest? You've been at it for weeks."

"I'm hoping I find something that Tornik might have overlooked."

"Don't you think you would have found it by now?"

It was a sopping hot evening in early August when I returned from the baseball game in Bridgeport. I swung through the south end of town and drove through the little patch of floodplain where Travis lived. I drove through the alley behind his house and saw him on the back stoop of his house, a bottle of Mountain Dew at his side, listening to WDEV in Pittsburgh and reading the report. With Big Frank somewhere south of the Mason-Dixon line, Travis felt comfortable reading the report outside.

I pulled my car alongside his house. As I exited, Travis opened up the report and splayed it on a concrete step, facing me. "Come here and look at this," he said.

"Did you find your missing golden nugget?" I asked.

"You tell me." Travis pointed to a name that was hardly legible, printed and circled in the margin on a page of handwritten notes. The photocopier had barely registered the name, and while it was faint, it was unmistakable. "I've read this report fifteen times and never saw that until tonight."

Beneath the scrawled name were the fading initials, "BF???" and "S to D."

"Holy shit," I said. "BF is boyfriend?"

"That's my guess. What's 'S to D'?" Travis asked.

"Scared to death?"

Travis smiled and leaned back against the steps. "How interesting," he said. "How very interesting. Well, that's one mystery solved."

From the beginning of August through the first of November, the Blue Devil Touchdown Club held meetings at the high school every Monday night. Prior to football season they met to prepare for the various fundraisers they held on home Saturdays—ball raffles, fifty-fifty raffles, concessions, and program sales. After the season began, they met to watch game films and, in the words of my dad, "painfully review the debacle that had unfolded before them" the previous weekend.

This was our senior year, and we were hoping to revive the past glory of Brilliant football. Brilliant hadn't fielded a decent football team since Alex Harmon's senior year. At one point the Blue Devils lost twenty-three straight games and won just once in three years. We had been mercilessly pounded my freshman year, losing every game, improved to five and five when I was a sophomore, and seven and three, our first winning season in six years, as a junior. Nobody was giving us much of a chance to win more than three games my senior year. On this Monday in mid-August, we had finished our first day of conditioning and I stayed late to work on my placekicking, which wasn't going well. My legs were wobbly from the workout, and I was shanking balls all over the field. It didn't seem to matter how hard you worked during the summer, your legs were never quite ready for the first day of conditioning. I had set my orange "Boomer" kicking tee on the twenty-five-yard line and was working on field goals. Each scuffed kick brought a groan from the members of the Touchdown Club, who were giving the home bleachers a fresh coat of royal blue and white paint.

They didn't dare groan too loudly, however, without risking the ire of their president, Clay Carter, who was my kicking tutor. Clay was the closest thing to a living legend in Brilliant, having quarterbacked the Blue Devils for three years when they posted a 28–1–1 record and were three-time Big Valley Athletic Conference champions and state champs in 1948 and 1949. Clay had been first-team All-State twice in football, twice in basketball, and once in baseball, which may have been his best sport. He had been a rising star in the Boston Red Sox organization, a hard-hitting third baseman, when he collided with a catcher and tore up the shoulder in his throwing arm.

The injury quickly ended his baseball career, and Clay went to work for his father, learning the ropes at Carter Chevrolet and Buick in Steubenville. Clay was just twenty-six when his dad dropped dead of a heart attack. He took over the business, and he'd made the operation a bigger success than his dad could have ever envisioned. He lived outside of Brilliant in a sprawling ranch home that sat atop a knoll overlooking Beach Flats.

Clay was in his early forties and, except for a few flecks of gray around the temples, looked like he could still suit up for the Devils. His shoulders were broad on his six-foot-five frame, his stomach flat, and his muscles solid. Clay was a successful businessman and a little embarrassed by the attention that his high school feats continued to earn him. Rarely could the Touchdown Club get through a meeting without someone asking him to recount some past heroic feat. I often felt he liked working with me on my kicking simply because it gave him an excuse to get away from the attention.

He walked down out of the stands. "How's the height?" he asked.

"The height isn't the problem," I said. "It's the width that's killing me."

He frowned. "The width?"

"Yeah. Everything's going wide right by about twenty yards. My kicks have more slice than my golf drives."

"Tee 'er up and let's have a look," Clay said.

I did, and promptly choked under the pressure of Clay's critical eye. The ball sailed off the side of my toe and skidded to rest in the end zone, never getting more than about five feet off the ground. He chuckled and said, "Yeah, we're going to have to work on that a bit." He took one of the loose balls and squeezed it between his big hands before squaring it up on the tee. "You're trying to kick the air out of the ball. You don't have to kill it. It's all about making solid contact. Your heel comes down and you drive your toe between the stripe and the middle of the ball and follow through." Clay approached the ball, wearing dress loafers, and buried his foot into it with a resounding thud. The ball lifted and slowly rolled end-over-end, splitting the uprights. "It's like the sweet spot on a baseball bat," he explained, setting up a ball for me to kick. "You have to find just the right spot on the ball. When you do, it'll sail. Keep your heel down and your toe up, and follow through."

I did. We had been over it dozens of times. My next kick cleared the uprights with just inches to spare.

"Lower on the ball," he said. "Drive through it. Don't poke it."

Travis was just coming through the gate at the far end of the field as my kick came to rest near the fence. He scooped up three of the balls and started jogging toward us. With the footballs he was carrying a brown paper bag under his left arm. Travis had that ornery look in his eyes. He awkwardly tossed one ball at me, and said, "Hey, Mitch; Mr. Carter."

We both nodded. I wanted to run and hide, for I knew what was coming. "What's going on, Trav?" I asked.

"Aw, not much." He dropped the other two balls. "You know, same old stuff. Oh, here, Mr. Carter," Travis said, handing him the sack. "This is yours."

Clay's brow furrowed. "Mine? What is it?"

"Something you've probably been looking for."

Clay Carter peeked into the sack and promptly turned the shade of a fish belly. It was a sick white, as if the blood had drained from his face so fast that it made him nauseous. He laughed a nervous laugh and asked, "What's this?"

"It's your right dress shoe," Travis answered. "The one you lost in the cemetery when you and Mitchell collided."

Clay looked at me, then averted his eyes, staring somewhere across the river into the hills of West Virginia. It had been his name—Clay C.—that was the faded notation on the page margin that Travis had found. Once I saw the name, it made sense. It had felt like I had tackled a tank, and that was Clay Carter. He tried to swallow, and it looked as though he had a dishrag in his throat. "Travis, I don't know what you're talking about," Clay said. "This isn't my shoe."

The muscles tensed in Travis's neck and face. It took a lot of nerve for a kid to stand up to an adult, particularly one of Clay Carter's legendary stature. But Travis was tired of the games. "It's yours, Cinderella," he said. "Mitchell pulled it off your foot when he tackled you that night. How many people around here wear a size-fourteen shoe?" Travis pulled a sheet of paper from his hip pocket, unfolded it, and held it up for Clay. "Even if it's not your shoe, maybe you can tell me why your name is on the homicide investigation report concerning my mother's death?"

Clay took the paper and read it. By the time he handed the paper back to Travis, he was looking anything but legendary. In fact, he looked pitiful, like a schoolboy caught with a cheat sheet. "Frankly, son, this isn't the kind of thing that I'd like to become public knowledge," Clay said.

"Mr. Carter, the last thing I want is for this to become public. I just want to know what you know about my mom."

I gathered up an armload of footballs and lined them up next to my tee, trying to avoid Clay Carter's glare. It was a safe bet that my kicking instruction was over for the evening.

"You couldn't have approached me privately?" Clay asked, agitated. "Did you have to humiliate me in front of your friend?"

"Mitchell already knew. I figured if I approached you in private that you'd deny everything and blow me off. Mitchell won't say a word."

His eyes narrowed, and he peered at me. "You knew about this?"

I nodded. "Yes, sir. Travis and I have been working on this for a long time."

Clay scanned the field and glanced up toward the dozen Touchdown Clubbers who were painting the bleachers. None seemed to have noticed the encounter. "I can't talk here."

"Why not?" Travis asked.

"Because I'm standing in the middle of the football field with a spare right shoe," he said, a stinging tone in his voice. "Stop by my dealership tomorrow afternoon and fill out a job application. I've got an opening for part-time janitor. That way nothing will look suspicious."

"Mitchell, too?" Travis asked.

Clay Carter did not answer. He turned and walked off the field, passing by the workers he had been organizing, and headed straight for his car.

"Big mistake," Travis said, as I drove him up Stony Hollow Boulevard to Carter Chevrolet and Buick, which was located in the Pleasant Heights section of Steubenville. "I should have just grilled him right there on the football field last night. I caught him off guard; he was on my turf; I had my nerve up. There he was, looking at his name on that report, holding that shoe in his hand. I was dealing on my terms. Now we've got to go see him in his office. It's like going to the principal's office. Goddammit. I'll bet he won't even talk now. He's had too much time to think about it."

"He asked you to come up. Of course he'll talk to you. But let me ask you something. Why is it that everything is a frontal assault with you? Why couldn't you have approached him in the parking lot? Why did you bring the shoe and make a scene of handing it to him?"

"He's Clay Carter."

"So, what's that got to do with anything?"

"He's a legend in town and a successful businessman. Do you think if I called him on the phone he would give me the time of day? If there's going to be a fight, you have to take it to him."

"That's exactly my point. Why does it always have to be a fight? You've got some balls on you, Travis, I'll say that, but we're going to have to work on your approach." I moved into the passing lane and blew by a coal truck that was making the long trudge up the hill and belching out exhaust that left a black plume a quarter-mile long. "If you had walked up to him in the parking lot, handed him the shoe, and said, 'I need to talk to you about this,' he would have done it. Otherwise, he would be worried that you'd start shooting off your mouth all over town."

"I wouldn't do that. I can't. If I did, word would get back to Big Frank and he'd kick my ass up around my shoulders."

"Mr. Carter doesn't know that. As far as he's concerned, we're holding all the cards and believe me, it's not your ass he's worried about. He has a family, a reputation, and the biggest car dealership in the Ohio Valley. He doesn't want to see his name dirtied up in this affair."

The realization that Clay Carter had much to lose seemed to buoy Travis a bit. "Are you sure you want me going in with you?" I asked.

We turned onto Brady Avenue and then made a left onto Sunset Boulevard, pointing the car back toward downtown Steubenville.

"Absolutely. He knows you. It'll make him more comfortable."

"I doubt that." I was nervous, but frankly, I didn't want to miss it. The mystery man revealed. "Do you think it was Mr. Carter in the boat with your mom?"

Travis shrugged. "Maybe we'll find out."

We parked on a side street, then hustled across Sunset Boulevard ahead of a bus, ducking into the front door of the dealership. "Service department?" Travis asked a salesman in a short-sleeve white shirt and a wide, red-and-yellow tie. He sized us up in an instant. Seeing no buying potential in either of us, he nodded toward a heavy steel door in the rear of the showroom. I opened the door, allowing the whirl of the air wrenches and the clanging of tools to escape into the quiet showroom.

The service center was divided down the middle by a yellow stripe that separated the cluttered repair side from the cleaner, seemingly less hectic side where new cars were being cleaned and prepped for their owners. On the repair side, seated behind a brown particle-board counter, was a prim, silver-haired woman with her eyeglasses dangling around her neck from a gold chain, who appeared to have applied red lipstick following a three-martini lunch. She was working feverishly at the Steubenville *Herald-Star*'s crossword puzzle, but still looked as much in charge as anyone. "I was told to come back here to get an employment application for part-time janitor," Travis said. The woman spun in her chair and reached for an application. "We need two applications, please."

"There's only one opening," she said.

"I know," Travis said. "The competition between the two of us should be fierce."

She didn't appear amused. "You can sit over at that picnic table and fill this out."

"I think Mr. Carter wants to see us when we're done," Travis said.

"I've already been informed as much," she said, her eyes dropping back to her puzzle.

We went to the picnic table next to the pop, coffee, candy, and cigarette vending machines. Travis searched out a spot that wasn't covered with grease and sat down. It was too gross for me, so I stood and filled out the application against the side of the candy machine. As I did, Dicky Cole, the preparation supervisor at the dealership and an offensive guard on Brilliant's championship football teams with Clay Carter, walked by and nodded at me. I returned the nod and said, "Hey, Dicky." The creases in Dicky's hands looked like little road maps, filled with grime, and he smelled of sweat and grease. I tried to act nonchalant. I knew Dicky and Big Frank were occasional drinking buddies at the Hillbilly Bar in Riddles Run.

"Whatta you boys doin' up here?" Dicky asked.

"Putting in applications for the part-time janitor's job," I said.

"Long way to drive to push a broom for a couple of hours, ain't it?" Dicky asked, slipping two dimes into the Coke machine.

Neither of us answered.

"Got shit in your ears?" Dicky asked, looking at me.

"It's not that far," I said. "It's hard to find a job in Brilliant."

Dicky sniffed, wrapped his filthy hands around his can of Coke, and started across the floor. Travis kept his head buried until he was out of earshot. "That's great. He'll tell Big Frank he saw me up here."

"So what?" I said. "You're filling out a job application. What's the big deal?"

"How do I explain why I'd want a job up here when all I have to do is walk across the street to the bakery?"

"Tell him you wouldn't give up your bakery job, but you wanted another job for some extra hours to buy a car."

Travis nodded. "That's good. I like that. You have good ideas. It's too bad your Adam's apple wiggles so bad when you lie."

It was a simple application, and we had them completed in a few minutes. I handed mine to Travis, and he passed them over the counter to the woman, who took them as she spoke unhappily on the telephone to a clerk at a parts store. "Really? Well, sir, I can assure you that it won't be *my* tit that gets caught in the wringer if this isn't taken care of. It's a bad water pump. It was bad when you sold it to us and bad when we put it on our customer's car. Don't expect us to eat this or we'll just take all our business to Genuine Parts, where they don't give me a bunch of static about replacing a defective part." She listened and after a moment began nodding. "Very fine. We'll expect it delivered before the close of business." She passed the applications back to Travis. "Keep them," she said. "Mr. Carter will see you now. Take the applications with you—top of the steps and to your right."

Extending from the middle of the floor to a second-floor landing was a well-worn set of wooden stairs, its green paint nearly rubbed away and replaced with years of grease and oil. I followed Travis up the stairs. On the right side of the landing, down a short hall, was an oak door with a frosted glass window. On the door in black paint that was faint and chipping away was:

Eugene V. Carter
President

Clay's father had died fifteen years earlier, but he had never bothered to have the glass repainted.

Travis trudged down the short hall, his tongue clicking against the roof of his mouth. "What's wrong?" I asked.

"Nerves. I can't work up any spit."

"You're in charge of the situation. Don't talk to him like you talked to Tornik and everything will be fine. Remember, all we're trying to do is find out what he knew about your mother."

He rapped twice lightly on the glass.

"Come in."

Travis pushed the door open. Clay Carter was sitting behind his desk, a pair of half-glasses on the end of his nose and piles of invoices and assorted papers stacked around him. "Come on in," he said, waving us into the office. "I expected to see you two here first thing this morning."

"I had to work," Travis said.

Clay Carter stood and lifted the glasses off his nose. He looked tired, and I imagined that he hadn't slept well the previous night. "Where are you working?"

"At the bakery."

"That's a good job. It's right across the street from your house, isn't it?"

"Yes, sir."

Clay was in a white dress shirt, his sleeves rolled up on his muscular forearms, a scarlet and navy striped tie hanging loosely around his neck, wrinkled khaki slacks cinching up around his thighs. "Sit down," he said, motioning toward two leather chairs and a couch in the corner that surrounded a battered coffee table, on which were a half-dozen car magazines.

Travis sat in one chair; I sat on the couch and scanned the office. It was large, but quite modest. Steel file cabinets lined one wall. Files and books, all related to the dealership and selling automobiles, filled bookshelves on the other. The maroon area rug that was stretched under the chairs and coffee table was faded and tired, worn to the burlap by the thousands of shoes that had rested on it over the decades. I said, "I gotta tell you, Mr. Carter, I was expecting something a little more, uh . . ."

"Palatial?"

"That's a good word, I guess."

"I've got my den at home for escaping and relaxing. This one is for work. I try to spend as little time in here as possible. You can't sell cars sitting behind a desk, so I don't want to make it too comfortable." He settled into the open chair. "So, where are we starting here?"

Travis dug his elbows into the padded armrests and pushed himself upright. "I, uh, I don't really know exactly where to start."

Clay's brows arched. "You didn't seem to be having any trouble yesterday."

"Yes, sir, I know. I'm sorry for that. I could have handled that a little better. It's just that Mitchell and I have been on this mission for the past couple of years trying to find out about my mother. That's all it was at first. I just wanted to know who she was, what she was like. But after a while that wasn't good enough. I wanted to know the identity of the mystery man from the boat and how she died. After that night in the cemetery, we figured if we could find out your identity, the mystery might be solved."

He sat for a long moment, his fingertips pressed together. He took a deep breath, exhaled, and asked, "So, you want some answers, huh?"

"Yes, sir," Travis said.

"I must say I admire your determination. If it had been anyone else, I would have told them to go piss up a rope. However, since you're Amanda's son, I feel I owe you this much. So you've been working on this since when—the night at the cemetery?"

"Before that," I said.

Travis nodded. "About three years, give or take," he offered. "We've heard the rumors and we've read the old newspaper articles, but I want to know more about her. We heard there was a memorial to her at the cemetery, and when we were checking it out we saw that someone had been putting fresh flowers on the grave."

Clay frowned. "You heard about it? You mean you didn't know about your own mother's memorial until a few years ago?"

"No, sir. My mother is not a topic often discussed at my house."

"I see. So, you saw the flowers and that's why you were staking out the cemetery?" We nodded in unison. A faint smile crossed Clay Carter's lips. "Good detective work," he said. "You scared the hell out of me." He grinned at me. "That was a nice tackle."

"Thanks, but I paid the price. My balls were the size of lemons for two weeks," I said.

"Sorry about that." He didn't sound the least bit sincere.

Travis said, "We had no idea that you were somehow involved in this until I saw your name on the investigator's report."

"Okay, so what do you want to know?"

"Everything," Travis said. "Everything you can tell me from the day you met my mom until the night in the cemetery."

Clay Carter's brows arched. "That covers quite a bit of territory, son." His fingertips came together in a steeple-like tower in front of his nose. After a moment he stood and called down to the woman at the parts counter. "Edna, hold my calls, please." He slid back into the chair. "Okay, do you want to ask the questions or do you want me to just start talking?"

"How about you just talk?" Travis said.

He nodded. "Before we start, I think we need to discuss some ground rules. I need your word that anything discussed in this room stays in the room. I have a family and would prefer that my wife not know that I'm putting flowers on another woman's memorial."

"I won't say a word," Travis said.

"Me, neither," I said.

"Okay, I'm taking you at your word." He took a breath, straightened himself, and began. "I had been playing baseball in the Boston Red Sox organization—double-A ball in Birmingham—when I tore up my shoulder. We rehabbed it for almost a year. When I went to spring training the next year they moved me from third to second base for the shorter throw. It didn't matter. I couldn't even make the short throw from second to first. They cut me and that quick . . ." He snapped his fingers. ". . . I went from being the future phenom to pushing a broom down in the garage. I was just kickin' around, trying to figure out what to do with my life. I thought about having another surgery and trying to make a comeback, but every doctor I went to said the shoulder was shot. I took a few accounting classes at the Business Institute of Pittsburgh, but ultimately decided to stay on here. Dad wanted me to learn the business and take over for him when he retired; I decided that was my best option. I spent most of my time learning to sell on the floor and reading management manuals in a little office at the other end of the landing. That was my life for the next year. In truth, I was hiding more than anything. I didn't have any control over the injury, but I always felt like I was a disappointment to everyone in Brilliant. They thought I was going to be the first guy out of Brilliant to make it to the big leagues. When my career went belly up, I thought I was a failure. I buried myself in work until I met your mother, which was the spring after I washed out."

"Where did you meet her?" Travis asked.

He smiled. "Church. Easter Sunday, 1951. I was a twice-a-year man as far as church was concerned—Easter and Christmas Eve, and the only reason I went that often was because my mom would have had a coronary if I hadn't. I didn't actually meet her that day. I just stared at her from across the church. God, she was the most gorgeous woman I had ever seen. I was in love with her from the instant I laid eyes on her. She made me a church-going man." He laughed. "I didn't miss any Sundays after that. A couple of weeks after Easter they had a dinner in the basement after church—one of those potlucks—and I finagled a seat across from her."

"Wasn't my dad there?" Travis asked, then immediately realized the folly of his question. "Right. Silly question. Sorry. Go on."

"I had asked a couple of my buddies about her. I knew she was unhappy in her marriage, and there was a rumor going around that she was going to leave your dad and move back to Virginia. I was afraid that if I didn't tell her how I felt that she would leave and I would never see her again. We hadn't had many opportunities to talk, but when we did I thought there was something there, a little spark. You know, hardly anything goes on in that church that someone doesn't see. So I wrote her a letter and slipped it to her in a hymnal at church." He took a moment to compose his thoughts. "I asked her to call me at the office, and she did." Clay shrugged. "That's how it started. We were seeing each other when your father was out of town. It was all very innocent. This went on for about a year. She was trying to summon up the courage to leave your dad when she got pregnant. I was crushed, and that's when we quit seeing each other."

"Whose decision was that?"

"It was mutual. We both knew it couldn't go anywhere as long as she was pregnant."

"She wasn't pregnant when she died," Travis said. "Were you seeing each other again?"

"I was hoping that we could get it rekindled, and I stopped by one night to see her. We talked, and there was no doubt in my mind that her feelings for me were as strong as mine were for her."

"Were you the mystery man on the boat?" I asked.

Clay winced. "No. Of course not."

"Who was it? Do you know?"

"I wish I did. It was very confusing, because your mom was definitely going to leave your dad. Did you know that?"

"I'd heard."

That was a lie, I thought. Travis had never heard any such thing, but he wanted Clay to think he knew most of the story.

"Your mom loved me, Travis. I'm sorry if that hurts you. But the plan was for her to take you and move out. I had already found her a little place not far from here, someplace where she would be safe while she started the divorce proceedings. She was going to wait until your dad was out of town on a trip and then make the move. We were planning to make a life for ourselves and you. That's why I will never believe she was out on that boat with another man. For a long time I thought maybe she had faked her death to get away from your dad. You know, when it's someone you love, you'll hold on to any shred of hope."

Travis nodded. "Trust me, I know exactly what you mean."

"I'm sure you do. I prayed that she was alive somewhere and in time she would get in touch with me. But, obviously, she didn't." Clay stood and walked to the lone window in the office, squinting into the late afternoon sun. "We kept our relationship a secret. I couldn't even mourn her when she was gone. I was crushed. In my heart, I knew she was dead, and I believed that your dad did it. Years after your mom died, maybe ten or so, I ran into the detective that investigated your mom's case . . ."

"Chase Tornik?"

"Yeah. That's his name. He was out in the used-car lot looking around. You know he went to prison for faking some evidence, or something like that?"

Travis nodded his head. "Yeah. I'd heard."

"I hadn't seen him in years, but he interviewed me not long after he started his investigation. Apparently, your mother and I weren't as secretive as we thought. When I saw him on the lot, he told me that he had always suspected your dad. In fact, he told me he was certain your dad had killed her. I've never been able to get that out of my head. It was maddening. I couldn't sleep, couldn't concentrate at work. My dad had always kept a revolver—a thirty-eight—in his bottom desk drawer. He kept it there for protection. I don't think it had been out of that drawer in thirty years. I got it, loaded it, and I was driving to Brilliant." He shook his head. "By that time, I was married, had kids, and I asked myself, 'What the hell are you thinking, Carter?' I turned around and went home—stopped on the way and tossed the gun in the river, just in case I ever started thinking stupid again." Clay walked back and sat down. "And I do. Every time I see your dad driving around in that Chevy, I want to strangle him."

Travis frowned. "The Chevy? Why?"

"Oh, I assumed you knew that story, too. You don't, huh?"

"I guess not."

"Well, the letter I gave your mom in church, professing my love, wasn't the only one I gave her. In fact, there were many. I told her to burn them after she had read them, and she said she would, but she didn't. After your mom disappeared, six months or so later, I guess, your dad found the letters. My dad was still alive, and Frank walked into his office and told him about the letters—showed him a couple of them. Frank was threatening to spread the word all over the valley that I was screwing his . . ." Clay caught himself in mid-sentence, suddenly remembering who he was talking to. "I'm sorry. I shouldn't have been so crass."

"Don't worry about it. Go on, please."

"He was going to tell everyone about me and your mother. Dad was afraid that it would ruin the business and my reputation, so he gave your dad that car to buy his silence." He forced a smile. "Your dad came back to the dealership after my father died, demanding five thousand dollars for the letters. I hit him square in the mouth. I said, 'Go ahead, show the letters. Let everyone know that you couldn't keep your wife happy, so she went looking for a man who could.' I was pretty certain that Italian pride of his would keep him from ever showing them to anyone."

Travis smiled, partly at the thought of his dad getting punched in the mouth, but mostly at the fact that someone had called Big Frank's bluff and won. "He never gave you the letters, did he?"

"Nah. He used to keep them in his car and hold them up for me to see whenever we passed, but I don't think he ever showed them to anyone."

"Do you think he threw them away?"

"No. No way. Not Frank. He would hold on to them, just in case he ever got the opportunity to use them against me."

"At least he didn't find them while Travis's mom was still alive," I offered. "That would have been bad."

Clay Carter's eyes had the sorrowful look of a wounded animal. It was as though my comment had exposed Clay's deepest fears. "Frank said he found the letters after Amanda's death, but I'm not so certain. I think he might have found them before she could get out of the house. There was a lot of damning stuff in those letters. Maybe he read 'em and just went nuts. You know your dad. He might have thought, 'If I can't have you, no one will.' Who knows what happened? It just about kills me to think that I could have been the one who caused your mom to be killed."

"But he was out of town when she died. How could he have killed her?"

"Nobody knows for sure that she was on the boat. They never found her body."

"That's not unusual. That river can be very unforgiving."

Clay shrugged. "I think your father is the embodiment of evil, son. I don't know how he did it, but I just can't believe he didn't have something to do with it."

"Are you sure she was going to leave my dad?"

Clay took a long, cleansing breath. "She wanted desperately to leave him, but she was afraid—not so much afraid of what Frank would do to her, but afraid that he would try to take you. You were the most important thing in her life."

Tears welled in Travis's eyes. He pushed himself out of the chair and extended a hand toward Clay Carter. "Mr. Carter, just to reassure you, I'll never say a word to anyone about this."

They looked at me. "Oh, me neither."

Travis continued, "I really appreciate your time."

Clay stood and draped his left arm around Travis's shoulder. "I know your mom would be proud to know that you care enough to do what you're doing. She was a special lady."

Travis nodded and muttered, "Thanks."

"Either of you boys want that janitor's job?" Clay asked.

"No, thanks," I said. "It's too far to drive."

As we headed south out of Steubenville, Travis asked, "Do you think it was him on the boat?"

"No," I said.

"Why? He could easily lie, and there is no way we could prove him wrong."

"I don't think either of them were on the boat."

"Someone was on the boat," Travis said. "The captain pushing the barge said he saw them jumping in the river."

I shrugged. "I don't have an explanation, Travis. Why would she go out on the river to see someone? Big Frank was out of town. If they wanted to see each other, he could have gone to her house. And no way she leaves you at home and runs out on a boat."

"Do you think she's alive?"

"I didn't this morning. Now, I'm not so sure."

The remainder of the ride home from Carter Chevrolet and Buick was silent. There are times when you know that nothing should be said, no questions asked, and that was one of those times. When Travis got out of the car he muttered "thanks" and shut the door behind him. I didn't see him for more than a week. When he next stopped by the house, he said nothing about the visit with Clay Carter, and I wondered if this signaled the end of Project Amanda. With the cemetery mystery apparently solved, perhaps he now had all the answers he wanted.

CHAPTER TWENTY

I was on my way home from football practice the week before school began when the car pulled up alongside me. It was a brown AMC Javelin, with the wide wheel wells. Behind the wheel was Hushpuppy Harmon, Alex's cousin, whose real name was Delmar. He was a year out of high school and an arrogant punk. I had a hard time believing that he and Alex shared the same bloodline. He was thin, with kinky yellow hair and a lame moustache that he had been trying to grow out since his sophomore year.

He pulled the Javelin to the curb and yelled at me through his open passenger-side window. "Malone!"

I didn't say anything, but walked up and leaned into the open window. "Nice ride, Hushpuppy," I said. He gave me a look of disgust, then handed me the envelope that had been tucked above his sun visor. "Alex asked me to give you this."

It was a plain white business envelope. On the back was my name and the word PERSONAL, which also was underlined. Alex had signed across the flap in ink, then covered it with clear tape. "This is great. Thanks, Hush. I really appreciate it." I started to walk away.

"Hey, Malone, what is that?"

"It's just something from Alex."

"No shit, Sherlock. What?"

I tucked the envelope into my gym bag. "It's kind of personal, Hush."

"Yeah, well I'm not going to be your personal mailman anymore. Got that?"

I kept on walking, and Hushpuppy squealed his tires as he pulled away.

The house smelled of cube steaks and fried potatoes and onions. My dinner was in a cast-iron skillet, a sheet of aluminum foil wrapped over the top. Dad asked me how practice had gone, and I said okay. I scraped the contents of the skillet onto a plate and went up to my room. Despite my name being on the envelope, I knew it was for Travis. But I was going to open it anyway. I had earned that. I tapped the envelope against my left palm several times before carefully tearing it across one end. I blew into the envelope and pulled from it a single sheet of paper. The missive had been typed, but unsigned.

> *Mitchell:*
>
> *Sorry this took so long, but it turned out to be quite a project. I may start a new career as a private investigator.*
>
> *I think the man you are looking for is Ronald E. Virdon. He retired in 1963 after a distinguished career in the Navy.*
>
> *The best I can tell, he is very much alive. His checks are being sent to 771 Easter Avenue, Asheville, North Carolina. All the information adds up.*
>
> *Hope this helps. Good luck.*

It did. I slipped the letter back in the envelope, ate my dinner, and headed out to find Travis.

Jimmy Jagr left for the three-block walk to the Coffee Pot at fifteen minutes after eight each morning. He would have a cake donut and a cup of coffee, one cream, extra sugar, and one refill while he read the morning Wheeling *Intelligencer*. He would get another coffee in a paper cup to bring back to the office. The routine never varied. He would be back a little after nine.

From a side window, Travis watched his boss waddle down LaGrange Avenue until he disappeared on Risdon Avenue. When

Jimmy was safely out of view, Travis pushed open the side door of the bakery warehouse and let me in. We hustled into Jimmy's office at the rear of the cement block building and pounded out the eleven digits that connected him to a home in Asheville, North Carolina.

I leaned over the desk and put my ear near the handset. It rang twice before a male voice, cheerful, picked up the phone. "Hel-lo."

Travis swallowed, but didn't speak.

"Hello?" the voice repeated.

"Uh, yes, is this Ronald Virdon?"

"It is. Who's calling, please?"

"Uh, I'm . . . are you . . . are you the father of . . . ?"

"What? The father of who?" The voice was changing from pleasant to irritated. "Who is this?"

The old man was still waiting for an answer when Travis slammed the phone back in the cradle, and the line in Asheville, North Carolina, went dead.

"Why didn't you tell him who you were?" I asked.

"No guts. I was afraid of what he might say, or might not say."

CHAPTER TWENTY-ONE

Travis and I were walking down Second Street on the first day of school of our senior year—September 1, 1970—when he asked, "Remember the letters Clay Carter said he sent my mom?"

I nodded. "I remember him telling us about them."

"I want to find them."

"Why doesn't that surprise me? Where are they?"

Travis rolled his eyes. "If I knew that, Einstein, I wouldn't have to *find* them; I'd just go *get* them."

I looked over at him. "You are such a smart ass. You're lucky you don't get your ass beat four times a day." He walked on as though he hadn't heard me. "Clay said Big Frank used to flash them at him when he was out in the Chevy. Maybe they're still there?"

Travis shook his head. "No, I checked all through the car the last time he was out of town. No luck. I figure Big Frank's got 'em stashed somewhere in the house. We've just got to figure out where."

I turned to him and said, "We?"

"We. You know, me and you. Us. Dos amigos."

"Travis, mi amigo, just so we're very clear on this point, there is no way on God's green earth that I am searching through your house for those letters. No. I won't do it. Sorry. No, wait, I'm not sorry. This is the kind of thing that could have tragic consequences. You remember, of course, the last search we made of your house?"

"Yeah, you got so scared that you pissed yourself."

"I pissed myself because you left me straddling the rafters atop your sleeping father for three hours in hundred-degree heat!"

Travis frowned. "You're being a puss. What are you afraid of?"

"Oh, well, let me think—Big Frank. Bodily harm. Death. All of the above. Pick one. If you find those letters and want to hide them in my bedroom, fine. But I'm not going to be anywhere near Big Frank's bedroom."

He grinned again. "I know you want to."

I paused to take a breath. "When were you thinking of undertaking this expedition?"

"Friday night. Frankie's got a new girlfriend, and you know how he gets when he's got a new girl. He's never home."

"Who is it?"

He shrugged. "Beats me. Angel Somethingorother. She's from Follansbee and giggles a lot. That's all I know. I'm sure she has a last name, most of them do, but I prefer to lump them into the category of the most recent winner of the Frank Baron Punch-of-the-Month Contest. He spends every Friday and Saturday night at her house. It'll be a piece of cake."

"Where, precisely, were you going to look?"

"Under his bed, in his trunk and dresser drawers, I guess." I covered my ears and began singing the national anthem. He removed my right hand. "Come on, be a buddy and help me."

"Travis, it doesn't take two guys to rifle an underwear drawer. My mom does it all the time. No way. This is where I'm drawing the line. You're crazy for even thinking about it. The letters are not going to help you find out anything substantial about your mom, except that Clay Carter was crazy in love with her. You don't need them to prove that Big Frank used them to blackmail Clay's father. You know he's capable of that, and it's probably true. Only bad things can come from this. Big Frank will catch you, and when he does, you're meat. He'll stomp you to dust."

"Come on, where's Sir Mitchell the Bold? I know that brave knight would help me."

"Trav . . ." He smiled and arched his left brow.

"What would I have to do?"

"Sentry. Easiest job in this man's army."

The target date was the last Saturday in September. Travis competed in a six-team cross country meet at eight in the morning, which he won by eighteen seconds and set a school record, then sold programs for the senior class at the football game against Yorkville that afternoon. He stopped by my house after the game for a Reuben sandwich with my extended family. Travis hung around the living room with me and the cousins and replayed the win over the Ductilites.

My cousin Johnny said, "You guys don't suck nearly as bad as you used to."

"We're undefeated," I countered.

"Yeah, but you're still not very good."

"Yeah, and you're not very smart, and that's not likely to change."

He raked his fingers under his chin at me. I walked into the kitchen. No one could get under my skin like my cousin Johnny.

Travis left without stating his plans for the evening. As he walked out the door, Mom shoved an uncooked Reuben wrapped in aluminum foil into his hand and gave him instructions on how to heat it in the oven. He looked a sad figure walking down the street, alone, a sandwich in one hand, the first-place medal he had won at the cross country meet in the other. He had been quite proud of the medal, which he had worn under his jacket at the football game, pulling it out to flash at me as we took the field for warm-ups. The athletic director had made a big deal of the school record and brought Travis out on the track at halftime to announce the accomplishment to the crowd. It should have been a big day for Travis, the cap to the kind of day most kids just dream about— breaking a school record and being recognized in front of the entire town. I'm sure he would have liked to have someone to share his success with, but we all knew he was heading to an empty house.

An hour after he left the house, he called, and I slipped out. He was standing behind the sagging screen door when I arrived. "Where do you want me stationed?" I asked.

"Come on up. I just wanted some company."

"You just want a witness so Big Frank won't kill you if he finds you snooping in his bedroom."

"Nah, that doesn't matter. He'd just kill us both."

"That's hilarious."

Following a systematic search plan that he had worked out in his head, Travis began dissecting the room, starting with the cardboard boxes under the bed. The contents ranged from used automobile parts to more of Big Frank's collection of hard-core porn magazines, but there were no letters, or anything else connected to Travis's mother. It was a time-consuming process, and when he had finished going through his dad's dresser, darkness had taken over the room.

"How do you know Big Frank didn't put them in a safe deposit box?" I asked.

"He's too cheap. Besides, the sonofabitch carries that forty-five with him everywhere. Who would want to try to steal something from him?"

"Think of what you just said."

Using a flashlight that he pulled from his hip pocket, Travis began searching Big Frank's closet. It was small and cramped, and the floor was littered with clothes.

"Why don't you turn on the light?" I asked.

"Too dangerous. If he came back, he'd see the light before I ever heard the car." The darkness made me nervous. I never feared the nearby railroad tracks or the trains during the day, but they were terrifying at night, when their cycloptic head beam eerily cleared their path, and their very passing vibrated the house and made my bedroom windows rattle in their frames. The closet revealed nothing of interest and the search seemed fruitless. Travis had searched under the bed, the closet, and both dressers. All that remained was the steamer trunk in the corner. It was unlocked, and Travis scooted the trunk away from the wall and pushed back the lid. The trunk was jammed full of Big Frank's junk—medals, ribbons, and plaques from auto shows, a few car magazines, his parents' brittle obituaries from the Steubenville *Herald-Star*, and assorted items that held no interest for Travis. Quickly, he pulled the items out of the trunk, setting them in a circle around him so he could return them in the same order.

The sound of a car passing by in the gravel behind the house was followed by a creak from downstairs. We both froze and listened. Nothing. It had been nothing more than the sighing of a tired house and the coincidental passing of a car. Still, it had given my nerves a jolt. "Come on, Trav, hurry up," I said.

He hurried though the rest of the trunk. With everything scattered on the floor, he could see nothing that resembled a letter. "Crap. Nothing here, either." As Travis put the contents back in the trunk, trying his best to remember the order in which they had left, he found a faded, four-page brochure: *Installation and Operation of your Hide-a-Safe.* Travis looked at the brochure, finding a series of numbers on the back page.

"Run down to the kitchen. There's a scratch pad and pencil on the table. I need you to write something down." I did as he asked and was back in seconds. He said, "Nine, sixteen, fourteen . . ."

"Nine, sixteen, fourteen," I repeated.

"Thirty-eight, one."

"Got 'em."

For the next thirty minutes, we scoured the house, basement to attic, looking for the safe. "How can you hide a safe like that around here? This place isn't that big," Travis complained. "We've checked every wall in the place—basement, bedrooms, living room, everywhere."

"Maybe he didn't put it in a wall," I suggested. "Maybe he buried it in a floor."

Travis looked at me, that crooked grin stretched across his face. "It's in the garage."

I shrugged. "Maybe, or in the basement."

"No. It's in the garage. I know right where it is—under his tool chest. He's got it covered with a piece of concrete. I asked him about it once when I was little and he blew me off—wouldn't answer. That's exactly where it is."

I was excited by the prospects. "Let's go."

Big Frank kept an extra key to the side door of the garage hanging on a nail just inside the basement door. The key unlocked both the door lock and the two deadbolts. "Let's get in there, get the letters, and take them back to your place," Travis said. "After I've read them, I'll put 'em back."

"Sounds like a plan."

We slipped through the door and pushed it nearly closed. The Chevy, buffed and gleaming in the dim light of the neon clock on the wall, rested in its usual spot. Travis shined his flashlight against the large, red tool box against the back wall. "I'm getting nervous. Maybe we should abort," I said.

"You're kidding, right?" Travis asked.

"Maybe we should wait until he's out of state on a trip," I offered.

"No. It's safe. Come on, let's do it." The tool box was on wheels and we easily moved it away from the wall, exposing a square block of concrete. Buried in each side of the concrete were two threaded receptors. Travis grabbed a handful of bolts from a coffee can on the workbench and worked them at the receptors until he found two that fit; they were nine-sixteenths. Using them as handles, he pulled the concrete block out of its resting place, revealing the face of the safe. It was gray, about a foot square, and resting in a cocoon of cement, a patina of rust developing along its exposed edges. The combination dial was off-center to the left, the handle to the right. I held the flashlight on the dial and read the combination aloud. It took Travis several tries before the handle moved freely. He took a nervous breath, opened the door to the safe and shined the light inside. There were only a few items lying on the bottom of the safe—the deed to the house, the title to Frank's prized Chevy, and a packet of envelopes wrapped in a rubber band.

The envelopes were tattered and yellowing badly around the edges. There were about twenty in the bundle, each marked in block letters, "Amanda." Each had been carefully opened by being slit across the top. Travis crouched down, leaning against the wall with the envelopes resting in his lap, the beam of the flashlight throwing a hazy light. He took the top envelope and held it between his fingers, gently, like an archaeologist might cradle a precious find. "I feel like I'm invading her privacy," he whispered.

"If Big Frank has read them, it was invaded a long time ago."

"I'm sure she never dreamed that her son would be reading letters from her lover."

"I'll give you that one." The adrenaline rush of sneaking into Big Frank's garage had masked the fact that my bladder was about to explode. "I thought you were going to take the letters and leave."

"In a minute."

"Well, if we're not getting out of here right now, I need to whiz." He used the flashlight as a pointer, throwing a beam of light on the little bathroom that Big Frank had built into the corner of his garage. I followed it into the room.

I stood in front of the toilet for a minute, allowing my eyes time to adjust to the near total darkness. When I could finally make out the rim of the toilet, I started to fumble with my zipper. I thought of how Travis's life would have been different if Clay Carter had been his father. I envisioned Travis with a normal, happy family. In my mind's eye I could see Travis as a youngster, maybe four years old, playing on the beach with the mother that I knew only from a photograph, and a younger Clay Carter. They were all smiling and laughing as they built a sand castle on the shore. That was the image in my mind as I grabbed my dick to relieve myself, the same instant that the overhead light to the garage came on.

"Find anything interesting, boy?" Big Frank Baron asked.

"Shit," Travis said.

"Thought I'd bring Angel down for some fish at the American Legion, and as I was driving by I wondered, why is there someone in my garage with a flashlight?"

I tried to stuff myself back into my jeans and stem the flow of urine. I succeeded in getting it in my pants, but failed miserably at stopping the flow. Again, hot piss ran down my front, soaking my jeans and running into my socks. I froze, concealed in the darkness of the bathroom. I turned, and through the slit in the door I could see the scene unfolding.

Big Frank was standing in front of the door, blocking Travis's only escape route. "Come here, boy," Big Frank said.

"What are these?" Travis asked, standing and holding the letters in his right hand.

Lord, but I admired his guts.

"They're mine and none of your fuckin' business, that's what they are." He pointed to the safe. "Put them back and come here."

Travis shook his head. "You said you didn't know who her boyfriend was."

"I said, put those letters back in the safe and come here."

"I'm through taking orders from you. Why do you have these?"

"That ain't none of your concern, either. Give 'em to me."

"Why would you keep them? Huh? Why would you keep Mom's love letters from another man? Unless, of course, you were hoping you could blackmail someone. Maybe get another car out of the deal? But if you tried to do that, Clay Carter might kick your ass again."

Travis, shut up, I thought.

It was too late, though. Big Frank had all he was going to take. He moved away from the front of the Chevy and started toward Travis. In the illuminated doorway, Big Frank's girlfriend appeared and hollered, "Frankie, what are you doing?"

He turned his head and yelled back, "I'll be back in a minute. Go sit in the car."

As he turned his head, Travis tried to dash past his dad, hoping to leap the hood of the Chevy and escape into the night. Despite his quickness, the garage was too small and Big Frank too close. Before Travis could jump, Big Frank threw a forearm into his son's ribs, driving him off his feet and sending him flying into the edge of the work bench. The envelopes flew out of his hand and fell like confetti. The air rushed from Travis's lungs as his ribs hit the bench. Before he could stagger to his feet, Big Frank grabbed him by his ears and lifted him up. The fight was over. All that remained now was punishment. "Don't ever let me catch you in this garage again," Frank Baron said in an eerily calm voice. He released the ears and backhanded Travis across the side of his head, his ring opening up a gash over Travis's right ear and sending him to the floor. "I hope you understand me, boy," Big Frank said, grabbing

Travis by the back of his shirt and carrying him like a bitch with a pup. He hauled Travis just outside the door and threw him face first into the dirt and gravel. Angel backed away from the scene, her hands behind her feeling for the car. "I told you to go wait in the car, goddammit."

Frank Baron crouched down over the limp body of his son. I was expecting a kick to the ribs or face. Apparently, Travis was expecting it, too, because he curled and covered. "Now, this is the last time I'm going to tell you this: Knock it off. I know what you've been doing, snooping around, trying to find out shit about your mother—you and your fuck buddy Malone. I want it to stop, and I want it to stop now. This is a small town, boy, and you'd be surprised what all I hear. I know you talked to Clay Carter, and I heard that you been talkin' to that cocksucker Chase Tornik. I don't know what you think you're looking for, but it's over. You think you want to know about your mom, but you really don't. Trust me. You might find out things you wished you didn't know, like that she was a cheating, fucking whore." Frank took a few sucks of breath. "You best let it go. And if I ever find you snooping around in my shit again, it'll be the last time, son or not."

I remained still as Big Frank walked back into the garage and picked up the scattered letters. He got them all, except for one that had neatly slid between the windshield and the wiper arm on the passenger side. It looked like a parking ticket pressed against the glass, but he didn't spot it. He took the wad of letters in his fat hand and flicked off the lights as he walked out of the garage. A few seconds later I heard the locks click. About ten minutes later, Travis rapped on the door. "Hey, fuck buddy, the coast is clear. You can come out."

I plucked the envelope from the windshield as I passed and slipped it into my back pocket. "Glad you haven't lost your sense of humor," I said, pushing the door open.

I looked at his swollen face. He looked at the stain covering the front of my jeans. "What is it with you and your bladder?" he asked.

I had no desire to explain. "How're your ribs?"

"I don't know. My head hurts so bad that it won't allow me to think about my ribs."

"Did you get to read any of the letters?" He shook his head. "Here you go," I said, gently slipping it from the pocket.

Travis smiled, which caused him to wince. He sat down on the back steps, blew gently into the envelope, and removed a single page of stationery, folded twice and, like the envelope, yellowing at the edges. He looked at it for a minute in the dim light of the kitchen. He began to read.

My Dearest Amanda:

I cannot tell you the exhilaration I am feeling at this moment. Only minutes ago you left me. While already I miss you more than you can imagine, I have never felt so alive. Never has a woman made me feel the way you make me feel. I love you, my darling, and I cannot wait until the day when it will be just you and me together forever.

I know you are under a terrible strain as you try to maintain your life at home. I am so sorry for this. Please, I beg you, leave him soon. Say the word and I will arrange everything. You and your son will be safe with me. This, I promise.

My heart aches for you, now and always. I cannot imagine a life without you, for I know that there is no other who could give me the happiness that you have given me. You, sweetheart, belong in my arms—now and forever.

I love you deeply.

Clay

CHAPTER TWENTY-TWO

It was the last week of football season and we were working over-time getting ready for the game against our big rival, the Mingo Indians, who were quarterbacked by my cousin, Duke Ducheski. With eleven seconds to go in the game, I reached the pinnacle of my high school athletic career when I intercepted a deflected pass in the end zone. We beat Mingo 14–13 and captured the first Big Valley Athletic Conference football championship since the days of Alex Harmon. Here's something I've never before admitted: I was totally out of my position, and that interception was nothing but dumb luck. Doesn't matter. I was the hero. After the game, I shook hands with Duke and he had tears in his eyes, and I felt bad for him . . . but only for a second.

The Blue Devil Touchdown Club had a victory parade through town and a celebration in the high school gymnasium. It was great fun, and early the following morning Travis was back at the house. "Okay, hero, time to get back to work on Project Amanda," he said.

He had healed quickly from his encounter with Big Frank. The cut over his ear had mended, and he could once again breathe without pain.

"All and all, that night wasn't as bad as I thought it was going to be," Travis explained. "When that light flipped on, I figured it was all over. I was sure he was going to kill me. And I don't mean that figuratively. I really thought he was going to kill me. When he said, 'Find anything interesting, boy?' I swear, Mitch, I believed it was the end of my life."

"I wouldn't have let him kill you."

He grinned. "What were you going to do, run out and piss on him?"

"Kiss my ass, Travis. I couldn't see in there."

"If I could have gotten past him and out the door, I would have kept running and never come back."

I raised one brow toward him. "And where, exactly, would you have gone?"

"I probably couldn't have made it in one night, but I was thinking of Asheville, North Carolina."

I smiled. "Really. That's interesting." Travis hadn't mentioned his grandfather, or the man we believed to be his grandfather, since the day he had made the aborted call. "So, you're thinking that Ronald E. Virdon might actually be your grandfather?"

"I'm thinking he is, yeah."

I laughed. "You should have just asked him when you had him on the phone."

"Hell, with the way my luck has been running, he'd probably get so excited he'd have a heart attack. Hopefully, that doesn't happen when I see him."

"See him? When are you going to see him?"

"As soon as you can get the car. I'm thinking next weekend, before wrestling season starts."

On Monday, Travis came over for dinner and I called for an executive committee meeting of the Malone family. Mom came in from the kitchen, where she was cleaning up from dinner. Dad was in his recliner, smoke from his pipe swirling up over the sports pages of the Steubenville *Herald-Star* and filling the room with the faint aroma of cherries. I had decided to take the direct approach. I had given this a lot of thought. I was a teenager, and there were certain things that I would try to slip past my parents. However, a weekend road trip to North Carolina was not on that list. Either I did this with their blessing, or I didn't do it. Neither of my parents held Frank Baron in high esteem, and I hoped this would play in my favor. We would tell them about Project Amanda—to a point—and hope that they would allow us to complete the mission. Frankly, I was harboring major doubts. Travis was hoping to play upon my mother's soft heart, which could work. Trying to slide one past my dad, however, was an entirely different issue.

There was no school on Friday because of a teachers' workshop. I had the weekend off before basketball practice began on Monday. That gave us three full days, which was all we needed. We planned to drive to Asheville on Friday, meet with his grandfather on Saturday, and drive back Sunday. I was hoping that my newly found status as football legend for the interception in the Mingo game would give me an edge in the negotiations. "I need a favor," I told my parents. "Actually, we need a favor. There's no use in pussyfooting around, because it's all going to come back to the fact that we need a favor. A big one."

Mom and Dad looked at each other. "What is it?" Mom asked.

Travis interjected. "Mrs. Malone, do you remember about three years ago, Mitchell and I were sitting out on the porch, and I asked you if you knew how my mother had died?"

Mom nodded. "Yes."

"Well, since then, Mitchell and I have been conducting our own investigation. I asked Mitchell to help me because I wanted to know about my mom. So we started Project Amanda." My dad's brows arched. "We've done a pretty good job, actually. We gathered up old newspaper stories, police reports, interviewed people, stuff like that."

"But why?" Mom asked.

"Because I wanted to know about my mom, Mrs. Malone. Before we started, I didn't know anything. I didn't even know what she looked like. Imagine if the only thing you knew about your mother was what you overheard people whispering about her. Big Frank would never tell me anything, and I really wanted to know. So, to make a real long story short, I snooped around and found out that I have a grandfather—Mom's dad."

Travis stated this as fact, even though we didn't know for sure that Ronald E. Virdon was his grandfather. Any doubt about this "fact" would have prompted my parents to immediately nix the plan.

"Where does your grandfather live?" Dad asked.

"Asheville, North Carolina," Travis said, as though it were just two miles down the road.

"Are you planning to go there?" Mom asked.

"I was hoping I could drive us there," I said.

My dad put his paper on his lap and removed the pipe from his mouth. He and Mom looked at each other without speaking. "I don't know about that," Dad said. This wasn't a defeat. My father never agreed to anything right out of the blocks. If he said no, he could always change his mind. If he said yes, he was stuck with his decision.

We both sat in silence for several moments, until Travis said, "I know this is a lot to ask, because there's nothing in it for you. I know you're taking all the risk. But I really need your help. Short of hitch-hiking, I can't get there. You guys do a lot to make me feel a part of your family, and I really appreciate that. But I'm not a part of your family. All I have is Big Frank, and you know what that's like. This might be the only other family I have. I don't want to wait any longer. I've waited my whole life, and I just don't want to wait . . ." Travis was choking up and couldn't complete the thought.

My mom, too, was tearing up.

Dad turned to me. "Do you think you're responsible enough to handle this?"

"Yes, sir. There's no school Friday. We could leave early Friday morning. Visit with his grandfather on Saturday, and drive back Sunday. And we've got money. I've got a hundred dollars I've been saving. Travis has . . ." I looked at him.

"Eighty-eight dollars."

"So we can cover our own expenses," I added.

"What about your dad, Travis?"

"He's going to be out of town or with his girlfriend. He never knows where I am most of the time, anyway."

Dad took out his pocketknife and started cleaning the bowl of his pipe. "I'll talk to your mother about it and let you know."

We left Brilliant at six a.m. Friday. It was still dark and spitting snow in the Ohio River Valley, which made my mother even more nervous than usual. We had washed the car—a 1968 Buick Wildcat—and Dad had added an oil change and a tank of gas. In the backseat was a cooler that my mother had packed. It contained enough food to sustain a division of Green Berets for a week. Dad gave me a credit card for an emergency. We were ready to roll.

"Call collect as soon as you get there," Mom said just once more as we pulled away from the curb. We were on a mission to locate Travis's grandfather, and it was the greatest adventure of our young lives. The radio was cranked and so were we, as we turned off Third Street and headed south on Ohio Route 7, which we would follow along the Ohio River to Marietta. The highway had been cut out of the eastern Ohio hills, and staggering cliffs climbed from the berm of the road. The last orange and yellow leaves stubbornly clung to the trees that covered the tops of the hills and the lowland plains between the highway and the river.

From Marietta we cut across to Charleston, West Virginia. As we cruised past the West Virginia capital, Travis pulled out a notebook and began scribbling notes.

"What are you doing?" I asked.

"Trying to figure out what I'm going to say to him."

"You have to write it down? How about, 'Hi, I'm your grandson, Travis'?"

"I'm writing down other things. I've never talked to the guy. I want to be able to tell him everything I've been doing for the past seventeen years."

"I see. Here's one. Tell him about the time in the sixth grade when you stuffed the sanitary napkin up the milk machine, and Miss Peniwinkle got an extra surprise with her milk purchase."

Travis failed to conceal the grin. "I was thinking, since this is the first meeting and all, that I'd try to keep it positive. You know, the highlights—honor roll, cross country, wrestling, stuff like that. That's why I thought it would be good to write it all down. I don't want to start stammering around and look like a stooge."

"Why don't you just relax? You've never had any trouble talking before, why would you think you would choke up now?"

"I don't know, Mitch. Maybe because it's the most important meeting of my life? Maybe because for the longest time I thought he was dead?"

"Just relax," I said.

We gassed up twice and ate while we drove. The adrenaline was surging, and there was no need to stop and rest. We hit the restrooms at the gas stations as we continued south, while performing the near-impossible task of scanning for a radio station that wasn't hillbilly.

The further south we drove, the more nervous Travis became. By the time we got to Asheville, at seven-twenty p.m., he was barely talking.

"You nervous?" I asked.

"Kind of."

"You think maybe he's not your grandfather?"

"No, actually, I'm pretty certain it's him. That's reason enough to be nervous."

"How so? You've found him. The hard part's over."

"The hard part hasn't even started. What if he doesn't want anything to do with me?"

"Good lord, Travis, why would you think that?"

"How do I know he's not going to take one look and see not his daughter's son, but an extension of Big Frank Baron? I might just be a reminder of the fact that his daughter is dead."

It was just a few minutes beyond seven-thirty when we checked into the Tar Heel Lodge on the city's eastern outskirts. I called home immediately. I was hungry for hot food, but Travis wanted to take a drive and find the address on Easter Street. "Let's run a brief reconnaissance mission, then we can eat," he said. We had been given directions by the desk clerk at the motel and cruised through the business section of town to a residential development pressed into a soft hill. We drove through an entrance of red brick pillars that were partially hidden by the low branches of guardian pines. A stone in each pillar was engraved with the words, "Gloaming Estates."

Easter Avenue was the first street that angled off to the right. The numbers began low and we started the long loop to the left. It was a half-mile drive to 771, a ranch-style home on our left. It had brick and cedar siding and a side-entry garage. The trim was painted light green and cream. An overhead light burned in the living room, visible through the sheer curtain covering the picture window just to the left of the front door. I slowed the car. "Do you want to stop by tonight?"

"No," Travis said. "Not tonight. Let's get some rest and come back fresh first thing in the morning."

I was up at seven, awakened by a bright Carolina morning that was bursting through the only window in the room. Travis had already showered and been to the pancake house across the street for breakfast. He was sitting at the tiny table next to the door, reading the newspaper.

"What time did you get up?" I muttered.

"One o'clock. Three o'clock . . . three-fifteen, four, four-twenty, four-forty-five, five. I didn't sleep very well. At five, I was lying there staring at the ceiling, and I knew I wasn't going back to sleep, so I got up and went out for pancakes."

I kicked off the covers and stretched, but made no move to get out of bed. "You're not planning to go knock on his door right now, are you?" I asked.

"Not with you sporting a morning boner like that. Shower up."

I did. Travis sat with me while I ate breakfast—steak, fried eggs, and hash browns. It was twenty minutes before nine when we headed back toward Easter Avenue, and just before the hour when we drove through the brick pillars of Gloaming Estates. It was a beautiful, brisk morning under a cloudless sky, and the air smelled of damp earth and pine. Jacket weather, my mother would call it. The neighborhood was up and moving. Children were riding bicycles on the sidewalks, and several men busied themselves in garages. As we closed in on the ranch house, we both spotted the man with silver hair working in the front yard.

"Hey, he's out," I said.

As we neared, the man bent over the dead and dying remnants of a flower bed that ran from the porch along the front of his house to a rose trellis that lined the side of the ranch. He knelt on a blue rubber pad, wearing work gloves, white painter's pants, and a gray sweatshirt, and wrestled with the dreary remains of what that summer had no doubt been a beautiful bed of annuals.

"This is great," I said, turning to look at Travis.

The only other time I had seen that expression on his face was when he had walked into Mrs. Tallerico's yard to fetch our baseball, only to find her German shepherd unchained and headed toward him in a full gallop.

"Keep driving," he said.

I had already started to slow and pull to the curb. "What?"

"Drive, goddammit, drive. Keep going."

It was like a pilot aborting a landing at the last second and jerking back into the sky. I hit the gas too hard, causing the Buick to rumble in the quiet neighborhood, and out of the corner of my eye I saw the old man turn to look. "What the hell was that all about?"

"Sorry. I need a minute. I'm just not ready. Take a lap around the block. Let me build up my nerve. I gotta get psyched up for this." He was breathing as though he had just finished a cross country meet. "Once around the block, just one, and I'll be ready."

It took three more laps, and he still wasn't ready.

"Travis, this is a nice neighborhood, and we're circling it in a car with Ohio license plates. Someone has probably already called the cops because they think we're staking out a house for a burglary. I didn't drive halfway across the country for you to bail on me. Now, this time I'm stopping the car and your ass is getting out."

I pulled to the curb across the street from 771 Easter Street and cut the ignition. Travis had gone white. The man had worked himself in toward the porch, tossing dead plants as he went. "Approach him while he's outside. That way you don't have to knock on the door."

Travis sat and looked, swallowed, and said, "Okay, I'm ready." He got out, crossed the street and cut across the yard, hands in his pockets. I could tell he was terrified. The man heard him coming and squinted into the morning sun. "Morning," Travis said.

"Morning."

"Uh, I'm looking for Ronald Virdon."

The man put the steel claw he was working with down and stood, pulling off his gloves. "I'm Ron Virdon." He was a little shorter than Travis, but still possessed straight, strong shoulders. He had a wide smile and friendly eyes. "What can I do for you, son?"

"Well, this is a little hard to explain." From his breast pocket Travis pulled a photo he had gotten from the attic. It was a wallet-size, black-and-white graduation photo of his mother, wearing a black gown and mortarboard. Without a word, he handed it to the old man, who squinted at it, his seventy-plus-year-old eyes taking a minute to focus. When they did, his smile disappeared and his gray eyes turned quite serious.

"Where did you get this?"

"Out of my attic." Travis swallowed. "Is it your daughter?"

The man looked back at the photo, then back at Travis. "Why do you want to know?"

As they stood, Ronald Virdon's wife came out the front door with a glass of water. She could not see the photo, nor did she know the gist of the conversation. But she stared hard at the young boy and smiled. It seemed as though she was staring at someone she thought she should know, but just couldn't quite put a name with the face.

"What's this all about, son?" the man asked, his voice neither hostile nor friendly. "Why do you want to know?"

Travis swallowed again. "Because that's my mother."

It took a moment for the words to register with the old man. The eyes that had a second earlier been so intense softened and relaxed. He looked at Travis, then his wife, then Travis again. His hands were shaking when he finally showed the photo to his wife. She dropped the glass and put her hands to her face. "Oh, my sweet Jesus. Are you Travis?" she asked.

Travis nodded. "Yes, ma'am."

She shrieked, began crying, and threw her arms around the grandson she had not seen since he was a baby. "Oh, my God, oh, my God. I don't believe it," she cried. The old man, too, had tears rolling down his face, and after a moment and a silent prayer, he draped an arm over Travis's shoulder. Forty feet away, I was bawling, wishing I could jump out of the car and be part of the celebration. But it wasn't my place. However, the exhibition that was unfolding before me had made the past three years of Operation Amanda worth the effort—the fear of being stranded in the attic above Big Frank, the nauseating pain of taking Clay Carter's kick to my groin, the embarrassment of pissing myself not once, but twice. It was all worth it. But for all Travis and I had shared, this moment belonged to him, alone. I watched for several minutes as they hugged and cried and finally disappeared into the house.

Travis was finally getting the one thing for which he had searched all his life—unconditional love. It had been instantaneous. He was their daughter's son, and that was enough. They took him into their home as though they had always been destined to do so. Travis had lived his life without the affection of a loving parent, or any relative who had truly cared for him. My mother had hugged Travis a lot because, she said, he needed hugging. I don't think I ever understood just how much he needed it until the moment he walked through that front door.

Twenty minutes after they went inside, a car pulled up in front of the house and a couple with three children jumped out and sprinted for the door. The man stopped on the sidewalk and picked up the shards of glass. It was Travis's aunt, uncle, and cousins. I was thinking that I might be making the return trip to Brilliant alone. Fifteen minutes later the uncle came out of the house and walked up to my car. "Come on in," he said, in a friendly tone and a mild Southern drawl. "In all the excitement, Travis sort of forgot that you were sitting out here."

"Not a problem," I said, stepping out. "That was family time."

"Heck, sounds like you and Travis are just like brothers. It was nice of you to drive him all the way down here."

When I got inside, Grandma Virdon was already orchestrating a family feast for that evening. As I entered the living room, she abruptly stopped talking, ran across the room, and threw her arms around my neck. "Thank you, thank you, thank you for bringing Travis back to us," she said, pecking at both cheeks. "This is such a blessing." She then went about her plans, sending her daughter-in-law to the Piggly Wiggly for groceries that included a turkey and hams and sweet potatoes. It was a day of celebration, of thanksgiving, at the home of Ronald and Esther Virdon.

The scene was chaotic for the first hour, and Grandma Virdon couldn't begin to settle down or keep her hands off her newly discovered grandson. She kept holding his face in her hands and looking into his eyes and seeing, I'm sure, the reflection of her daughter. She didn't begin to relax until the turkey entered the oven and her daughter-in-law and eldest granddaughter were busy in the kitchen, having ordered Grandma to retire to the living room with a glass of lemonade. And there, with Travis on the couch, the process of educating actually began.

"Everything," Grandma Virdon said. "We want to know everything."

Travis grinned. "How much of everything?"

"Absolutely everything," his grandfather said. "Start from your earliest memory and tell us all that you can remember. Everything you've done—school, interests, sports, hobbies, just everything. We want to know all you can tell us about yourself."

And so he began. It took hours, and there seemed to be few details that escaped him. His first day of school. Little League. Sneaking off to fish in the river. The death of his Grandmother Baron. The death of his Uncle Tony. His high school wrestling and running accomplishments. His academic prowess. He told them how Alex Harmon had helped us track them down. He told them everything, but nary a word about his father until his grandmother finally asked.

"He's around," Travis said. "We don't get along very well."

"Does he know you're down here?" his grandfather asked.

"Oh, God, no. He wouldn't be happy about that in the least."

They nodded and didn't press the issue. It was uncharted territory, though it would seem that Ronald and Esther Virdon's unspoken opinion of their former son-in-law was very similar to that of the rest of the free world. "You said this man in Pittsburgh helped you locate us?" his grandfather questioned. Travis nodded. There was an obvious look of concern on the man's face. "Why did you go to all that trouble? Didn't you get the mail we sent you?"

Travis looked as though he had been hit in the gut with a sledgehammer. They never had mail delivery to the house. For years, Big Frank had rented a post office box, the combination to which had always been a mystery to Travis. He had assumed that his dad used the box for his porn-by-mail collection. Never had he imagined that it was simply a way to keep him from being contacted by his grandparents. "No. Never. I've never seen anything."

"Not a single birthday or Christmas card?" his grandmother asked.

"I've never seen any cards," Travis said.

Ronald Virdon's jaw muscles tightened, and his hands clenched the arms of the rocker in which he sat. There was a fire in the eyes of the old man, hatred, but Travis's grandmother simply looked confused. "Oh, sweetheart, we've sent you birthday and Christmas cards with money every year. I feel so bad now, because I used to get upset that we never got a thank-you note or a letter. I guess you couldn't have known. We wanted to call, but there's never been a listing."

"Our phone number is unlisted," Travis said.

Travis looked away and blinked back the tears. I wondered how many times Big Frank was going to break his son's heart. There didn't seem to be any limit. Fortunately, the old man couldn't break his spirit. "I'll give you Mitchell's address before I leave. You can write to me there."

Travis's grandmother insisted that we check out of the motel and ordered me to go pick up our things. We would spend the night at their home. They couldn't have been nicer, or more excited. Mrs. Virdon gave thanks to Jesus no fewer than two dozen times, and she continually hugged and kissed Travis, and cried. The evening meal was a feast. All the while, Travis was the center of attention, and he basked in the spotlight. He didn't tire of answering their questions.

They were all disappointed that Travis and I couldn't stay for church services the next morning, as they wanted to show off their rediscovered grandson. However, I explained that we had to get on the road early, as that was part of the deal with my parents. At nine p.m., Travis's uncle and his family left for home, promising to be back for breakfast. I had stuffed myself and was heavy in the eyes when Grandmother Virdon entered the living room with a box, the contents of which were the various remembrances they had kept of their daughter. Travis had spent the entire day talking about himself. He was now going to get a chance to learn about his mother from those who knew her best.

I excused myself and retired to one of the spare bedrooms. There was nothing Travis could tell his grandparents about himself that I didn't already know. But the discussion that was about to take place was for the family, for Travis. If he chose to tell me later, fine, but I didn't want to be there for what would be an emotional discussion. It would be a long drive tomorrow, I explained, and I needed to get some sleep.

This evening, I assumed, was the fitting end of Project Amanda. I was happy for Travis, but I knew that I had just lost my best friend. We would drive back in the morning, but I knew he was not long for Brilliant, Ohio.

We were on the highway headed north out of Asheville at a few minutes after nine the next morning. Mr. Virdon had gotten up early and gassed up the Buick, then pressed forty bucks into my hand for gas on the return trip. They forced Travis to take two hundred dollars and promised to make up for all the gifts and money they had sent, but he had never received.

They had stayed up well into the night talking about his mother, and Travis fell asleep a half-hour after we were on the highway. He did not wake up until we were almost out of Virginia. "You're a hell of a traveling partner," I said.

He blinked, yawned, and said nothing. How much his life had changed in the last twenty-four hours. He had gone from having virtually no family to a family who couldn't wait for him to return. As we left, his grandparents were making plans for a holiday visit to Wheeling, where they could rent a cabin at Oglebay Park and see their grandson.

"Unbelievable, huh?" he finally said, fifty miles into West Virginia.

"Absolutely. You couldn't have scripted it any better."

"No doubt."

We stopped and ate lunch at a diner just outside of Beckley. "I'm buying," Travis said, flashing the wad of twenties that his grandfather had given him. We sat in a corner booth and Travis showed me a few snapshots of his mother during her high school years.

"It's kind of sad to see it come to an end," I said.

"See what come to an end?"

"Project Amanda. I figure that there's little else left to do. You've found your family. You probably know more about your mom than you ever thought you would."

He sipped at his water and looked out a window streaked with a drizzle that had followed us most of the trip home. "You're probably right."

The waitress stopped and took our orders. Travis had the meatloaf, and I had the fried chicken and coffee. I was not ordinarily a coffee drinker, but I was charging up for the stretch drive home. "Things were going so well, I half expected to get up this morning and have you tell me you were staying in Asheville."

He smiled. "I would have liked to have done just that. Man, what great people." He sipped his Coke and frowned. "Why do you suppose Big Frank's been hiding my mail?"

"Wouldn't it be hard to explain why two dead people were sending you cards and presents?"

"Oh, yeah. I forgot he told me they were dead. Jesus, what a son of a bitch. Why did he do that?"

I shrugged. "Once again, you're looking at me to explain Big Frank? If I had to guess, I'd wager he knew your grandfather suspected him in your mother's murder." I paused for a moment, wondering how many times in the history of mankind someone had spoken similar words to his best friend. Damn few, I hoped. "He probably didn't want your grandparents putting that idea in your head."

"Just when you think he couldn't be any more despicable, he proves you wrong."

"Why didn't your grandparents come up north to see you after your mom died? Did they say?"

Travis nodded. "Yeah. They said they tried, but Big Frank made it miserable for them. They came up to see me about a year after my mom died. They arranged this vacation and visit, and when they got there Big Frank had apparently taken me and left town. He told them he had the dates mixed up, but he did the same thing on the next visit. After that, Grandpa said he and Big Frank got into a big argument on the phone, and Big Frank told him not to ever come to Brilliant again. He said that Mom was a cheating whore and he didn't want his son to have any contact with a family who raised a daughter like that."

"A pure charmer, that father of yours."

"I know. Big Frank told Grandpa that he was friends with the cops and if they ever came back he would have them arrested for harassment or something. Big Frank moved us into the new house and had the phone number unlisted. They said they wanted to come up and see me, but they were afraid it would cause problems for me. And since I never got their mail, I had no idea that they wanted to have any contact with me. Hell, I didn't even know they were alive."

"What do they think happened to your mom?"

"They don't know. For a long time they thought Big Frank had killed her. They said they would like to believe she drowned, that she was so miserable in her marriage that she really was out on the boat with her boyfriend."

"Do they know about Clay Carter?"

"I don't know. I didn't bring up his name, but they seemed to know she was planning to leave Big Frank." Travis quit talking while the waitress set the meals on the table. Travis slathered his meatloaf with ketchup.

"So, she wanted to get away, but your dad killed her before she got the chance?"

Travis shook his head. "Remember, Mitch, he wasn't even in the state." There was a hint of aggravation in his voice. "I know you think Big Frank was involved, but I'm just not convinced that he had anything to do with it. I know he's a bastard, but that doesn't mean he killed her and had her dumped in the river."

It was strange to hear the words come so easily from Travis's mouth. It was his mother and father he was talking about, and the likelihood that a murder had been committed had so long been a possibility that Travis could talk about it very matter-of-factly, discuss it in detail as easily as he poured his ketchup. It gave me a chill. I wondered how many sleepless nights this had caused.

"I can tell you one thing—Big Frank had better never smack me again," Travis said. "He does and I'm outta there. I'll go to Asheville and live. I don't have to put up with that shit anymore."

"Just try to get along with him until the end of the school year, Trav; then you can do what you want. You don't want to leave before graduation."

"Yeah. I'd like to finish out the year at Brilliant, but he isn't going to beat me anymore. He's been beatin' my ass since I was old enough to walk, and it's going to stop."

"You know how he is. Just try not to aggravate him."

"The mere fact that I'm breathing aggravates him. You never know when he's going to go ballistic. Hell, you've seen him explode. It doesn't take anything to set him off. Say the wrong thing, look at him wrong . . ."

"Write in his cement."

Travis frowned. "Write in his cement?"

I cleared my mouth of fried chicken. "It was something Alex Harmon told me about when I was talking to him. Big Frank caught Alex and Jimmy Kidwell writing in some fresh cement up at the old place on Shaft Row. He grabbed a switch off a tree and beat their asses."

"Writing in what cement?"

"Alex said he was just a kid, six or so, and he and a buddy had been down in the creek trying to catch crawfish to sell to the bait shop. They came up over the hill and your dad had just poured a cement cap on the cistern. Alex said they found a stick and started writing their names in the cement when Big Frank caught him. Alex never knew he was there until Big Frank lashed him across the ass with a switch from a mulberry tree. He said he jumped three feet in the air, and ran back over the hill with Big Frank stingin' their butts all the way." I was laughing at my own story, but Travis just stared, unamused. "What? That was funny."

"What was he doing again?"

"Catching crawfish."

"No. Big Frank. He poured cement over what?"

"The old cistern."

"What's that?"

"I didn't know either. Alex said it's like a well to catch rainwater off the house. People had them before they got city water so they had water for their gardens. We used to have one in the side yard and Dad capped ours, too."

"Why would you do that?"

"So you didn't have a hole in the ground that some kid could fall in, I guess."

"That's why your dad capped his. If every kid in Brilliant fell in Big Frank's cistern, he couldn't give a shit less. Remember, I'm living in a house that Big Frank is letting crumble around us. Why would he go through the trouble of capping a cistern?"

I shook my head. "When Brilliant got city water, everyone capped or filled in their cisterns, Trav."

"Sure you would, especially if you were trying to hide a body in the bottom of it."

I set down my fork, wiped my mouth and began massaging my temples. "You know, sometimes you give me a migraine right behind my right eye. For the love of God, Travis, please, try for two minutes to enjoy the great weekend you've just had. There is no body at the bottom of that cistern. Your mom drowned."

He stuffed his mouth with meatloaf. "Doesn't make sense to me."

"Everything isn't a conspiracy, Travis. There is no body. He capped the cistern so no one would fall in. End of story."

He shrugged and stared back out the window beyond the orange neon *EAT* sign. "You're probably right. But doesn't it make you wonder?"

"No, it doesn't." I pointed at his plate with my fork. "Eat your meatloaf and think about how incredibly lucky you were this weekend."

CHAPTER TWENTY-THREE

In its day, Shaft Row was the home to the elite of Brilliant. It was simply a road that extended from Labelle Street up the hillside toward the entrance to the deep shaft mines of the long-defunct Thorneapple Coal Company. The road had been the home of the executives and owners of the Thorneapple Coal Company and the Thorneapple Nail and Rail, a nail and railroad spike manufacturing company and the predecessor of the Ohio Valley Steel Corporation. The homes had wooden siding and elegant gingerbread and lattice, and had to be painted every summer because the acrid smoke from the factories scoured the houses and caused the paint to peel in big chunks. The homes built on the north side of Shaft Row were tucked into the hillside, built on foundations that required the removal of tons of earth and were subjected to flooding from the run-off from every big rain. On the south side, the hill was tapered and homeowners had sprawling yards that led down to Thorneapple Creek.

The sidewalks and streets were made of red brick from a pottery near Amsterdam. When the wives of the executives complained about having to walk down the hill—all of a couple hundred yards—to catch the streetcar to Steubenville, the Brilliant & Steubenville Trolley Company put rails into Shaft Row with a turnaround at the dead end, near the entrance to the company offices.

Thorneapple Nail and Rail prospered through the early part of the twentieth century, with Shaft Row as the town's opulent thoroughfare. But by the 1930s the deep shafts were mined out, and Thorneapple Nail and Rail was sold to the Ohio Valley Steel Corporation in 1935.

Meanwhile, Shaft Row evolved from Brilliant's showplace to an eyesore. The trolley car abandoned its line and the brick street and side-walks were pulled up for use elsewhere, leaving it little more than a mud path that washed away with every storm, leaving Labelle Street covered and packed with gravel and mud. The homes along Shaft Row were claimed by those much less affluent. By the early fifties, only a handful of dilapidated, sun-bleached homes remained.

At the back of the row, tucked in behind a grove of elms and maples, was the location of the home purchased by Frank and Amanda Baron in the spring of 1950 for thirty-one hundred dollars. It was from this home that Amanda Baron mysteriously disappeared in October of 1953. Less than nine months later, on July 16, 1954, while Frank was allegedly having dinner in Steubenville with a woman he met, married, and divorced all inside of four months, the house mysteriously went up in flames. There was little evidence as to the cause of the blaze, though everyone with a minimum of cognitive power suspected Big Frank had it torched. He collected the insurance money—nearly eight thousand dollars—and bought the house across the street from the bakery.

On a sunny day in the early spring of 1971, Travis showed up at my back door and waved me out to the back porch. "Put on some old shoes; I need you to help me do something," he said.

"What?"

"Nothing major. Come on."

I did as he requested, though I was wary of Travis's interpretation of "nothing major." Although sunny, it was early April and the temper-ature was just a few degrees above freezing, the ground still soggy from the thaw. We walked toward the north end of town and turned up Shaft Row. "What's this all about?" I asked, though I instinctively knew.

"I just want you to see something," he said.

"You're just not going to let it go, are you?"

I followed him up the gravel road to where his first home had been. The trees had grown up in a bowl around the old property, which was now covered with a thick bed of desiccated weeds and thistles and thorny locust trees. The village had filled the old root cellar years earlier, using it as a dump for debris from street cleanings. A clear path, new, had been beaten down to where the house had stood, and parts of the concrete foundation were exposed. It wasn't, I knew, his first visit to the old homestead.

"So, what have you been up to?" I asked.

He turned sideways to slip through a thicket of thistle. He knelt and pulled at the corner of a piece of canvas, revealing a shovel and a garden hoe. "I want you to help me find that cistern."

"I knew it. For the love of God, Travis! Why?"

"Because . . . I just want to find it, that's all."

"No, you don't. You want to find it so you can see what's in it. I could just kick myself in the ass for ever bringing that up. You can't possibly believe your mother's body is in there. She was seen jumping in the river, remember?"

"I know, I know. But something's just not right."

"I agree. It's your brain that isn't right."

Travis had met with his grandparents in Wheeling at Christmastime. He spent three days with them, and he couldn't have been happier. For weeks, all he talked about was graduating and moving to North Carolina. But the cistern had obviously been on his mind since the moment I mentioned it in the diner near Beckley.

"The cistern in your side yard is thirteen paces from your house—I stepped it off," Travis said. "I figure this one wouldn't have been in the front yard, and the backyard is uphill. The other side of the house is too close to the trees, so it has to be out here somewhere," he said, pointing toward a gentle, weed-covered slope that ran down to where Thorneapple Creek circled behind the old company headquarters.

"It could be covered with a lot of dirt," I offered.

"There were parts of the foundation still exposed. We ought to be able to find it."

I stopped at ten paces and began working the ground with the hoe. Travis continued another five paces and scraped the ground with his spade. The thistles were snagging my clothes and jabbing me with every step; the mud worked up over the edge of my new Chuck Taylor All-Stars, which was going to make my mom furious. "That's why I buy you boots," she would say. We worked in an oval, moving inward one step with each lap. We had made three laps when Travis struck cement; it was the cap on the cistern. It was covered by a four-inch layer of coal chips, gravel, and dirt. "It looks like it was covered up intentionally," he said.

"Oh, please," I said, rolling my eyes. "The hillside has simply moved down and covered it. Everything isn't a conspiracy, you know."

"That's what they want you to think," he said, taking the hoe and scraping the dirt from all around the concrete cap. It was circular and eight inches high. I smiled and pointed to the rim on the far side. In rough print was: "Alex Harmon" and "Jimmy Kidwe."

"Big Frank must have switched Jimmy's ass before he could finish his name," I said.

Travis said nothing. He took his hoe and began moving the earth from around the disk. After a few minutes the entire cement cap was exposed. Travis took the spade and wedged it between the stone base and the cement cap, using the shovel as a lever. It budged, but the wooden spade handle was cracking under the pressure. "It must weigh a ton," he said.

"Once we get this off, then what?"

He looked at me. "We've got to go down and see what's in there."

Chills raced up my spine. He didn't mean "we." I knew what he was thinking. "You want me to go down there?" I said. "Down there—God only knows how far—and see if your mom's body is buried in the bottom of this cistern? That's your plan?"

Travis nodded. "Look, Mitch, I know you don't want to do it, but if my mom is buried down there, I don't want to be the one who finds her."

"I understand," I said.

"Good. Besides, you owe me."

"I owe *you*! How do you figure?"

"You stayed in the bathroom that night while Big Frank kicked my ass."

"That's not fair."

"Nothing is fair; nothing is free," he said, staring at the cap. "How deep do you figure it is?"

"Too damn deep for a ladder."

"I'll figure it out," he grinned. "Come by about ten."

Travis was sitting on the front porch steps waiting for me. He motioned me around the side of the house where he had a six-foot length of heavy pipe, a pair of two-by-eight planks, a car battery, and the winch and a length of a cable that were remnants of Big Frank's unsuccessful attempt to open a tow truck business. A flashlight was stuck in his hip pocket. I looked at the pile of materials and asked, "Can I assume that you've developed a plan?"

"You can."

"Can I also assume that I won't like it?"

"Oh, most assuredly. In fact, you're going to hate it."

We placed the pipe, winch, and battery on the planks and carried them like a stretcher. From the alley behind Travis's house we cut across the back of the lumberyard to Thorneapple Creek and walked along its soggy bank a quarter mile up the hill to the rear of Shaft Row and the foundation of the old Baron home. By the time we were able to drop the load, my arms and shoulders ached from slogging along the creek bank. Causing me more angst, however, was the fact that I believed I had figured out Travis's plan for placing me inside the cistern. And he was right. I didn't like it. Not even a little bit.

Travis used the steel pipe to wedge the three-foot cement disk off the cistern opening. Once the cement cap was clear of the rock base, we were able to rotate it to its edge and balance it in the weeds. We then placed the two-by-eight planks over the opening with a two-inch gap between them. The winch was placed on the middle of the planks with the cable running between them. At the end of the cable was a loop, a foot in diameter, held together with cable crimps. Travis hooked the winch to the battery with wiring that he had carried over his shoulder, then tested the winch, both up and down.

Unfortunately for me, it worked like a charm.

"We're ready," he said, handing me the flashlight. "The batteries are fresh; I just put 'em in."

I took the flashlight and shined it down the hole. The beam was faint. "I thought you said these batteries were fresh."

"Fresh to that flashlight. They've been in the kitchen drawer for a while."

I guessed that it was sixteen feet to the bottom of the cistern. I shined the light to the cistern floor. The beam was faint, but bright enough to see the cistern floor. There was no body, just the dark and dank earth. "I suppose you want me to dig around down there."

"Yeah." He took a deep breath and peered into the cistern. "Look, if I were you, I wouldn't want to do this, either. But I have to know if there's anything down there. There's probably not, but I have to know for sure or it will always bug me. Once I know, I'll be okay. We can put Project Amanda to rest and I swear that I'll peacefully go on with the rest of my life. But I can't have this gnawing at my gut forever, and I can't go down there and poke around where my mother might be buried. I just don't have the guts to do it. So I really need your help on this one. Do this for me, and I promise I won't ask for any more favors."

I looked him in the eyes and said, "Liar."

He laughed. "But this will be the last *big* favor I ask."

"Qualify 'big,'" I said, putting my right foot in the cable loop. He lowered the cable until I could stand free of the edge of the hole. He tucked the shovel under my arm, then he slowly lowered me into the abyss. The winch whined as my head disappeared beneath the rim of the opening, I was overtaken by fear unrelated to the possibility of unearthing the skeletal remains of Amanda Baron. "Travis, that battery isn't going to die when I'm at the bottom of the hole, is it?" I asked, my words echoing off the walls of the cistern.

"I'm hoping it doesn't die when you're halfway down."

"Goddammit, Travis, that's not funny."

"It's funny if you're not the one being lowered into the hole."

"Travis, if I . . ."

"It's fine. Quit fussin', grandma. And if something happens, I'll run home and take the battery out of the Fifty-Seven."

"Yeah, great. As I recall the last time you tried to take something out of Big Frank's garage it wasn't exactly a sterling success."

"Try to remember who's controlling the winch, would you, smart ass?"

The drop was slow, just a few feet a minute. Once I got comfortable with the trip down, I held the shovel below my feet so I could feel for the bottom. When the shovel hit, I reached down with my left foot for the earthy floor.

It was darker than anyplace I had ever been. I could see nothing. I was certain that as soon as I moved some dirt a boney hand was going to reach up and pull me into the grave, or I would turn on the light and shine it into the decaying face of a miraculously back-from-the-dead Amanda Baron. She would arise from her grave to avenge her death and mistakenly confuse me for Big Frank, and of course the battery would go dead and leave me stranded in a hole with the walking corpse as hunks of flesh fell from her body. I realized these were all unreasonable fears, but I was the king of unreasonable fears. And, at that moment, I was trapped in a black, sixteen-foot pit with my vivid imagination.

The cistern had a diameter of about four feet, which didn't leave much room to maneuver. I turned on the flashlight and wedged it between two stones on the wall. I pressed my back against one wall, pinning the dangling cable behind me, and shoved the spade into the ground across from me. The dirt was soft and the spade easily sunk to its top edge. I pulled back on the handle until it hit the stone wall, then flicked the dirt to one side. I decided to scrape dirt away on one half of the cistern floor, then the other half. After taking a few scoops, I began using the spade like a hoe, raking the soft dirt away from the other side of the cistern.

"How's it going?" Travis asked, his voice echoing through the hole.

"Helen Keller digs a ditch," I said.

The dirt was building up around my feet, and I had hit nothing but the soft dirt bottom. I had skimmed a foot of dirt from the cistern floor when the shovel scraped against something hard. I froze for a moment, then gently used the shovel to remove more dirt from the area.

"What was that?" Travis asked.

"I don't know."

I pulled the flashlight out of the wall and slowly dropped the beam toward the floor, following the light down with my eyes. When the hazy yellow beam reached the floor, I took a breath and lowered my eyes, certain that a skull would be staring back at me. Across the floor was a grayish material, lumpy and solid. I kneeled and brushed the dirt from the concrete base of the cistern. I had hit nothing but the end of the line. Confident that a body could not be hidden beneath the dirt and the concrete bottom, I moved to the other side of the cistern and sank the spade into the undisturbed dirt. It took but a few tries to confirm that nothing but dirt and concrete lay at the bottom of the cistern. I was overcome by my own bravery and relief.

I put my foot in the loop and told Travis, "Bring 'er up." I was at the surface and resting ten minutes later.

"Anything?" Travis asked.

"Nothing," I responded.

"What was that scraping noise I heard?"

"Nothing. Just my shovel scraping the bottom of the cistern."

"Rocks?"

"Concrete."

"Concrete?"

"Yeah, the concrete floor."

Travis didn't have to say it, for I already realized my folly, but he did anyway. "Why would there be a concrete floor in a hundred-year-old cistern?" He pointed to the outcropping of limestone that extended over Thorneapple Creek. "Wouldn't you just dig down to the limestone and use that as your foundation?"

"Maybe it was just the concrete left over from making the cap. They just poured it down the cistern."

"Sure," Travis said. "They poured the cap, then after it hardened they reopened it and dumped what was left down the cistern. Makes perfect sense to me."

My jaw started to tighten. "Might I remind you that you're lipping off to the only guy in the free world who would allow himself to be lowered into a cistern, at night, to look for a body?"

That brought a grin. "Was it just in a pile, or was it completely covering the bottom?"

"It was higher in the middle than around the sides, but it covers the entire bottom of the cistern."

"Mitchell, we've got to see what's under that concrete," he said.

"Your use of the word 'we' continues to amaze me."

"Can you break it up with a sledgehammer?"

"I don't know. Maybe. I don't know how thick it is, and I don't have any room down there to swing it. I'll have to use it like a tamp."

"Okay. Wait here. I'll run home and get a sledge."

"And flashlight batteries. These are about done."

Travis ran off through the brush to the creek bank. I could hear him for only a minute until his footfalls were drowned out by the sounds of the stacks clearing at the power plant south of town. He was back in twenty minutes, puffing for air. He handed me two new batteries, and I put them in the flashlight. The beam was bright against the wall of the cistern. "Much better." I slipped the light back in my pocket and my right foot back in the cable loop. Travis lowered me a few feet, handed me the sledge, then sent me on my final descent. I was a little more comfortable with the drop and the darkness. I kicked the dirt from one side of the concrete, then straddled the area, allowing the head of the sledge hammer to dangle between my legs. I lifted my hands to eye height, then slammed the sledge straight down. The head hit crooked and the handle jerked out of my hands. I stumbled forward and smacked my knuckles against the rock wall, scraping them clear of skin. "Yowl!"

"You okay?" Travis echoed.

I shined the flashlight on them. Skinned, but not a lot of blood. "I'll be fine."

The concrete was several inches thick at the center of the cistern. The second hit struck closer to the wall. It sounded hollow and seemed to give a little. I hit it several more times, each strike a little harder than the one before. On the sixth hit, the cement cracked. I set the sledge to the side and lit the area with the flashlight.

"What'd you find?" Travis asked.

"Nothing."

The light was still strong, and it easily lit up the bottom of the cistern. There were two cracks in the concrete, creating a rough, pie-shaped wedge. I moved a few small chunks of concrete that had broken loose at the point and wedged an index finger under the concrete and lifted, carefully standing it against the wall and turning my light on the floor.

I would have expected to have panicked, but it wasn't scary, actually. In fact, there was something oddly serene about the tiny bones lying in the black earth beneath the yellow beam of my light. It was a browned wrist bone and the delicate bones of a pinky, ring finger, and middle finger, resting in the dirt lengthwise along the top of the opening. I stared at the skeletal remains for several minutes, hunching over it to block Travis's view. How would I tell him? In his heart, he had wanted desperately to believe his dad had not been involved. He still held faint hope that she was alive. Now, there was no doubt as to her fate. For a minute, I pondered sliding the concrete wedge back into place and telling him I had found nothing. "Goddammit, Travis. Why didn't you just leave well enough alone?" I muttered.

"What'd you say?" he asked.

"Talking to myself," I said.

He had found his grandparents. He could have just walked away. I took hold of the concrete wedge and was ready to recover the grave when the beam of my flashlight caught the glint of metal. I took my pen knife from my pocket and used the smaller of the two blades to gently move some of the dirt. On the ring finger, pushed down on the first knuckle of the hand, was a ring. I slipped the blade between the ring and the bone, lifting it free, then used the knife to slide the bone back to its resting place. The light on the ring gave me chills, much more so than the sight of the bones. It was gold—a crescent of rubies around a small, marquis diamond. It was the ring from the journal, the ring that Amanda Baron had accepted as a testament of Big Frank's love. The concrete I had moved was, without question, the cover of Amanda Baron's crypt.

I pushed the ring and the knife deep into my pocket and slid the concrete back into place.

"What the hell's going on?" Travis asked. "What're you doing?"

"Comin' up." I put the head of the sledge in the crease of my elbow and my foot in the loop. "Bring 'er up."

I could hear the whine of the motor as it lifted me toward the opening. It was a long, slow ride—a trip to the dentist, the long walk to the principal's office, but worse. I wondered what he would do when he realized that his dad, in fact, had killed his mother?

Travis stopped the winch as my head neared the two planks and grabbed the sledge. I put my left hand on the top rim of the cistern and the right on the nearest plank, and Travis winched me up until I could step away from the hole.

"Nothing?" Travis asked.

I turned on the flashlight and handed it to him, then reached into my pocket and pressed the ring into his open palm. "I'm sorry I busted your chops about looking down there." I think he knew what it was before it was hit by the light. I stood beside him as he inspected the ring. There was nothing to say. His dad was a murderer, and the remains of his mother lay beneath a concrete slab at the bottom of an abandoned cistern on Shaft Row. Travis sat cross-legged at the edge of the cistern and tried to fight back tears.

CHAPTER TWENTY-FOUR

Travis bought a rusting 1958 Rambler from Keltenecker Used Cars for a hundred dollars, and I would argue that even that was too much. It was an oil-burning heap with a dog of a push-button transmission that you had to continually monkey with to get into reverse. Snookie was working at McKinstry's Sunoco, and every other day he would fill a gallon jug of used crankcase oil for Travis to use in the Rambler.

"You can't put that used oil in your car," Snookie had protested when Travis first made the request. "It'll ruin it."

"Snook, it burns oil so fast, it won't be in there long enough to hurt anything."

The Rambler had been on Mr. Keltenecker's lot for months, and I'm sure he was glad to get rid of it. Despite the plume of white smoke that followed us everywhere, and the fact that Travis couldn't get it into reverse—I had to push it backward out of his parking space at school—Travis was happy for the cheap transportation.

It was early May when Travis eased the Rambler into the gravel parking lot on the river side of the main entrance of Ohio Valley Cement and Masonry Company. When he cut the lights, the security guard's flashlight came on and he walked toward the car, not shining the light directly on Travis until he stepped out of the car. As soon as he recognized Travis, Tornik holstered the flashlight and walked up to the chain-link fence. "Well, well, if it isn't the intrepid detectives."

Tornik looked bad. It had been ten months since we had last seen him, but he seemed to have aged dramatically. He was grayer, and the lines that creased his forehead and cheeks ran deep through his face, giving it a reptilian appearance. The rough life and booze appeared to be overtaking him at a gallop. The omnipresent cigarette wasn't doing him any good, either, and he was developing a deep smoker's cough that was painful to hear. Travis leaned against the fence, clinging to it above his head. "Can we talk? I promise not to be a smart ass."

Tornik checked his watch. "Sure. I've got a few minutes." He walked through the open front gate and pointed toward his car, which was just a few spaces down from Travis's. I got into the back seat and let Travis have the front.

Spring had been slow creeping into the Upper Ohio River Valley. Travis was wearing a denim jacket and jeans. Despite the chill, he rolled down the window of Tornik's Pontiac to vent the cigarette smoke. "Didn't expect to ever see you again. What's up?" Tornik asked.

"You were right," Travis said. "All along, you were right." He turned and looked at Tornik. "He killed her. My dad murdered my mom."

Tornik took a long drag on his cigarette and slowly allowed the smoke to escape his mouth. "Sounds like you're convinced. What made you change your mind?"

Travis held up the ring. "Among other things, this."

Tornik took it from Travis and inspected the ring. "I'll bite. What's this have to do with anything?"

"That's my mother's ring, the one my dad gave her when they were dating, just before they got married. She wrote about it in her journal, and she was wearing it the night she died."

Tornik turned on the dome light and examined the ring a little more closely, trying to see if there was something particular about it that he was missing. "So, where'd you get it?"

"Off her finger," Travis said.

He turned his head and frowned. "Excuse me?"

Travis nodded. "Off my mom's finger. We found her body."

"Who found it?"

Travis nodded toward the back seat. "Me an' Mitch. We found it at the bottom of the cistern at the old house—the one they were living in when Mom disappeared. It burned down later."

Tornik nodded. "You mean the one your dad torched for the insurance money?"

"Given everything I've learned in the past year, that wouldn't surprise me in the least."

"Tell me about the body."

"He must have killed her and put her body in the cistern, and then hid it under some concrete."

"What on earth prompted you to look in the cistern?"

"It's a long story. I had a hunch she was there, and she was. Just bones, now, but she's there."

"Jesus Christ." Tornik pinched the bridge of his nose between his index and middle fingers. "Have you told anyone?"

Travis shook his head. "No, not yet."

"How about you, slick?" he asked, turning his head to the back seat.

"No, sir. It's not the kind of thing I'd want getting back to Big Frank, at least not yet."

You could almost see the wheels turning in Chase Tornik's head. I imagine he was feeling like a cop again, proud that his instincts had been right—Amanda Baron had been murdered.

"I'm thinking of going to the cops, but I wanted to talk to you first," Travis said. "I want to know what information is in those other pages you tore out of the report. I've come to terms with this. He killed her. Period. But now I need to know what you know. If my mom didn't die in the river, who was on that boat? Who were the man and woman who jumped into the river?"

"Jesus, kid, you've really thrown me here. You're sure? You're absolutely sure that it was a human skeleton? You actually saw the body?"

"Yeah," I said. "The ring was still on the finger."

Tornik put his cigarette between his lips and reached across the car and unlocked the glove compartment. Inside were four pages, neatly folded and attached by a paper clip. "I figured you would be back," he said. Tornik smoothed them out and quickly read them over before passing the top two sheets to Travis. I leaned forward to read them by the dim glow of the dome light.

The pages had been typed and, though the copy was light, it was still legible.

> *On October 3, at about 2 a.m., Mrs. Florence Sabo was standing on her back porch at 400 Dillonvale Road NW, after letting her dog outside. The dog began barking. Mrs. Sabo said she saw a man and a woman running along the fence line behind her house. (The fence is near the bank of Thorneapple Creek.) Mrs. Sabo had not turned on the back porch light and was not spotted by the man, whom she identified as Tony Baron, the younger brother of Frank Baron. She could not identify the woman, but assumed it was his wife, Trisha, since she watched as they cut across the ravine to the house trailer where they lived. Mrs. Sabo said the neighbor has a bright light in the backyard that was on that night, which illuminated the creek behind her house. She said she got a good look at the couple and has absolutely no doubt that it was Tony Baron.*

> *At about noon, October 2, a pleasure craft matching the description of the boat owned by Frank Baron was seen anchored along the shore of Goulds Creek, near Hickerstat Road. A witness stated that he was taking his small craft up the creek to fish for rock bass and he took particular notice of the pleasure craft as it was highly unusual for a boat that size to be that far up Goulds Creek, which is no more than a few feet deep and with a rocky bottom. A man appeared on the deck of the boat and stared briefly at the fisherman. The fisherman realized the significance of this after seeing the description of the Baron boat in the newspaper. He identified a police mug shot of Tony Baron as the man he had seen on the deck of the boat.*

> *Mr. Earl Tomassi is the president of the Brilliant Boat Club. He said he stopped by the club twice on October 2—at 10 a.m. and 3 p.m. He said*

the Baron boat was not at its dock either time. He was at the club from 3–8 p.m. and said the boat was not at the dock during that time. When questioned about the whereabouts of his boat, Frank Baron could not explain why his boat was not at its dock, but blamed it on his wife, who he believes was out on the boat all day with her boyfriend, Clay Carter. This does not hold water, as this investigator has documented the whereabouts of Clay Carter for nearly the entire day of October 2.

The whereabouts of Clay Carter for Oct. 2:

7 a.m.—He bought coffee and two dozen doughnuts at JoAnn Bakery in downtown Steubenville, which he took to his workers. Mrs. Ida Mae Bishop waited on him at the doughnut shop. He had a receipt for the purchase.

7:25 a.m.—Carter purchased a Pittsburgh Post-Gazette paper at the South Side News & Tobacco in Steubenville. None of the employees remember Carter on that particular day, but stated that he regularly stops and purchases newspapers at the shop.

About 7:45 a.m.—Carter arrived at work at Carter Chevrolet and Buick. Employees Bruce Kowoloski and David Davis were already at work. They remembered that particular morning because Carter had asked them to concentrate on repairing an oil leak in the engine of Henry Ullrich's Buick. They recalled this because Carter told them that Mr. Ullrich purchased a new Buick every other year and he wanted to keep him happy. Kowoloski and Davis, as well as seven other Carter employees, remember seeing him in the garage that day until at least 11 a.m. (He claims he was there until noon. He had completed his work by 10 a.m., but said he waited until noon because he was hoping to receive a telephone call from Amanda Baron to set up a rendezvous. The call never arrived.)

12:30 p.m.—Carter had lunch at Isley's. Carter said Stella Hansen waited on him, but she doesn't remember that specific day. She said Carter is a regular customer and could have been in on the day in question. Carter said he sat next to Nick Nikodemus at the food counter and talked to him. Nikodemus said he remembers the day specifically because he stopped at Isley's for lunch on his way to Williams Funeral Home for the calling hours for Gladys Longley, the widow of his friend Glen Longley.

2 p.m.—Carter reported back to the garage after receiving a phone call at Isley's that Bruce Kowoloski had been injured at the garage. He had broken his thumb after pinching it between the new engine and manifold. Kowoloski was taken to the hospital and Carter ordered work on the Buick halted until Monday a.m. Carter then telephoned Mr. Ullrich to inform him of the accident and stated that it would be Monday afternoon before the car would be ready. Mr. Ullrich remembers receiving the telephone call, but doesn't recall the time. Mr. Carter said it was between 3 and 3:15 p.m. Carter stopped by the hospital on the way home. This was confirmed by Mr. and Mrs. Kowoloski, and Dr. Homer Pittman.

5:30 p.m.—Carter spoke to a neighbor, Sheila Swoboda. Swoboda said she had just gotten home from the A&P in Steubenville and remembers the date specifically because Carter spoke of the accident at the garage.

Mr. Carter's whereabouts after 5:30 p.m. on October 2, 1953, cannot be accounted for. Carter claims to have spent the evening at home, reading and listening to the radio. However, it should be noted that his whereabouts can be accounted for after the time when the Baron boat was gone from the dock, and when it was seen docked along the shore of Goulds Creek.

Travis looked over the documents, then, with complete puzzlement, turned to Tornik. "I'm not sure I get it. Did my uncle kill her?"

Tornik shook his head. "No. Your dad killed her, but your uncle helped him get away with it. Some of this is conjecture on my part, but I think I had it nailed down pretty solid. Your mom was probably killed on the night of October 1. The last time anyone saw her alive was earlier that day, but she spoke to Clay Carter that afternoon. My guess is that she finally told your dad she was leaving him the evening of the first. This enraged him, and he killed her."

"On purpose?"

Tornik shook his head. "I don't know. If I had to guess, I'd say it occurred in a moment of rage. I don't think he plotted to kill your mother, but he couldn't take the thought of her leaving. It would have been too damaging to his ego. Maybe he hit her with a fist, maybe he picked up something and hit her. I don't know. Whatever his intentions, she was no less dead. Here, look at this," he said, handing Travis the final two pages of the report.

> *Sherman Grodin, an employee of Strausbaugh Scrap and Iron in Steubenville, said he had been told by a customer that Amanda Baron had been killed by her husband.*
>
> *He identified the customer as Harold "Turkeyman" Melman.*
>
> *Mr. Grodin said he was violating a confidence by contacting this investigator, but believed it was his civic duty to do so. I interviewed Mr. Melman at his home, 901 Simpson Ridge Road, on January 10, 1954. Mr. Melman was very nervous at the time and said he didn't want to assist in the investigation. He claimed that he feared retaliation by Mr. Baron. However, after being promised that we would protect his identity until trial, he agreed to be interviewed.*
>
> *Mr. Melman is well known around Brilliant as an eccentric. He has no regular job, but works at the dump collecting scrap for resale. His property is littered with junk cars and used appliances. He sells and repairs used appliances out of his basement.*
>
> *In the late afternoon of September 30, 1953, Mr. Melman said he was scouring the area near the old Thorneapple Mine No. 2. He had been told that several coils of heavy copper wire could be found near the site of an old storage unit that had been uncovered by heavy rains earlier this year. Mr. Melman said he was searching the area when he heard loud arguing coming from the home of Frank and Amanda Baron. Mr. Melman watched from the woods and stated that he could not understand what was being said, but could tell Mr. Baron was very upset. From his vantage point on the hillside, Mr. Melman said he could see inside the kitchen windows of the Baron home. Several times Mr. and Mrs. Baron moved past the windows. Each time, Mrs. Baron was walking backward as Mr. Baron pursued her. This went on for several minutes.*

Mr. Melman said the arguing stopped for several minutes. He heard Mrs. Baron yell once more. A few minutes after he heard her yell, Mr. Melman witnessed Frank Baron run out of the house, slam the door behind him, jump into his car and drive off. Mr. Melman crept up to the side of the house and peeked into the dining room window. He could see the legs of Mrs. Baron extending through the doorway from the living room into the dining room. She was not moving. Mr. Melman entered the house through the back door, which remained unlocked. There was a baby crying upstairs and Mrs. Baron was lying on her side on the living room floor. Blood was seen coming from her head and forming a puddle on the linoleum floor.

Mr. Melman became very scared and ran out of the house. He said nothing of this to anyone until he told his friend at the scrapyard. Mr. Melman is very upset that his friend violated his confidence. According to Mr. Melman, and several independent sources, Mr. Baron has a history of thuggish behavior and Mr. Melman fears for his life if he is forced to testify. He was promised protection from Mr. Baron.

June 3, 1954: Sheriff Stuart DiChassi: Interview of Harold Melman at Ohio Valley Hospital in Steubenville.

Mr. Melman was brought to the hospital March 16, unconscious, the result of a beating he received from an unknown assailant. He received facial lacerations, a broken jaw and extensive dental damage, a fractured skull, a broken nose, and a fractured orbital socket. Mr. Melman was attacked in his home, 901 Simpson Ridge Road in Brilliant, and was beaten with a blunt instrument, perhaps a pipe or a baseball bat. Mr. Melman said he cannot identify his attacker. It is this investigator's belief that Mr. Melman knows his attacker, but is afraid to identify him.

Mr. Melman had previously been interviewed by former detective Chase Tornik. During that interview, Mr. Melman claimed to have extensive information about the death of Amanda Baron. However, when interviewed at the hospital by this detective, Mr. Melman said *he had no personal knowledge of Mrs. Baron's death, nor would he ever testify in court. When he was questioned about the information he had given to former detective Tornik, Mr. Melman said the report was completely false. In light of former detective Tornik's recent problems, it is the opinion of this investigator that the prosecution could not present Mr. Melman as a reliable witness as his previous statement to former detective Tornik would not hold up in court.*

There is some question as to whether Mr. Melman will ever be able to make a full recovery. Since the attack, he has become extremely nervous, and has frequent nightmares. Mr. Melman also suffered mild brain damage, and the beating has left him with a severe speech impediment and hospital personnel have a difficult time understanding him. At times of duress he chants a cry that doctors say sounds like: Nomo-teemo-nomo.

I remembered the day Turk Melman died, July 4th the previous summer, and the reports that in his hallucinogenic final hours, Turk supposedly repeatedly cried out, *Nomo-teemo-nomo.*

Travis folded the report and looked at Tornik. "Big Frank beat him up."

Tornik nodded. "That's what I suspect."

"No, he did. There's no doubt in my mind. Big Frank did it. Nomo-teemo-nomo."

"Gibberish," Tornik said.

"That's what I thought when he died last summer. Word went around town that when he was loony with the fever, that's what he was chanting—nomo-teemo-nomo. Everyone thought it was some kind of directions to a treasure trove of gold that he supposedly had buried on the property."

"Maybe it was."

Travis shook his head. "No. I understand it. I spent years listening to Turkeyman. Let me see your pen."

On the back of the paper he wrote:

Nomo-teemo-nomo

And beneath that:

No more, Tino, no more.

He showed it to Tornik. "My dad's full name is Francis Martino Baron. When he was younger, when he and Turk were in high school together, my dad's nickname was Tino. It wasn't gibberish. He was crying for mercy. No more, Tino, no more." Travis shook his head. "I can hear him saying it, 'nomo-teemo-nomo.' He wanted Big Frank to stop beating him. All these years, people have believed that Turkeyman was beaten by someone trying to find his gold, but it was Big Frank making sure he never testified."

"Melman was already afraid of your dad. Imagine what it was like after that beating."

"I wonder how Big Frank found out that Turk had seen my mom dead."

Tornik shrugged. "If you tell one person, you might as well put it in the newspaper. That guy at the scrapyard who called me probably told someone else, swore them to secrecy, then they told someone and swore them to secrecy, and so on until it got to one of your dad's friends."

"But the boat? What's this about Uncle Tony and Trisha running up the creek?"

"My theory is that your dad killed your mom, panicked, and went to ask your uncle for help. I always believed they put the body in the river and then staged the accident so authorities would find her and it would look like an accident. But, based on what you just told me, they obviously dumped the body in the cistern. They panicked, buried her, then realized it was a likely place to look. They probably figured that if she just disappeared, the cops would search the property and find the body, so they came up with the scheme for sinking the boat and making it look like she drowned. Your dad called and got a shipment, then left town. That eliminated him as a suspect. Your uncle and aunt, the precious flower that she was, got the boat out of the dock in the middle of the night and docked it up Goulds Creek so no one would see them take it out. They probably went downriver after dark and waited for a barge. They drove into the path of the barge, which was on the Ohio side of the river. Remember, it didn't drift, because when we found the ignition switch it was still in the *on* position. They headed it toward the barge and jumped naked into the river and swam to shore. The captain sees two naked people—a man and a woman—dive in the river while he's trying to avoid a crash; he doesn't get a good look, really. They have clothes stashed on shore, then run home up the creek bank, which was when Mrs. Sabo saw them. They shower up and are in bed sleeping, or waiting, when the cops knock on the door. They feign sorrow and go up to the house and get you. Your dad is out of town, so no one suspects him of anything. They're dredging the river for the bodies, which, of course, aren't there, so the rumors begin that your mom and her lover ran off together, but no one suspects any foul play. This gives your dad time to play the role of the grieving spouse. Later, he puts a cement cap on the cistern. Case closed."

"Until now," I said.

Tornik looked back at me, then at Travis, and slowly shook his head. "If you're thinking of going to the cops with this, that's honorable, but it's too late. It will cause you nothing but heartache."

"How do you figure?" Travis asked.

"It's been too long. There's no proof whatsoever that your dad killed her. He has an alibi. He was out of town, and he'll testify that your mother was alive and well when he left. I know he did it and you know he did it, but a prosecutor would never take the case before the grand jury. Never. There are no witnesses or physical evidence linking him to the murder. Mr. Melman was the only witness who could slam the door on your dad, and he's dead. The only other witnesses that could put your dad away are your Uncle Tony and his wife, and they're both dead. They were the ones seen running up the creek bank the night the boat was hit, which would make them prime suspects in the murder. Mrs. Sabo's report would be turned over to a defense attorney and he would use that to deflect all attention away from your dad. On top of that, the defense attorney also would get reports linking Clay Carter as your mother's lover. They'll finger him as a possible suspect." Tornik lit a cigarette. "Then, Mr. Carter gets dragged through the mud. You don't want to do that."

Travis shook his head. "No, I don't. And Big Frank's got the love letters that Mr. Carter sent my mom. I'm sure he would use them against him. Big Frank would claim that mom was trying to break off the relationship and that it was Mr. Carter who killed her in a fit of rage."

Tornik frowned. "I didn't know about the letters."

"A recent development," Travis said, staring out into the night.

"Besides, what happens between you and your dad when you turn him over to the cops? He'll obviously know that you ratted him out. That could get extremely ugly."

Travis was silent as Tornik worked on his cigarette. "Maybe I'll take care of it myself," Travis finally said, turning toward the detective. "That cistern's big enough to hold another body."

Tornik pointed at Travis with the glowing stub of a Camel. "I hope that's just bluster on your part. I know you'd like to kill the old man and get away with it, but you wouldn't. You'd get caught; sure as shit, you'd get caught. Yeah, your dad got away with it, but that was because I couldn't finish the job. If I stayed on the case, your dad would have gone to prison for a long time."

"And now?" I asked.

Tornik sent a stream of smoke out the window and shrugged. "Now? We go on with our lives."

"That's it?" Travis asked. "He gets away with murder?"

Slowly, Tornik nodded his head. "Unfortunately, yes."

Under the cover of darkness, Travis and I returned to the old family property the following Saturday night with a garden rake and a rusting, steel-wheeled wheelbarrow that had been forgotten in the weeds behind Big Frank's garage. In the wheelbarrow, which Travis slowly and silently worked up the banks of Thorneapple Creek, was a flat stone that he had picked out of the creek bed earlier in the day. On it he had painted in black letters:

> Beneath this stone lies the body of Amanda Virdon Baron.
> Born: April 2, 1931
> Murdered by her husband, Frank Baron: September 30, 1953

He moved the cement cap from the cistern and dropped the handmade tombstone inside. He said a prayer for his mother and apologized to her and God for not being able to seek for her the justice she deserved. When he had finished, we began the task of filling in the cistern, hauling dirt and scrap and stones from the property to the hole. We worked into the early morning hours, filling the hole a little more than a third of the way.

We returned the next Saturday to continue the fill. While Travis pushed dirt into the hole, I scavenged the hillside for pieces of pipe and board, a tree stump, two old car tires, and the rusting remains of a girls bicycle, all of which were dumped in the opening. Around the base of the foundation of the old house were loose stones that easily came out. I rolled them down the grade to Travis, who guided them into the hole. By midnight, we could see the bottom of the hole, not five feet deep. There were enough pieces of crumbling concrete and stones around the foundation of the house to fill in the rest of the way to the rim. When the hole had been filled to near ground level, we rolled the cement cap back over the opening, sealing forever the tomb of Amanda Baron.

CHAPTER TWENTY-FIVE

With only finals week left before our graduation, Travis had a death grip on the Ohio Valley Steel Scholarship. He would finish the year with a perfect 4.0 grade point average and as our class valedictorian. Margaret Simcox would be our salutatorian, finishing her high school career with an average of 3.96, four one-hundredths of a point behind, the "B" she had received in driver's education dooming her to second place.

There seemed to be little chance of Travis blowing the lead. He was excused from the trigonometry final by virtue of having an average of one hundred for the year. The College Prep English class final was a term paper, which he had completed three weeks earlier and received a score of one hundred and six out of a possible hundred, collecting all six bonus points. Chemistry had been an in-class demonstration and talk, which he aced. Mr. Jankowski, our journalism teacher, graded us on the quality of the school newspaper over the course of the year, and he rarely gave anyone less than an "A." The only class that remained was American Government, which was Travis's strongest subject. Margaret had resigned herself to the fact that Travis would breeze through the exam and claim the scholarship, though it made her blanch to think he would use it to attend welding school, to which he had yet to apply.

Travis had been particularly quiet since the night we talked with Tornik in his car, which I deemed understandable. He stopped by the house the night we were eliminated from the regional baseball tournament. Artie Drago had been daydreaming in center field and let a lazy fly ball drop just ten feet away. It was one of those embarrassing mistakes that we would be reminding him of at our twenty-fifth class reunion. I was on the back-porch swing, savoring the last few minutes that I would ever wear any kind of uniform for the Brilliant Blue Devils. It had been a good run, I thought.

He came up and sat down on the swing. "Tough way to end a season," he said.

I nodded. "No doubt. Glad it wasn't me. That's the kind of thing I'd wake up in the middle of the night and think about fifty years from now. Fortunately, I guess, it was Artie." Travis smiled and nodded, the implied message understood. Artie Drago didn't have the brain power to agonize over his mistakes. While such a mistake would haunt me for years, Artie had probably already forgotten about it. "So, what's going on with you? You haven't killed Big Frank in his sleep, have you?"

"That son of a bitch isn't getting off that easy. If I kill him, it's going to be while he's awake. I want to make sure he knows who's doing it."

"Have you heard anything about . . ."

"No, Mitchell, I haven't heard anything about welding school and let's preserve our friendship by not discussing it any further."

"Cheesus, who pissed in your oatmeal?"

"You bring it up every time we talk."

He was trying to bait me. Over the years, I had become very astute at understanding when he was trying to pick a fight. "Bank on this: I'll never bring it up again."

He crossed his ankles and jammed his hands into the pockets of his shorts, the pressure he was exerting causing the fabric to stretch tight. "I can handle myself, you know. I practically raised myself," he said after a few moments.

"I know you can handle yourself, Trav. That's not the point. I know this whole thing is a mess, and I know it's pinging around inside your head like a pinball, but I don't want it to ruin your future."

He got up to leave. "Don't worry about my future," he snarled. "I know exactly what I'm going to be doing. You don't have to worry about me."

I worried. It was my nature.

The American Government test was given on Friday, the last period before lunch. Once it was taken, our classroom obligations at Brilliant High School were officially completed. The test was easy, a basic review of the class highlights, and certainly nothing that Travis couldn't handle. I had been working on the test for twenty minutes when Travis stood, shoved in his chair, and started for the front of the room. As he passed Margaret, he leaned down, draped an arm over her shoulder, and whispered a few words that sounded like, "Always speak kindly of me." Then he winked and left the room.

Our final exam grades and our career averages were posted the next Tuesday afternoon. On the American Government test, I had gotten an A, Urb a B, and Travis a D. The D on the test gave him a B for the grading period. The full-credit B dropped him in the standings below Margaret's half-credit, driver's education B. His name appeared second on the career grade point average chart, behind Margaret Simcox, our valedictorian.

I tracked him down at the bakery warehouse, where he was still working a few hours a day. "You tanked it. Why?"

"What are you talking about?" he asked, poorly feigning ignorance.

"Don't give me that. I heard what you said to Margaret. You said, 'Always speak kindly of me.' You threw the government test so Margaret could be valedictorian and get the scholarship."

He continued to unload the empty metal racks from the back of the truck. "Mitchell, I don't have the faintest idea what you're talking about. I thought that government final was a bear."

"I don't get it, Travis. Even if it's welding school, you could have used the money."

He shrugged. "Margaret Simcox, for all her arrogant, self-centered faults, has some direction in her life. She's going to college. She can use that money. I don't know if I'm even going to welding school, let alone college. And I checked. Either the valedictorian uses the money within one year, or it's defaulted. The salutatorian can't have it. So why let it go to waste?"

I took a seat on the edge of the loading dock as Travis moved to the next truck, unloading and stacking racks of trays. "Does this mean you're going to make a career of loading and unloading bread trucks?"

Travis arched a brow. "Hardly," he sneered.

CHAPTER TWENTY-SIX

I imagine they felt relatively safe. The only person they were concerned about hadn't seen them in eighteen years, and Big Frank Baron had never been attentive to details, anyway. With the dozens of grandparents and aunts and uncles showing up for graduation in the crowded auditorium, Ronald and Esther Virdon slid right in, virtually unnoticed. They took a seat in the corner of the auditorium. Ronald sat stoic, eyes forward, shoulders straight, a look in his eyes that said he almost hoped Big Frank Baron saw him. The more-animated Esther sat away from the aisle, hunched, peering around her husband's shoulders for a glimpse of her former son-in-law.

Travis had not told them of our discovery at the bottom of the cistern. If he did, he was certain his grandfather would kill Big Frank. Travis was so grateful for the new family, he didn't want to chance losing it. Tornik, we were confident, would never say a word. Beyond that, the truth behind the mysterious disappearance of Amanda Baron was buried as deep as her remains.

When Big Frank entered the auditorium, attending the only function that involved his son's high school career, Esther spotted him immediately. He was dressed in black slacks, pointy black boots, and a silver polyester shirt that stretched tight over his droopy belly. He had a gold chain around his neck that intertwined with his mat of chest hair. He needed a haircut; his locks were slicked back into a ducktail that hung over his collar, and a slick of sweat coated his jowls and neck.

From the lobby, I could see the look on Esther Virdon's face when Big Frank entered the gymnasium. "Look how fat he's gotten," she mouthed. Ronald never budged, keeping his head, eyes, and erect shoulders forward. Big Frank walked past the couple without noticing them.

The Brilliant High School orchestra began playing *Pomp & Circumstance* as we entered the auditorium from the rear. We split, with Margaret Simcox leading half the graduates down the left aisle, and Travis leading half down the right. He saw his grandparents, but made no sign of recognition. I winked at Mrs. Virdon, who smiled. We sat in the first three rows of the auditorium. Folding metal chairs were set up on the stage to accommodate Margaret, Travis, and the local dignitaries, all of whom felt obligated to tell us how the worlds of industry, commerce, and higher education were anxiously awaiting our arrival. We, too, were certain that the Brilliant High School class of 1971 was destined for greatness. However, what we wanted most at that point was to get to the graduation parties, and thus paid scant attention to the principal, superintendent, or class advisor.

Then it was Travis's turn to speak as class salutatorian. He stood before the hushed auditorium, and I got a chill. He was smirking, and I wondered if perhaps he would use this opportunity to tell all present of our adventure, and end the biggest mystery in the history of Brilliant, Ohio. It would be the most memorable speech in Brilliant High School commencement history, that's for sure. Then again, maybe that was what he wanted me to think, just to rattle me a little. Even as we prepared to graduate, Travis continued to play me like an Ohio River bullhead.

Thus, as I nervously gripped the armrests, he began.

Do we fear the future? Does the class of 1971 know what awaits it beyond tonight? No, we most certainly do not. Too often, it is not the future that we fear, but the darkness in which it lurks. We fear what we cannot see. The future is not bleak, but it is dark, for we can only imagine what lies ahead.

As graduates, we have been told that the future awaits. Certainly, that is true. But the future awaits everyone, not just the graduates of 1971. What is out there? Only the unknown.

Some of us will not meet that challenge. We will shirk and give in to the future. Simply, we will give up. Why? I don't think we know. Perhaps the future is simply more than we can bear.

To those members of my class that meet the challenge of tomorrow, Godspeed. It will be those people who shape the future. But there will be those who, for whatever reason, fail to step up to the challenge. Not because they are weak or lazy, but because they cannot, for whatever reason, summon the strength to face tomorrow.

Travis paused for a long moment, looking out into the crowd and allowing his words to sink in. His was not the typical, upbeat speech generally delivered by the number two honor student, and the crowd was captivated.

It may be your son or daughter that fails to meet your expectations. Encourage them if you can. Help them. Love them. Be there for them. Many of you know that life is difficult. Help each other along the path of life. For when a family fails to meet the needs of their loved ones, they can be lost in an instant, and lost forever.

The auditorium, save for a smattering of polite applause, was silent. Travis went back to his seat, and Principal Fishbaugh stuttered through an introduction of Margaret Simcox, who had prepared a speech comparing her graduation to the joy of watching her beagle, Daisy-Doo, giving birth to a litter of puppies. She hurried through the speech, accepted her scholarship from the president of Ohio Valley Steel, and took her seat.

"That was a very uplifting speech, Travis," she said through clenched teeth.

Travis grinned. "As was yours, Margaret. I particularly liked the part where the puppy you named Apple Strudel kept biting your shoelaces."

"Bite this," she said under her breath, smiling as Principal Fishbaugh thanked the two speakers and began introducing the 1971 graduates of Brilliant High School.

As the families of the graduates came together after the ceremony, two figures slipped unnoticed out the back of the auditorium. They were pulling away from the high school parking lot before any of the others left the auditorium. At the foot of the stage, where graduates posed with teachers and relatives, Big Frank Baron stood until he caught his son's eye. "I gotta go," he mouthed, tapping his wristwatch. Travis nodded.

Earlier in the evening, as Big Frank dressed for the graduation, he had complained that it would make him late for his run to Buffalo. As Big Frank left the auditorium without so much as a congratulations directed toward his son, Travis walked over and joined my family. I wrapped my arm around his shoulder and we mugged for the school photographer. "We made it, buddy," I said.

"We sure did." He kept his arm wrapped around my waist and squeezed.

Travis posed for my mom with his honors diploma and his salutatorian trophy. Urb, Snookie, Johnny Liberti, and Brad Nantz came over for more group photos. My parents had a small open house after graduation, and I had to spend a few hours there doing face time with my relatives and family friends. My cousins Duke and Johnny were there. Duke planned to attend college and play basketball. Arrogant Johnny had signed a minor league contract with the Baltimore Orioles and, following his graduation, would be heading to one of their rookie league teams. He was there with Dena Marie Conchek, whose eyes were all red and watery from her crying over Johnny leaving. I stood and wondered what it would be like to have a woman as gorgeous as Dena Marie cry over me. Meanwhile, Johnny was scoping out every girl in the house and talking incessantly about someday making it to the major leagues with the Orioles, which made her cry even more.

Meanwhile, Urb, Snookie, Travis, Johnny, and Brad ducked out and hit the party trail. I wanted to be with them, but there was college money waiting in white envelopes in hands that had to be shaken. I told them I would catch up with them later at Dwayne Robinson's house.

It was 1971, and the cops in Brilliant gave all seniors an unofficial drinking waiver for graduation night. There was to be no drinking and driving, but drinking at the graduation parties was perfectly acceptable. Parents, too, went along with this. For many of my fellow graduates, it was truly a night to celebrate, as it ended a journey of twelve years, or, in the case of Johnny Liberti, thirteen. For several of my classmates, high school graduation must have seemed the educational equivalent of space travel to the ancient Greeks. For some, the right to receive their diploma hinged upon their final six-week grading period. Johnny Liberti, I believe, was passed along more out of pity than academic achievement.

The Robinsons were hosting a graduation party that was, in a sense, more of a celebration for them than their son Dwayne, who was the last of nine Robinson siblings to graduate from Brilliant High School. The Robinsons lived at the foot of Simpson Ridge, just up from the United Methodist Church. As I left my open house, my dad lectured me on the evils of drink and automobiles, and I promised both parents that I would not do anything that would enhance the possibility that I would become a statistic.

The Robinson party was held in their side yard, which sloped dramatically from the side of the hill toward Grant Avenue. Paper Chinese lanterns were strung across the yard. Lawn chairs and spent beer bottles were lined up around a makeshift volleyball court. Mr. Robinson was manning a grill full of burgers, brats, and hot dogs, which he offered to anyone who passed. "Mitchell, brat? Burger? Dog?" I wasn't hungry, but Mr. Robinson was looking a little hurt that no one was eating, so I took a burger and a scoop of potato salad just to be polite.

Dwayne Robinson was a freckled redhead with a bad overbite and a perpetual smile. He was one of the most well-liked kids in our graduating class. He played three sports—football, basketball, and track—but none well. He just loved being part of the team and was the most upbeat kid I had ever known. He had enlisted in the Navy and was scheduled to leave for basic training in early July. Those of us who had grown up fearing we would be drafted and shipped to Vietnam thought Dwayne had completely lost his marbles. We were stretched out on a pair of chaise lounge chairs in the front yard—me with an RC Cola, Dwayne with an Iron City longneck. To the north I could see the tops of the few homes still lining Shaft Row, and then the river and the expanse of West Virginia hills beyond. Dwayne and I talked about the future, and there was an almost Christmas-like feeling to the day. There had been so much anticipation about graduation day, so much build-up, and here we were, sitting in the gloaming, the sun fading over the ridge. In an instant, it seemed, the big day had passed.

I had been accepted into the journalism program at Indiana University and offered a chance to walk on to the baseball team. I was excited about my prospects. While I harbored no fears of the academic challenges before me, I did question my ability to hit a Big Ten-caliber curveball. I was equally concerned about Travis. The sentimental part of me hoped that Travis and I would always be close friends. But I was enough of a realist to know that this night represented a change in our friendship. It was from this point that our paths would diverge. Our relationship, precious as it was to me, would never be the same. It couldn't be.

Whatever Travis's future held, it certainly would not involve me. It was sad to see it all coming to such an abrupt end. Operation Amanda had brought us so close that I felt as though I was losing a brother. I was privy to his most intimate feelings. Together, we shared an enormous secret. Now, it was over.

It was a warm, clear night, the amber glow of the mill lighting the sky far to the north. Our fellow graduates came and went, taking turns sitting in a semicircle of folding chairs and talking of the future and the past. At a few minutes before eleven, a brown Ford station wagon with dealer plates pulled to the curb just down from the Robinsons' and out poured Urb Keltenecker, Snookie McGruder, Brad Nantz, Johnny Liberti, and Travis.

Urb, having been given use of the car for the evening, part of his dad's plan to keep sobriety at the front of his son's consciousness, was sober. Brad Nantz, too, was sober. The other three were in various stages of alcoholic stupor, and Travis was virtually falling-down drunk. "Malone!" he yelled, waving a can of Iron City in his right hand. "It's the beer drinker's beer," he yelled. "When you're really ready to pour it on, pour on the Iron!"

Brad walked past me and said, "He's absolutely trashed."

Everyone within earshot turned to see Travis struggling to negotiate the steep concrete steps leading to the sidewalk that sloped up toward the Robinsons' front porch. I stood to help him make the last three steps. "Whoa, I didn't know if I could make it up," he said, staggering forward into my arms. "Thanks, pal." But he was dead weight and I couldn't hold him; he fell sideways into the yard, and rolled onto his back, laughing.

"How 'bout you babysit him for a while?" Urb said. "He's an obnoxious drunk. I've never seen him like this."

"I don't think he's all that bad," Johnny Liberti said, trying valiantly to help Travis to his feet.

"That's because you're almost as hammered as he is," Urb said, heading toward the side yard where Mr. Robinson was pleadingly waving a brat in his direction.

"Johnny, go get yourself something to eat. I'll help him," I said.

Johnny staggered off, and Dwayne and I rolled Travis upright as he giggled at his drunkenness. "I've got to get me a fresh beer," he slurred. "Whatta ya serving, Du-wayne?"

Dwayne looked at me and whispered, "No way my dad's going to let him have another beer."

"Trav, buddy, don't you think you've had enough?" I asked.

Travis's eyes closed to slits, and the corner of his lip curled. "You're not my father, Malone. Don't tell me what to do with my life, *Mister College Boy*." There was an uncommon, hateful tone to his voice.

"Come on, Trav, don't talk like that."

"Why?"

"Because you've been drinking and you don't want to say something that you're going to regret later."

"Screw you. I won't regret anything. Go on off to college, big man. Mister big man at Indiana University. Mister Hoosier. Come on back and visit your old buddies once in a while, okay? Grace us with your magnificent presence, Mister Joe Fuckin' College."

"You're drunk."

"Oh, you think? Very perceptive. Did you learn that at *college*?"

I put my hand on his shoulder and tried to lead him toward the steps. "Come on, let's get you home so you can sleep this off."

"Get your fuckin' hands off me," he said, jerking away.

"Very nice, Travis." My voice was rising, and I reached for the can of beer he still held in his left hand. "Give me the beer. You're acting like a jerk."

Travis dropped the beer from his left hand as he fired his right fist into my nose. I reeled back several steps but didn't fall. Everyone who had been sitting in the grass jumped up to get away from the commotion, and Dwayne stepped between us as I lunged back at Travis. "Mitchell, don't. You're only going to make it worse," Dwayne said.

"Come on, Malone, you fuckin' pussy," Travis goaded. "Come on, let's see what you've got, college boy."

I charged through Dwayne, knocking him to the left, and took two more steps, driving my right shoulder into Travis's ribs. I wrapped him up, and we fell into a heap in one of Mrs. Robinson's peony bushes. He shoved both hands into my face and my only punch was an errant one, which glanced off his cheek. Snookie and Urb pulled me off of him. A small amount of blood trickled from my left nostril. I said, "I'll kick your scrawny ass, Travis."

"Yeah, you and what Marine?"

This all brought Mr. Robinson down from his post at the grill. Urb handed me a paper napkin, and I dabbed my bloody nose. Travis was laughing. No one said anything. Everyone knew how close Travis and I were, and they were shocked that we would fight, even if he was sloppy drunk. Mr. Robinson said, "Travis, I think it's time for you to go home."

Travis squinted at Mr. Robinson. His jaw tensed, and he started toward the steps. "Fine. It's a shitty party, anyway."

"Dwayne, help him down the steps," Mr. Robinson said.

Dwayne tried to hold Travis's arm, but he shook free. "Get your paws off me. I don't need your help; I don't need anyone's help." He was yelling again. "I've made it eighteen years without anyone's help, why would I need it now? Enjoy your stinkin' party. Screw all of ya."

Mrs. Robinson came out of the house and handed me a damp

washcloth and everyone watched Travis as he ran, wobbling, across Grant Avenue and over the hill toward the United Methodist Church. "Don't you think someone should go with him to make sure he gets home all right?" Mrs. Robinson asked.

No one responded or offered to escort Travis.

"What a jerk," Urb said.

"He'll be okay once he sleeps it off," I said.

"I shouldn't have pulled you off him. I should have let you pound him," Snookie said.

I didn't respond. There was nothing to say. I sat down in the chair and pinched the bridge of my nose until the bleeding stopped, then thanked the Robinsons for the invitation and started toward my car.

"Are you okay to drive?" Mr. Robinson asked, assuming that I, too, had been a drunken participant.

"I'm fine, sir. I've just been drinking RC."

"Okay," he said, not convinced. "Are you heading home?"

"I'm going to swing out to the Hatchers' for a little while. If I know the Hatchers, things will just get hummin' around midnight."

He shook my hand, said congratulations, thanked me for stopping by, and asked me to please be careful.

My timing was good.

From what I was told later, I hadn't been gone fifteen minutes when the rumbling made its way up Grant Avenue, causing everyone at the party to freeze and peer down the road. Aside from the train horns, the barge whistles, and the high-pitched siren that summoned Brilliant's volunteer firemen, the single most recognizable sound in Brilliant, Ohio, was the rumble of the engine within the 1957 Chevy Bel Air hardtop owned by Francis Martino Baron. Before the car crested the knoll on Grant Avenue, Urb looked at Snookie and asked, "He wouldn't do something that stupid, would he?"

But he had.

The tires squealed when he crossed the railroad tracks at the bottom of the hill, and a pair of headlights headed up Grant Avenue. He burned rubber twice as he shifted up the hill, slowing the car at the last minute in front of the Robinson home. The black lacquered finish gleamed under the streetlights; the reverberation of the engine shook the asphalt. Urb and Snookie hustled down the steps, hoping to talk Travis out of the car. He laughed at them through the open passenger-side window. "How do ya like my new ride, boys? Better than the Rambler, huh? Big Frank gave it to me for a graduation present."

"Really?" Urb asked.

Snookie winced at Urb's naiveté. "Bullshit, Travis. Get out of the car," Snookie said. "When Big Frank finds out you took it from the garage he's gonna hang your balls from the rearview mirror."

Travis opened the lid on the case of longnecks he had placed on the passenger seat. "Care for a brew? They're Big Frank's, too."

"Please, Travis. Just get your ass out of the car," Snookie said.

Travis revved the engine; the roar was deafening and hot exhaust billowed up around the car. "I'm takin' her for a spin. It's a little graduation present to myself."

"Oh, shit," Urb said. "Mayday. We've got a Barney Fife sighting."

The Brilliant Police cruiser was heading down Grant and stopped next to the Chevy. Officer Cloyd Owens was in the cruiser. By the look on his face, it was obvious that he expected to see Frank Baron behind the wheel, not his drunken son. Travis grinned at Cloyd. "Hey, Barney, wanna beer?" he asked, holding a bottle out the window toward the officer.

Cloyd appeared to be in a momentary state of disbelief, not only because he had been offered a beer by a drunken teenager, but because the drunken teenager was behind the wheel of Big Frank Baron's prize Chevy. "Turn that engine off and get out!" Cloyd ordered, opening the door to the cruiser.

Travis dropped the beer on the pavement between the two vehicles, and an explosion of foam and amber glass spread over the asphalt. He turned to his buddies and grinned. "I gotta dash, boys. Gonna take me a little joyride," he yelled as he popped the clutch, leaving behind two strips of rubber and a haze of white smoke. Before Cloyd could exit the cruiser, the taillights of the Chevy disappeared over the knoll onto

Wilhelm Avenue. Cloyd closed his door, hit the lights, backed into the driveway, and took off after Travis.

There was little chance that the cruiser could catch the Chevy. Travis drove away, and he was already heading south on Labelle Street before the police cruiser cleared the knoll onto Wilhelm. Urb watched from the knoll and said Travis downshifted and fishtailed through the bend in the road as Labelle crossed Steuben Street. That's where he lost sight of him.

He stomped on the gas, burned rubber, and slid broadside onto Ohio Avenue, nearly clipping a car driven by Margaret Simcox. She later said that pieces of gravel pinged the side of her car as he passed. A trail of white smoke followed the Chevy. It was several seconds later before she spotted Cloyd in pursuit. "Travis was just running away from him," she said.

When he drove past my house, Mom heard the car and said it sounded like a fighter jet going down the street. She looked out the window, but only saw the taillights and didn't realize it was Travis driving.

He turned the corner at the Coffee Pot, and in seconds, Travis had the Chevy squealing through the soft left turn in front of Rudy Tarbaker's house. He passed the high school and stayed on Third Street, following it toward the south edge of town. He passed two southbound cars and whizzed by three others heading north. All five cars parted as the cruiser gave chase.

At the south end of Brilliant, Travis continued under the Route 7 overpass and past Ohio Ferro Alloy, turning right toward Riddle's Run Road, a four-mile gravel and pitch strip that connected with Ohio Route 151 just beyond New Alexandria. Travis slowed when he hit Riddle's Run Road. Cloyd would later say that he never lost sight of his target, but he couldn't catch the Chevy. When the cruiser turned onto Riddle's Run Road, nearly sliding off the asphalt and into the ditch, Travis floored the Chevy. He easily distanced himself from Cloyd, who was fighting darkness and the dust clouds the Chevy left behind. The final mile of Riddle's Run Road was a straight, uphill climb. Travis hit Route 151 just as Cloyd reached the bottom of the hill.

Travis continued through New Alexandria, jumping off 151 onto Jefferson County Road 19, known to the locals as New Alexandria Road. It is a winding, five-mile strip of asphalt that entered Brilliant at its northernmost tip, intersecting with Steel Road just north of Hunter's Ridge Park. The park was owned and maintained by Ohio Valley Steel and had once been the grounds of the Thorneapple estate. There were no turnoffs or other intersecting streets between New Alexandria and Steel Road. Cloyd had radioed the Jefferson County Sheriff's Department for help. A sheriff's cruiser was southbound on Route 7 and would set up a roadblock at Steel Road.

Travis again opened a huge gap between the Chevy and the cruiser as he homed in on the entrance to Hunter's Ridge Park. He hit the high beams and pointed the nose of the Chevy toward the wooden gate that extended across the main entrance to the park. The gate exploded into kindling when Travis rammed it. He spun through the gravel road, which cut under the railroad and highway overpass. The car slid on the gravel and clipped the concrete abutment of the highway overpass, but Travis continued on for a quarter mile to the main parking lot, which sat on the edge of the cliffs overlooking the valley far above the Ohio River. He brought the car to a halt. The siren behind him was closing in.

Cloyd locked up his brakes when he saw what was left of the splintered gate to the park. He jerked the wheel hard and pulled into the park, realizing it was the only exit. He drove slowly down the road, shining his spotlight along the berm, certain the Chevy was lurking in the shadows, like a caged animal looking for his path of escape. But there was nothing but silence; the path was clear except for the last flecks of dust raised by the Chevy. Cloyd put the car in park and stood beside the open driver's door, covering the parking lot with his spotlight. He feared he had somehow lost his quarry and was ready to leave when he saw the gaping hole in the white fence that rimmed the parking lot. On the asphalt before him were two thick strips of rubber. In the grass between the support posts were the rutted grooves that had been carved out by two hot-running tires.

Cloyd ran through the opening and carefully scooted down the sixty feet of grass that ended at the cliffs, a towering precipice that ran more than one hundred feet up from the river. At the bottom of the cliffs, rising out of the water, was a mound of jagged boulders that over the years had freed themselves from the rock wall. And just beyond that were the taillights of Frank Baron's 1957 Chevy, sinking into the dark waters of the Ohio River.

CHAPTER TWENTY-SEVEN

From the picnic area of Hunter's Ridge, located at the top of the hill, across New Alexandria Road and behind the cliffs, it had looked surreal. I watched the car stop, its headlights shining off into the darkness over the Ohio River. A few seconds later, the familiar roar of the 283-cubic inch V-8 echoed off the hills. It sat for a moment, quaking, like an angry bull waiting for the gate to open so it could rid itself of the cowboy on its back. And when the gate opened, the beast erupted forth, and a plume of blue-white smoke grew from under the tires and the squeal of rubber pierced the night. The car broke through the fence, darkening a headlight, and lurched down the embankment, launching itself from the cliffs with all the high drama of a Hollywood death scene. It became a dart in the Ohio night, its lone headlight shining a cycloptic beam on the black target below. It hit the water and slowly bobbed as it filled with water, pulling it under only seconds after I spotted Cloyd with his flashlight on the edge of the embankment.

Within minutes, the emergency siren blasted throughout Brilliant. One of the two emergency squad vans pulled into the parking lot. There was another at the Brilliant Boat Club, where the firemen were taking pleasure crafts up the river in search of Travis.

The siren blasted longer than usual. Firetrucks and other cars pulled into the parking lot. Flashlight beams were everywhere. Panic arrested Brilliant.

It was a full twenty minutes after the car hit the water before Travis emerged from the line of pine trees behind me. He had taken the precaution of walking around the access road at the rear of the park. "What's all the commotion about?" he asked.

"Buster, you've just caused more hell than you could imagine." I pointed out toward the river. "They've already got the boats out searching for you." We watched in silence for a long moment. "Anyone see you come up here?" Travis asked.

"Nope." After leaving the party at the Robinsons', I had pretended to be heading to another graduation party, but cut back on the gravel lover's lane that led to the picnic area at the park. I was seated on the bench overlooking the cliffs, our prearranged meeting place, before Travis pulled the Chevy out of the garage.

"We'd better take advantage of the confusion," he said, looking at his watch. It was eleven-fifty p.m. "We'll never make it by midnight."

CHAPTER TWENTY-EIGHT

The duffle bag and two suitcases had been wrapped in plastic dry cleaner bags and stashed in the brush early that morning. We threw them in the trunk of my car and drove down the service road and back onto New Alexandria Road, a half-mile west of the park's main entrance. Travis wore a Pittsburgh Pirates cap low on his brow, but that was his only attempt to conceal his identity. We were near New Alexandria in minutes and were passed by an emergency squad from the New Alexandria Volunteer Fire Department that was headed toward the park.

"Maybe you should lie down in the back," I offered.

He waved off the suggestion. "No one is looking for me in this car. I'll be fine."

We were silent for most of the trip. There was little to say. I was an accomplice in an unbelievable con, and my job was simple: Deliver Travis safely and keep my mouth shut forever after.

"I really don't want to know too much, Travis, but how'd you get it in the river?"

"Stood outside the door with my foot on the clutch, put it into gear and wedged the gas pedal down with a case of Big Frank's beer. Popped the clutch and let 'er go."

"You drive pretty well for a drunk."

"I kept going in the bathroom and dumping my beers down the sink all night. I only drank enough tonight to get it on my breath. How's your nose?"

It was swollen and sore. "I'll live. I can't believe I agreed to that."

"Nice touch dumping me in the peony bush."

We went north out of New Alexandria and jumped onto Gould's Road, following its namesake creek for several miles. It was all back-road driving until we connected with Fernwood Road near Wintersville. It was a quick jog to US Route 22, which we followed past Belvedere to the E-Z Winks Motel in Bloomingdale. The green Chevrolet—a rental with Pennsylvania plates—was backed into a corner. I pulled around, and my headlights shone briefly on the older couple sitting in the front seat. I backed up next to the Chevrolet and quickly handed the bag and suitcases to his grandfather, who shook my hand and loaded the luggage in the trunk. Tears were already running down my cheeks.

"We don't have time for a long goodbye, Mitch."

I shook my head. "I know."

"Look, Mitch, you know you can't . . ."

"I know, Trav. We've been over it before. I can't say anything to anyone, ever. I'll handle it."

"Okay. You know, I couldn't have done any of this without you."

"And don't ever forget that," I said. "You owe me." I extended my right hand. "Someday, figure out a way to track me down."

He squeezed my hand and nodded, then left without another word.

I drove straight to the party at the Hatchers' house on Dago Ridge. The Hatcher twins, Gerald and Harold, were a wild pair of wrestlers who would entertain us at lunchtime by running two steps up the gymnasium wall and doing backflips. The celebration at their place, as I had known it would be, was particularly riotous. There had been serious doubt, for roughly the entire twelve years of their formal education, that they would ever graduate.

The twins lived at the end of Dago Ridge Road, a two-story house covered in brown asbestos shingles. In their front yard was one of the finest personal junkyards in eastern Ohio. There were no fewer than thirty cars on their property, most sans tires, that would never again see a paved road. Mr. Hatcher made his living with a myriad of odd jobs that included doing auto body work in the barn behind the house, which was where the graduation party seemed to be centered.

I parked behind a pickup truck that was on blocks in the side yard and killed the lights. Gerald and Harold could be heard arguing above the din, and I deduced the twins, neither of whom were strangers to alcohol, were both quite drunk. While the party raged, I slipped by a growling mutt on the front porch and into the house, where I sat down in front of the television in the living room, waiting there until I was spotted by Harold on his way to the bathroom. "Malone, you sonofabitch!" He slurred and squinted. "When'd you get here?"

"Been here, dude."

"No shit? I ain't seen you all night."

"Harold? You got me a beer an hour ago."

He looked at me, then at the floor, then at me. "I don't fuckin' remember that."

I stood up and threw my arm around his shoulder. "That doesn't surprise me."

He laughed. "Wait'll I take me a piss and we'll go get another one, you sonofabitch."

We went out to the barn and Gerald, the less drunk of the two, asked the same question. "He's been here all goddamn night, you sonofabitch," Harold yelled. "Where the hell you been?"

Gerald shrugged. "Drinkin', I guess."

I laughed a forced laugh, then joined the Hatchers on the fender of a primer gray 1961 Caddy for a toast to the Brilliant High class of 1971. It was half an hour later that Spuds Hassler and Mindy Weems ran into the barn with the news of the death of Travis Baron. Mindy was near hysterics. Spuds seemed happy to be the one with the information. "He was runnin' from the cops and drove over the cliffs at Hunter's Ridge in his old man's fifty-seven Chevy," Spuds said.

Gerald and Harold listened, then turned to me. "Man, he was like your best friend," Gerald said.

"No way. No way," I said, a panic in my voice that was not total exaggeration. "I just saw him before I came out here. Oh, my God. Oh, my God. When? When did it happen?"

"Sometime around midnight, maybe a little bit before. I'm not for sure," Spuds said.

It was one-thirty a.m. If it ever came into question, my time was accounted for. Mr. Robinson had seen me leave their party. The twins would swear I had been at their place when the Chevy went into the river.

I handed Gerald my unfinished beer. "I gotta go," I said, running for the car. I took the back route down Riddle's Run Road, the same path on which Travis had led Cloyd. This would be the most difficult part of the entire scam. Travis was long gone. I had to appear devastated that my friend was dead. I also felt bad for what I had put my parents through for the past ninety minutes. I'm sure they weren't convinced that I hadn't been in the car and wouldn't be until they saw me. My mom was standing in the sunroom when I turned the corner in front of the house. She sprinted out of the house, her eyes red from crying.

"Thank God, you're all right."

"I'm fine. I was out at the Hatchers'. I came home as soon as I heard."

Again, the tears came. It had been an emotional week. Everything was coming to a head at the right time. My eyes were red and moist. I was sorry for scaring my parents, sorry that I had lost a friend, worried that I would be exposed, and terrified that Big Frank Baron would eventually figure out the scam. Dad appeared on the sidewalk behind us. He had just gotten back from the marina. "Urb and Snookie are up at the marina. You want to go up?"

I nodded and swiped at my eyes with my sleeve. "Sure."

We hopped in his pickup truck and started north along Labelle Street to the split at Penn Street. "Does anyone know how it happened?" I asked.

Dad shrugged. "I guess he got drunk and drove his dad's car over the cliffs. Your mother said he raced through town, went out the ridge and back on New Alexandria Road. No one saw him go in. Evidently he drove down through the park and couldn't stop when he got to the edge of the parking lot."

"Christ."

"It put quite a scare into your mother and I. We thought you were going to be with him tonight."

"I was, for a while. He was pretty drunk at the Robinsons', and we ended up getting into a little scuffle."

"So I heard. Where'd you disappear to?" he asked.

"Out to Gerald and Harold Hatcher's."

He looked at me, and I looked out the window. If Dad sensed that all wasn't as it appeared, he didn't let on. He turned into the marina and parked alongside the caretaker's shanty. There were a dozen boats in the area, all combing the river surface with spotlights. The fire rescue boat was dragging two grappling hooks. It was too dark and too dangerous to send divers into the water. That would begin at daybreak.

Urb and Snookie were standing at the far end of the dock. Their eyes were red and swollen. "We should have sat on his ass at the Robinsons'," Snookie said. "We never should have let him go. Now look what happened, goddammit. It's our fault."

"It's not our fault, Snook. How could we have known?" I said. He continued to sob. Already, I wanted to break my promise to Travis. I walked over to the bench that had been built into the end of the dock. I had to get away from them before my weakness overtook me.

Travis had come up with the plan before he began filling up the cistern. For several days, he said, he had seriously contemplated killing Big Frank. He planned to stab him at home, then drag his body up Thorneapple Creek, dump him in the cistern, and fill it up. No one would ever find the body. He said he wasn't so much worried about getting caught, but he didn't want his mother to have to share a grave for all eternity with Big Frank.

Ultimately, Travis decided on the plan to fake his death and destroy his dad's most prized possession. "After it's all over," Travis had said, "Big Frank won't know if I'm dead or alive, but he'll know one thing for sure. He'll know that I know what really happened to my mother."

I didn't press him for details. In this situation, the less I knew, the better.

Somehow, he was going to let Big Frank know. And when Frank found out, no one would be safe, not even his son. Big Frank was a shark on land, concerned only with his own self-preservation. If he thought Travis was alive, he'd hunt him down. The only way out was to "die." So far, it seemed to be working. Of course, by this time he and his grandparents were probably closing in on Breezewood, Pennsylvania, the self-proclaimed "Gateway to the South." I had overheard one of the firemen say that the state patrol had tracked down Big Frank somewhere east of Cleveland and he was now on his way home. I wanted to be nowhere near the river when Frank Baron came to survey the damage.

I watched throughout the rest of the night as the boat operators continued their search, an exercise in futility in which I was the only co-conspirator. Dad helped tie up the boats that one by one straggled to shore. There was talk of the tragedy of Travis's short life, of his mother, the irony of it all, and the hidden meaning of the graduation speech. The question wasn't whether Travis Baron had died. He had. There wasn't even the specter of doubt. The only question was whether it had been an accident or suicide.

The moon was at three-quarters and disappearing over Tarr's Dome, the last of its shimmering beam fading from the waters of the Ohio. Only two boats remained, and both were adrift—a vigil more than a search—not wanting to leave the body alone, as though leaving would signify the final surrender.

"How 'bout it, Bud? Ready to go home?" Dad asked.

The first faint hint of dawn was creeping into the valley. It would awaken to the news of a tragic death, a senior with his world unfolding, lost to the depths of the murky river. It was the kind of story the wire services would pick up on and distribute across the country. I wondered if Travis had bought a newspaper and read of his own death. I nodded to my dad and pushed myself off the bench. A very tired and rattled Cloyd Owens met us at the end of the dock. He nodded, solemn, and I returned the nod.

As we drove home, I glanced up the hill at Shaft Row and then across the railroad tracks to the house that was now Big Frank's alone. As we passed, the Kenworth was pulling alongside the house.

CHAPTER TWENTY-NINE

Reverend Horvath spoke of how only God could make sense of such a tragic death. I wasn't paying much attention. Nothing Reverend Horvath had to say was going to make me feel any better about losing my friend. Ever since the accident, people kept approaching me like I had lost a member of my family. And, in a way, I had. They offered their condolences, but ultimately they wanted to know if I thought our fight had caused Travis to commit suicide. No, I told them. It had been an accident. That's all. The fight had consisted of Travis popping me once in the nose and the two of us falling into a heap in Mrs. Robinson's peonies. Actually, he also gave me a head butt when we hit the ground, but that was all. I didn't even hit him back. In the six days since then, it had grown to a battle of Biblical proportions. I was tired of the questions and tired of the waiting. I just wanted it all to be over. The organ music was a drone in my ears, and Reverend Horvath's words had no penetration. After the final prayer, several adults went up to offer condolences to Big Frank, and Duke and I slipped out.

But once he had me in his sights, Big Frank was not about to let me go. He hurried past those lined up to speak to him and went out the side door, slogging through water in the parking lot that was over his shoes, his belly jiggling out of his dress shirt, and then running down Campbell Avenue after me. We were almost to Third Street when Duke said, "You've got company." I turned to see Big Frank lumbering down the road, and I stood at the corner of Campbell and Third, waiting.

He was sucking for air by the time he got to me. "You been duckin' me, boy," Big Frank said between breaths. "We need to talk."

Big Frank Baron was moving toward me like a man after a disobedient dog. He was angry that I had not been around, and he was right, I had been ducking him. His nostrils flared; he was out of breath from the short run down the hill. He stopped within a foot of me and thrust a fist in my face. "What the hell is this?"

In the moment before I answered, I remembered why I loved Travis Baron. Even in "death," he remained the master.

"That would be your fist, Mr. Baron."

His upper lip curled and his teeth showed, clenched. He was breathing as though he could barely control his rage. "Be a smart ass to me, junior, and I'll fuck you up." He allowed the fingers on his right hand to go limp, and with the thumb and index finger from his left hand, he pulled a ring off his pinkie—a gold ring with a crescent of rubies set around a marquis diamond in the center. "Now tell me, where did this ring come from?"

I looked at Frank, the ring, and Frank again. If I had learned anything from Travis, it was to exploit any opportunity in which I held the upper hand. And clearly, I was in control. I took a breath and said, "Is this a trick question?"

"You tell me where this ring came from, or I swear to Jesus . . ."

There was panic in the eyes of Frank Baron. He was more scared than angry, afraid that the truth would finally be known. It made him appear much less formidable. People filing out of the church were staring down the hill, looking to see why Big Frank had sprinted out of the church.

"Look, Mr. Baron, I don't know what you're talking about. How am I supposed to know where your ring came from? Where'd you get it?"

"I'll tell you where I got it. It was in the locked glove box of my Chevy when they fished it out of the river."

Oh, Trav. Good one.

"So? I don't understand why or how that concerns me."

Frank again raised the ring close to my face. "It concerns you because you and Travis were thick as fuckin' thieves, that's why. Now, why don't you take a real close look at this ring; maybe it'll refresh your memory and you'll be able to tell me where it came from."

I shrugged. "Mr. Baron, you're making me real uncomfortable here. I never saw that ring before two seconds ago, and I don't know what you're talking about."

Big Frank laughed a forced laugh and looked away. "I think you're a liar, boy." He spoke in a calm voice that belied the rage building within. He swiped at his sweaty brow with his jacket sleeve. "Where'd my kid get this ring?"

Duke stepped in close to me and said, "He already told you he doesn't know."

Big Frank glared at Duke. "This ain't your fight, junior. Unless you'd like to lose a couple teeth, I'd stay out of it."

"I'm afraid I can't help you, Mr. Baron." I squinted at the ring, then offered, "It looks like a woman's ring, though, if that helps."

"I'm going to find out what happened up at that park. You better hope to Jesus that your ass wasn't involved. I found one of my shovels up behind Shaft Row near our old house, and it looks like a lot of dirt's been moved lately."

I shrugged. "Really? You just happened to be taking a walk up behind Shaft Row and found your shovel, huh?" We stood for a moment, locked in a stare-down. "I'm very sorry for your loss, Mr. Baron. Travis was a great kid. Too bad you never took the time to know him." I nodded at the hand that was clenched around the ring. "I hope you don't lose any sleep worrying about that ring."

Big Frank was still standing on the sidewalk, his face reddened from anger and exertion, as we started north on Third Street. "Are you ever going to tell me what that was really all about?" Duke asked.

"Probably not," I said.

"Would I want to know?"

"Definitely not."

The cars were pulling out of the parking lot and driving past us on Third Street. Drivers and passengers stared. Behind the church, towers of gray clouds were roiling in from the west, ready to drop more rain on the Ohio River Valley.

EPILOGUE

On December 21, 1985, I returned home from the offices of the *Ohio Valley Morning Journal* shortly before five. My wife and daughters were baking Christmas cookies. The youngest, Michelle, the precocious five-year-old who was wearing a Bullwinkle the Moose cap, had spilled green sprinkles on the floor and was making a clumsy attempt to herd them up with a broom. The seven-year-old, Robyn, was covered with flour and delighted that I was there to witness the actual baking of the cookies. I volunteered to finish the sweeping job so the baking could commence.

My wife, Laura, was six months pregnant with our third child. She was as lovely on this day as she had been on that Fourth of July evening when I first discovered her beauty, though she had that exasperated, don't-ask-what's-for-dinner look in her eyes. I didn't. I had, after all, learned a few things after ten years of marriage. I grabbed the bag of pretzels from the top of the refrigerator and assumed that a large mushroom and sausage pizza was somewhere in transit between the pizza shop in Elm Grove and our home.

I slid onto a stool at the kitchen counter and began leafing through the opened mail—a phone bill, a half-dozen advertising fliers hawking last-minute Christmas specials, a pre-approved credit card application, and a small pile of Christmas cards: Jeff and Linda Sue Ekleberry; Coach Oblak; Urb and Alice Keltenecker and sons; J.C. and Becky Wagner; Dr. Maxwell Skinner and Staff; the Groats; Carson "Snookie" and Melinda McGruder, and the Randleman Insurance Group. I tossed them to the side as Robyn insisted that I watch her push the ceremonial first sheet of gingerbread men into the oven. I applauded wildly. The pizza arrived, and I paid.

The girls were much too busy to bother eating, even pizza. They further insisted that I watch because at any moment they would be removing the first batch from the oven. I opened a bottle of beer and munched on the pizza, and for no good reason that I can recall, flipped through the cards again until I got to the one from J.C. and Becky Wagner, whom I knew not to be anywhere in my Rolodex. "Who are these people—J.C. and Becky Wagner?" I asked Laura.

She was covering four tiny hands with oven mitts. "I don't know," she answered, looking back briefly. "I never heard of them. I thought they were friends of yours."

"Not that I recall." I tossed it back on the heap, finished my wedge of pizza, wiped off my hands, and picked it back up and examined the left-handed script that seemed oddly familiar.

"Daddy, look," Michelle squealed. "Mommy says we can put icing on 'em."

I looked at my girls as Laura helped them maneuver the hot tray to the kitchen table. "That's great, sweetheart." I looked back at the card. "Laura, where are the envelopes to these cards?"

"In the trash."

I fished the envelopes from the wastebasket, knocked off the clinging dust and sprinkles, but it was no help. There was no return address, but the cancellation stamp showed that it had been mailed from Los Angeles. I called directory assistance and found three potential candidates in the Los Angeles area. I called them from work the next week, but none of them was the former Travis Baron.

I knew it was him. I can't tell you how or why I knew, but I knew.

I had trouble sleeping for a month, wondering where he was and what he was doing, and when he would again get in touch. I said nothing to Laura. For years the secret had been dormant, though I constantly wondered about him. It wasn't until the next Christmas that I heard from him again. This time the card was signed: J.C. Wagner, Becky, and Lisa, and was accompanied by a photo of an infant in a Santa Claus sleeper. Again, there was no return address, and this one had a New York City cancellation.

It was maddening. I didn't even bother to check the telephone directory for New York City. I assumed he was mailing them from different cities to remain hidden. Perhaps he didn't want to get in touch but simply wanted me to know he was alive and well. Or, knowing Travis, he was enjoying tormenting me.

We went to the Outer Banks of North Carolina on vacation the following June. When I returned, there was a stack of mail on my desk. One of the envelopes contained a note complimenting me on a column I had written about a World War II pilot's efforts to rebuild a P-40 Warhawk. The letter and the signature were in the familiar left-handed script. It was signed "J.C. Wagner." There was no return address, and it had a Chicago cancellation. Two weeks later, another letter arrived.

> Dear Mr. Malone:
> Your column on the city's last remaining drive-in restaurant reminded me of a similar restaurant in my hometown—the Coffee Pot. Your column gave me pause to think of my own adolescent years. Nicely done.
> Sincerely,
> J.C. Wagner

We were living on Kriegers Lane in Wheeling, and Robyn was playing soccer in the Wheeling Youth Soccer Association, an activity that has best been described as bumblebee soccer because the kids hover around the ball like a swarm of bees, all kicking at something— sometimes the ball, but more likely the ground, teammates, and opponents. Mostly, the kids are playing ball because their parents think it's a good idea, not because they particularly want to be there. I wrote a column about bumblebee soccer and Robyn's team, the O.K. Carry-Out Little Buckaroos, and their Saturday morning games at Wheeling Park.

I received a postcard the following week cancelled in Asheville, North Carolina. The message said, simply, "Go Buckaroos!"

Robyn wanted to play soccer because her best friend, Anna, was playing. Surprisingly, it turned out that Robyn was one of the better players on the team. She was lightning. She could easily outrun any kid on the field, which I found astonishing, considering she got half of her genetic makeup from me, and I had never been a speedster. We were late in the second half of a one-to-one game with the Brandt's Pharmacy Raptors when Robyn broke loose from the pack, sprinted the length of the field, and scored. Parents and players were still celebrating when the guy standing behind my lawn chair said, "That little girl's got some good wheels."

The chills that had consumed me when I recognized the handwriting on the first Christmas card returned, though I didn't immediately turn around.

I nodded. "Well, she gets it honestly. Her dad was a rocket."

"Oh. Really? I thought that was Mitchell Malone's daughter."

I laughed, hoping to fight off the tears that were already welling in my eyes. I was oddly afraid to turn around and look into the eyes of someone who had been like a brother but had died nearly fifteen years earlier.

Laura turned and squinted into the sun at the man, assuming it was someone I knew from the paper. She smiled and turned back to the game. I stood, my knees barely able to hold my weight, and turned fully toward him before looking at his face. The man grinned and arched his brows. It was the late Travis Baron—a receding auburn hairline, thin crows' feet, a neatly trimmed beard and moustache. He was dressed in a golf shirt and shorts, and looked the part of a dozen other suburban fathers.

"Mr. Wagner, I presume?" I asked.

He nodded. "Indeed. J.C. Wagner," he said, extending a hand. "And you, sir?"

I walked past the hand and hugged the former Travis, tears rolling down my cheeks. He returned the hug and we both cried. This, of course, attracted the stares of many, including Mrs. Malone. We walked away from the crowd and talked until the game was in its waning minutes. I told Laura that I would meet her and the kids at home and went on ahead with J.C. When Laura arrived at the house a half-hour later we were on the back deck, trying to catch up on the years.

During that time, I had not shared the story with anyone, not even Laura, who had known Travis well. Laura got the kids lunch and put Matthew down for his nap before joining us on the deck. She was, I believe, a little perturbed that I had left all the child-wrangling to her and walked off with this stranger. As she came through the sliding glass door, he stood, and Laura smiled, though there wasn't the faintest hint of recognition. "You remember Laura, don't you?" I asked.

"Sure," J.C. said, "but it's been a long time." He extended his hand. "Good to see you again. I'm J.C. Wagner."

She frowned. "I don't believe we've ever met."

"We have, but it's been quite a while."

He looked at me. "You can trust her," I said.

He said, "You see, Laura, before I became J.C. Wagner, I was Travis Baron."

Laura nodded and smiled, and an instant later it all sank in and she shrieked and jumped backward. The lemonade she carried flew out of the glass like a geyser. "Oh, my God," was all she could say, and she said it about fifteen times.

The "J.C." stood for Jeremy Christian, who had been a seventeen-year-old high school dropout from Florida when he joined the Navy in 1970. Following basic training, Jeremy Christian Wagner was assigned to the USS *Iwo Jima* and killed February 18, 1971, on the Mediterranean Sea, when the jet catapult on which he was working accidentally released. Travis's grandfather secured a favor from an admiral with whom he had worked for years. Every bit of documentation on Jeremy Christian Wagner was appropriately altered, copied, and sent to Ronald Virdon. When Travis had climbed into his grandparents' car on graduation night, he was handed a manila envelope that contained his new identity. That fall, he enrolled at Jerome Township Senior High School outside of Asheville, North Carolina, as a transfer student with a D average and a history of behavior problems. That year, he earned a 4.0 average and varsity letters in three sports, enabling school officials to believe they were responsible for one of the most dramatic salvage projects in the history of North Carolina high school education.

J.C.—who from day one refused to be known as Jeremy Christian—enrolled at the University of North Carolina at Asheville, so he could continue to live with his grandparents. He was so enamored of his new family that he didn't want to move away. He graduated with a bachelor's degree in business administration. Following college, with seed money from his grandparents, he started Amanda Distribution, a service company in Asheville that handled shipping for clients in the textile and furniture industry. It had grown from a one-man operation to one hundred and thirty-six employees and three warehouses. He had met his wife, Becky, through work; she was the daughter of the owner of a trucking company that shipped the textiles. When we all met later that summer, she was pregnant with their second child.

Travis said he had planned never to contact me. He missed me, but figured it best that he didn't try to locate me for fear he would expose himself. "You know, I didn't think it would bother me, but for years after I left, the fact that I was no longer Travis Baron about killed me," he said. "One day I'm Travis, and I have friends, a past, experiences, trophies, and awards with my name on 'em. And the next day, I can't be him anymore. I can't call my friends or send anyone a letter. I've got my medals and certificates in a box up in the attic, but I can't show anyone or talk about them. I made new friends, but I can't tell them anything about my past. Nothing. If someone asks me about growing up in Florida, I have to completely fake it. I never thought of that before I left. I was anxious to get away from my dad, but I really missed you and the guys. And your mom. Jesus, I missed your mom. She was always so great to me. I can't tell you how often I've craved one of her Reuben sandwiches. But I knew I couldn't say anything. I was in Pittsburgh on business about three years ago, and I was really tempted to rent a car and drive down to Brilliant. But I couldn't take the chance. I had a wife, and I still believe that Big Frank would hunt me down if he knew I was alive."

"Do you think Big Frank suspects you're alive?" I asked.

"I don't know, but I hope it torments him every day not knowing for sure."

The break had been clean. He had made a wonderful life for himself with loving grandparents who treated him like a son. His grandfather had passed away a few years earlier; his grandmother was in failing health. He was close to his uncle and his family.

Travis had been in Charlotte on business when one of my columns, which were distributed by the Alpha-Omega News Service, was reprinted in the Charlotte *Ledger*. He called the *Ledger* and was told that I was working at the *Ohio Valley Morning Journal*. From there, it was a simple call to directory assistance to find me. Even then, it took a while to build up the nerve to make contact.

Travis said he had been following my columns for several years in the *Morning Journal*, which he received through the mail. "So, I could have tracked you down simply by checking in with our circulation department?" I asked.

He laughed. "Yep. Your investigative skills need a little work."

We've stayed in constant touch since, and we get together at least once a year. This caused J.C. to have to tell his wife the truth about his past, which she at first didn't believe. When she finally came to the realization that he was telling the truth, it made her irate that he had kept it from her. But, like me, she couldn't stay angry at him for long.

I'm glad to have my friend back. I missed him. Granted, our relationship isn't the same as it was, but we are no less close. During a vacation our families took together to Bracebridge, Ontario, J.C. and I sat out by one of the pristine lakes, the embers of a campfire glowing between us, a full moon reflecting off the lake. We had shared a six-pack of Molson and were relaxing in our lawn chairs, talking about the past, of Urb, Brad, Snookie, and Johnny Liberti, and of Project Amanda and Big Frank.

"It would make one helluva book," I said.

"Write it," J.C. said. "Just make sure Big Frank is dead before you start."

AUTHOR'S NOTE

Yes. Brilliant, Ohio, is a real place.

It is the Ohio River village in which I spent the first eighteen years of my life, and which helped shape the man I grew to be.

Brilliant sits on a soft bend in the Ohio River between Steubenville, Ohio, and Wheeling, West Virginia. Since that descriptor may not help those unfamiliar with the geography of the Upper Ohio River Valley, go to a map and find the point where Ohio, West Virginia, and Pennsylvania meet, and come down the river about thirty miles. You'll find Brilliant tucked hard between the Appalachian foothills and the river. It stretches for about two miles along the Ohio River but is only about five blocks wide, consuming the flood plain and the first row of hills. From my side yard, I could see both the hills of West Virginia beyond the river and the western edge of Brilliant, and there wasn't a half-mile between the two.

Until I left for college in 1974, all that I wanted in the world could be found in Brilliant. Although I love my hometown, there was nothing quaint or charming about the Brilliant of my youth, as the name might suggest. It was a hard-working, blue-collar town where alcohol was outlawed in the early 1900s because of the numerous bars and fights. At the time, Brilliant had just six hundred and forty-seven residents, but thirteen bars. By the late 1960s, when this story began, the town was dry and the population had swelled to a robust sixteen hundred.

The Brilliant of my youth was a wonderful place to be a kid, where the surrounding hills, river, and sand quarry in the south end of town provided a landscape ideal for an adventurous boy, and enough dangers to worry parents half to death. We were a self-sufficient community in those days, with gas stations, churches, grocery stores, hardware stores, a lumberyard, drugstore, diners, and barbershops. And jobs. The valley was flush with good-paying jobs, and the economy thrived.

Much has changed since then. Brilliant, like the rest of the Ohio Valley, struggles to find solid footing in an economy that has been devastated by the collapse of the steel industry and the loss of tens of thousands of jobs.

In *A Brilliant Death*, I took a few liberties with the topography and the commerce, but anyone from the area will clearly recognize it as Brilliant. It is a place where I roamed the hills, played ball and waited for the day when I would be able to don the uniform of the Brilliant Blue Devils.

It will live forever in my memory.

ACKNOWLEDGMENTS

Wwhen I was a junior in high school, an English teacher whose ire I had ignited said, "You, Mr. Yocum, will never amount to anything!"

It was 1972. Our society wasn't so politically correct, and teachers weren't that concerned about your self-esteem. Even so, I thought that was a rough shot and told her so. "That's a bit harsh," I said.

She came out from behind her lectern, her neck crimson. Pointing a finger at me, she said, "See, that's exactly what I'm talking about. You always have something cute to say."

That was true.

In spite of that, I had English and journalism teachers who stuck behind me and gave me a solid foundation that now enables me to make a living as a writer, and they deserve my thanks. They are Bill McHugh, who was my journalism teacher and football coach, and who had an enormous influence on my life; Pauline Grabosky, whom I probably gave every reason in the world to believe I wouldn't amount to anything; and the late Lillian Hesske and Andrew Suranovich. Mrs. Hesske lived to see me published. Mr. Suranovich did not. I am grateful to them all.

This book never would have seen the light of day had it not been for my agent, Colleen Mohyde, who saw the potential in the manuscript and urged me to take it out of mothballs and give it a rewrite. She is a gem, a unique combination of cheerleader and drill sergeant, and I am fortunate to have her in my corner.

I especially want to thank the team at Seventh Street Books for all their hard work. First and foremost, thanks to my editor, Dan Mayer, for seeing the potential in *A Brilliant Death* and putting it into print.

271

Dan's deft touch in editing this book made it a tighter, better read. Many thanks to my copy editor, Sheila Stewart, for her discerning eye, and to my publicist, Cheryl Quimba, who worked overtime promoting *A Brilliant Death*.

ABOUT THE AUTHOR

Robin Yocum is the author of five books, including the critically acclaimed novels *The Essay* and *Favorite Sons, the latter of* which was named the 2011 USA Book News Book of the Year for Mystery and Suspense. Yocum is well-known for his work as a crime and investigative reporter with the *Columbus Dispatch*, where he won more than thirty local, state, and national awards. He is the owner of Yocum Communications, a public relations consulting firm in Westerville, Ohio.